CW01390244

Malcolm Sage, Detective

Herbert Jenkins

Table of Contents

Malcolm Sage, Detective

Herbert Jenkins

Kessinger Publishing reprints thousands of hard–to–find books!

Visit us at http://www.kessinger.net

CHAPTER I. SIR JOHN DENE RECEIVES HIS ORDERS

"JOHN!"

"Yeh!"

"Don't say 'yeh,' say 'yes, Dorothy dear'."

1

"Yes, Dorothy de —" Sir John Dene was interrupted in his apology by a napkin–ring whizzing past his left ear.

"What's wrong?" he enquired, laying aside his paper and picking up the napkin–ring.

"I'm trying to attract your attention," replied Lady Dene, slipping from her place at the breakfast–table and perching herself upon the arm of her husband's chair. She ran her fingers lightly through his hair. "Are you listening?"

"Sure!"

"Well, what are you going to do for Mr. Sage?"

In his surprise at the question, Sir John Dene jerked up his head to look at her, and Dorothy's forefinger managed to find the corner of his eye.

He blinked vigorously, whilst she, crooning apologies into his ear, dabbed his eye with her handkerchief.

"Now," she said, when the damage had been repaired, "I'll go and sit down like a proper, respectable wife of a D.S.O.," and she returned to her seat. "Well?" she demanded, as he did not speak.

"Yes, dear."

"What are you going to do for Mr. Sage, now that Department Z is being demobbed? You know you like him, because you didn't want to ginger him up, and you mustn't forget that he saved your life," she added.

"Sure!"

"Don't say 'sure,' John," she cried. "You're a British baronet, and British baronets don't say 'sure,' 'shucks' or 'vamoose.' Do you understand?"

He nodded thoughtfully.

Malcolm Sage, Detective

"I like Mr. Sage," announced Dorothy. Then a moment later she added, "He always reminds me of the superintendent of a Sunday–school, with his conical bald head and gold spectacles. He's not a bit like a detective, is he?"

"Sure!"

"If you say it again, John, I shall scream," she cried.

For some seconds there was silence, broken at length by Dorothy.

"I like his wonderful hands, too," she continued. "I'm sure he's proud of them, because he can never keep them still. If you say 'sure,' I'll divorce you," she added hastily.

He smiled, that sudden, sunny smile she had learned to look for and love.

"Then again I like him because he's always courteous and kind. At Department Z they'd have had their appendixes out if Mr. Sage wanted them. Now have you made up your mind?"

"Made it up to what?" he asked, lighting a cigar.

"That you're going to set him up as a private detective," she said coolly. "I don't want him to come here and not find everything planned out."

"He won't do that," said Sir John Dene with conviction. "He's no lap–dog."

"I wrote and asked him to call at ten to–day," she said coolly.

"Snakes, you did!" he cried, sitting up in his chair.

"Alligators, I did!" she mocked.

"You're sure some wife;" he looked at her admiringly.

"I sure am," she laughed lightly, "but I'm only just beginning, John dear. By the way, I asked Sir James Walton to come too," she added casually.

"You—" he began, when the door opened and a little, silver–haired lady entered. Sir John Dene jumped to his feet.

"Behold the mother of the bride," cried Dorothy gaily.

"Good morning, John," said Mrs. West as he bent and kissed her cheek. She always breakfasted in her room; she abounded in tact.

"Now we'll get away from the eggs and bacon," cried Dorothy. "In the language of the woolly West, we'll vamoose," and she led the way out of the dining–room along the corridor to Sir John Dene's den. "Come along, mother–mine," she cried over her shoulder. "We've got a lot to discuss before ten o'clock."

Sir John Dene's "den" was a room of untidiness and comfort As Dorothy said, he was responsible for the untidiness and she the comfort.

"Heigh–ho!" she sighed, as she sank down into a comfortable chair. "I wonder what Whitehall would have done without Mr. Sage;" she smiled reminiscently. "He was the source of half its gossip."

"He was very kind to you, Dorothy, when John was–was lost," said Mrs. West gently, referring to the time when Sir John Dene had disappeared and a reward of 20,000 pounds had been offered for news of him.

"Sure!" Sir John Dene acquiesced. "He's a white man, clean to the bone."

"It was very wonderful that an accountant should become such a clever detective," said Mrs. West. "It shows—" she paused.

"You see, he wasn't a success as an accountant," said Dorothy. "He was always finding out little wangles that he wasn't supposed to see. So when they wouldn't have him in the army, he went into the Ministry of Supply and found out a great, big wangle, and Mr. Llewellyn John was very pleased. You get me, Honest John?" she demanded, turning to her husband.

4

Malcolm Sage, Detective

Sir John Dene nodded and blew clouds of cigar smoke from his lips. He liked nothing better than to sit listening to his wife's reminiscences of Whitehall, despite the fact that he had heard most of them before.

"Poor Mr. Sage," continued Dorothy, "nobody liked him, and he's got such lovely down on his head, just like a baby," she added, with a far−away look in her eyes.

"Perhaps no one understood him," suggested Mrs. West, with instinctive charity for the Ishmaels of the world.

"Isn't that like her," cried Dorothy, "but this time she's right." she smiled across at her mother. "When a few thousand tons of copper went astray, or someone ordered millions of shells the wrong size, Mr. Sage got the wind up, and tried to find out all about it, and in Whitehall such things weren't done."

"They tried to put it up on me," grumbled Sir John Dene, twirling his cigar with his lips, "but I soon stopped their funny work."

"Everybody was too busy winning the war to bother about trifles," Dorothy continued. "The poor dears who looked after such things found life quite difficult enough, with only two hours for lunch and pretty secretaries to be—"

"Dorothy!" cried Mrs. West reproachfully

"Well, it's true, mother," she protested.

It was true, as Malcolm Sage had discovered. "Let us concentrate on what we know we have got," one of his chiefs had once gravely said to him. "Something is sure to be swallowed up in the fog of war," he had added. Pleased with the phrase, which he conceived to be original, he had used it as some men do a titled relative, with the result that Whitehall had clutched at it gratefully.

"The fog of war," General Conyers Bardulph had muttered when, for the life of him, he could not find a division that was due upon the Western Front, and which it was his duty to see was sent out.

5

"The fog of war," murmured spiteful Anita McGowan, when the pretty little widow, Mrs. Sleyton, was being interrogated as to the whereabouts of her husband.

"The fog of war," laughed the girls in Department .P.Q., when at half–past four one afternoon neither its chief nor his dark–eyed secretary had returned from lunch.

"But when he went to Department Z he was wonderful," said Mrs. West, still clinging tenderly to her Ishmael.

"He was," said Sir John Dene. "He was the plumb best man at his job I ever came across."

"Yes, John dear, that's all very well," said Dorothy, her eyes dancing, "but suppose you had been the War Cabinet and you had sent for Mr. Sage–" she paused.

"Well?" he demanded.

"And he had come in a cap and a red tie," she proceeded, "and had resigned within five minutes, saying that you were talking of things you didn't know anything about." She laughed at the recollection.

"He was right," said Sir John Dene with conviction. "I've come across some fools; but—"

"There, there, dear," said Dorothy, "remember there are ladies present. In Whitehall we all loved Mr. Sage because he snubbed Ministers, and we hadn't the pluck to do it ourselves," she added.

Sir John Dene snorted. His mind travelled back to the time when he had been "up against the whole sunflower–patch," as he had once expressed it.

"But why did they keep him if they didn't like him?" enquired Mrs. West.

"When you don't like anyone in Whitehall," Dorothy continued, "you don't give him the push, mother dear, you just transfer him to another department."

"Like circulating bad money," grumbled Sir John Dene.

"It sure was, John," she agreed. "Poor Mr. Sage soon became the most transferred man in Whitehall. They used to say, 'Uneasy lies the head that has a Sage.'" She laughed at the recollection.

"But wasn't it rather unkind?" said Mrs. West gently.

"It was, mother—mine; but Whitehall was a funny place. One of Mr. Sage's chiefs went about for months trying to get rid of him. He offered to give a motor—cycle to anyone who would take him, it was a Government cycle," she added; "but there was nothing doing. We called him Henry the Second and Mr. Sage Becket, the archbishop not the boxer," she explained. "You know," she added, "there was once an English king who wanted to get rid of—"

"We'll have it the sort of concern that insurance companies can look to," Sir John Dene broke in.

"What on earth are you talking about, John?" cried Dorothy.

Whilst his wife talked Sir John Dene had been busy planning Malcolm Sage's future, and he had uttered his thoughts aloud. He proceeded to explain. When he had finished, Dorothy clapped her hands.

"Hurrah! for Malcolm Sage, Detective," she cried and, jumping up, she perched herself upon the arm of her husband's chair, and rumpled the fair hair, which with her was always a sign of approval. "That's his ring, or Sir James's," she added as the bell sounded.

"Now we'll leave you lords of creation to carry out my idea," she said as she followed Mrs. West to the door.

And Sir John Dene smiled.

* * * * *

"In the States they've got Pinkerton's," said Sir John Dene, twirling with astonishing rapidity an unlit cigar between his lips. "If you've lost anything, from a stickpin to a mountain, you just blow in there, tell them all about it, and go away and don't worry.

Malcolm Sage, Detective

Here you've got nothing."

"We have Scotland Yard," remarked Malcolm Sage quietly, without looking up from the contemplation of his hands, which, with fingers wide apart, rested upon the table before him.

His bald, conical head seemed to contradict the determined set of his jaw and the steel–coloured eyes that gazed keenly through large gold–rimmed spectacles. Even his ears, that stood squarely out from his head, appeared to emphasise by their aggressiveness that they had nothing to do with the benevolent shape of the head above.

"Yes, and you've got Cleopatra's Needle, and the pelicans in St. James's Park," Sir John Dene retorted scornfully. He had never forgotten the occasion when, at a critical moment in the country's history, the First Lord of the Admiralty had casually enquired if he had seen the pelicans.

For the last half–hour Sir John Dene, with characteristic impulsiveness, had been engaged in brushing aside all Malcolm Sage's "cons" with his almighty "Pro."

"We'll have a Pinkerton's in England," he resumed, as neither of his listeners took up his challenge, "and we'll call it Sage's."

"I shall in all probability receive quite a number of orders for shop–fronts," murmured Malcolm Sage, with a slight fluttering at the corners of his mouth, which those who knew him understood how to interpret.

"Shop–fronts!" repeated Sir John Dene, looking from one to the other, "I don't get you."

"There is already a well–known firm of shop–furnishers called 'Sage's,'" explained Sir James, who throughout the battle had been an amused listener.

"Well, we'll call it the Malcolm Sage Detective Bureau," replied Sir John Dene, "and we'll have it a concern that insurance companies can look to." He proceeded to light his cigar, with him always a sign that something of importance had been settled.

Malcolm Sage, Detective

Sir John Dene liked getting his own way. That morning he had resolutely brushed aside every objection, ethical and material, that had been advanced. To Malcolm Sage he considered that he owed a lot, and with all the aggressiveness of his nature, he overwhelmed and engulfed objection and protest alike. To this was added the fact that the idea was his wife's, and in his own phraseology "that goes."

Passive and attentive, his long shapely hands seldom still, Malcolm Sage had listened. From time to time he ventured some objection, only to have it brushed aside by Sir John Dene's overwhelming determination.

For some minutes Malcolm Sage had been stroking the back of his head with the palm of his right hand, a habit of his when thoughtful. Suddenly he raised his eyes and looked across at his would–be benefactor.

"Why should you want to do this for me, Sir John?" he asked.

"If you're going to put up a barrage of whys," was the irascible retort, "you'll never cut any ice."

"I fully appreciate the subtlety of the metaphor," said Malcolm Sage, the corners of his mouth twitching; "but still why?"

"Well, for one thing I owe you something," barked Sir John Dene, "and remembering's my long suit. For another, Lady Dene—"

"That is what I wanted to know," said Malcolm Sage, as he drew his briar from his pocket and. proceeded to fill it. "Will you thank Lady Dene and tell her that I am proud to be under an obligation to her–and to you, Sir John," he added.

"Say, that's fine," cried Sir John Dene, jumping to his feet and extending his hand, which Malcolm Sage took, an odd, quizzical expression in his eyes. "This Detective Bureau notion is a whale."

"The zoological allusion, I'm afraid, is beyond me," said Malcolm Sage as he struck a match, "but no doubt you are right," and he looked across at Sir James Walton, whose eyes smiled his approval.

Malcolm Sage, Detective

"It's all fixed up," cried Sir John Dene to his wife as she came out into the hall as the visitors were departing.

"I'm so glad," she cried, giving her hand to Malcolm Sage. "You'll be such a success, Mr. Sage," and she smiled confidently up into his eyes.

"With such friends," he replied, "failure would be an impertinence," and he and Sir James Walton passed out of the flat to return to what was left of the rapidly demobilising Department Z, which had made history by its Secret Service work.

In a few days the news leaked out that "M.S.," as Malcolm Sage was called by the staff, was to start a private-detective agency. The whole staff promptly offered its services, and there was much speculation and heart-burning as to who would be selected.

On hearing that she was to continue to act as Malcolm Sage's secretary, Miss Gladys Norman had done a barn-dance across the room, her arrival at the door synchronising with the appearance of Malcolm Sage from without. It had become a tradition at Department Z that "M.S." could always be depended upon to arrive at the most embarrassing moment of any little dramatic episode; but it was equally well-known that he possessed a "blind-side" to his vision. They called it "the Nelson touch."

James Thompson, Malcolm Sage's principal assistant, and William Johnson, the office junior, had also been engaged, and their enthusiasm had been as great as that of their colleague, although less dramatically expressed.

A battle royal was fought over the body of Arthur Tims, Malcolm Sage's chauffeur. Sir John Dene had insisted that a car and a chauffeur were indispensable, to a man who was to rival Pinkerton's. Malcolm Sage, on the other hand, had protested that it was an unnecessary expense in the early days of a concern that had yet to justify itself. To this Sir John Dene had replied, "Shucks!" at the same time notifying Tims that he was engaged for a year, and authorising him to select a car, find a garage, and wait instructions.

Tims did not do a barn-dance. He contented himself for the time being with ruffling William Johnson's dark, knut-like hair, a thing to which he was much addicted. Returning home on the evening of his engagement he had bewildered Mrs. Tims by seizing her as she stood in front of the kitchen–stove, a frying–pan full of sausages in her hand, and waltzing her round the kitchen, frying–pan and all.

Subsequently five of the six sausages had been recovered; but the sixth was not retrieved until the next morning when, in dusting, Mrs. Tims discovered it on the mantelpiece.

CHAPTER II. THE STRANGE CASE OF MR. CHALLONER

"PLEASE, sir. Miss Norman's fainted." William Johnson, known to his colleagues as the Innocent, stood at Malcolm S. Sage's door, with widened eyes and a general air that bespoke helplessness.

Without a word Malcolm Sage rose from his table, as if accustomed all his life to the fainting of secretaries. William Johnson stood aside, with the air of one who has rung a fire–alarm and now feels he is at liberty to enjoy the fire itself.

Entering her room, Malcolm Sage found Gladys Norman lying in a heap beside her typewriter. Picking her up he carried her into his own room, placed her in an arm–chair, fetched some brandy from a small cupboard and, still watched by the wide–eyed William Johnson, proceeded to force a little between her teeth.

Presently her lids flickered and, a moment later, she opened her eyes. For a second there was in them a look of uncertainty, then suddenly they opened to their fullest extent and became fixed upon the door beyond. Malcolm Sage glanced over his shoulder and saw framed in the doorway Sir James Walton.

"Sit down, Chief," he said quietly, his gaze returning to the girl sitting limply in the large leather–covered arm–chair. "I shall be free in a moment."

It was characteristic of him to attempt no explanation. To his mind the situation explained itself.

As Miss Norman made an effort to rise, he placed a detaining hand upon her arm.

"Send Mr. Thompson."

Malcolm Sage, Detective

With a motion of his hand Malcolm Sage indicated to William Johnson that the dramatic possibilities of the situation were exhausted, at least as far as he was concerned. With reluctant steps the lad left the room and, having told Thompson he was wanted, returned to his seat in the outer office, where it was his mission to sit in preliminary judgment upon callers.

When Thompson entered, Malcolm Sage instructed him to move the leather–covered chair into Miss Norman's room and, when she was rested, to take her home in the car.

Thompson's face beamed. His devotion to Gladys Norman was notorious.

The girl rose and raised to Malcolm Sage a pair of dark eyes from which tears were not far distant.

"I'm so ashamed, Mr. Sage," she began, her lower lip trembling ominously. "I've never done such a thing before."

"I've been working you too hard," he said, as he held back the door. "You must go home and rest."

She shook her head and passed out, whilst Malcolm Sage returned to his seat at the table.

"Working till two o'clock this morning," he remarked as he resumed his seat. "She won't have assistance. Strange creatures, women," he added musingly, "but beautifully loyal."

Sir James dropped into a chair on the opposite side of Malcolm Sage's table. Having selected a cigar from the box his late chief–of–staff pushed across to him, he cut off the end and proceeded to light it.

"Good cigars these," he remarked, as he critically examined the lighted end.

"They're your own brand, Chief," was the reply.

Malcolm Sage always used the old name of "Chief" when addressing Sir James Walton. It seemed to constitute a link with the old days when they had worked together with a harmony that had bewildered those heads of departments who had regarded Malcolm

Malcolm Sage, Detective

Sage as something between a punishment and a misfortune.

"Busy?"

"Very."

For some seconds they were silent. It was like old times to be seated one on each side of a table, and both seemed to realise the fact.

"I've just motored up from Hurstchurch," began Sir James at length, having assured himself that his cigar was drawing as a good cigar should draw. "Been staying with an old friend of mine, Geoffrey Challoner." Malcolm Sage nodded.

"He was shot last night. That's why I'm here." He paused; but Malcolm Sage made no comment. His whole attention was absorbed in an ivory paper–knife, which he was endeavouring to balance upon the handle of the silver inkstand. More than one client had been disconcerted by Malcolm Sage's restless hands, which they interpreted as a lack of interest in their affairs.

"At half–past seven this morning," continued Sir James, "Peters, the butler, knocked at Challoner's door with his shaving–water. As there was no reply he entered and found, not only that Challoner was not there, but that the bed had not been slept in over night."

Malcolm lifted his hands from the paper–knife. It balanced.

"He thought Challoner had fallen asleep in the library," continued Sir James, "which he sometimes did, he is rather a night–owl. Peters then went downstairs, but found the library door locked on the inside. As there was no response to his knocking, he went round to the French windows that open from the library on to the lawn at the back of the house. The curtains were drawn, however, and he could see nothing."

"Is it usual to draw the curtains?" enquired Malcolm Sage, regarding with satisfaction the paper–knife as it gently swayed up and down upon the inkstand.

"Yes, except in the summer, when the windows are generally kept open."

13

Malcolm Sage, Detective

Malcolm Sage nodded, and Sir James resumed his story.

"Peters then went upstairs to young Dane's room; Dane is Challoner's nephew, who lives with him. While he dressed he sent Peters to tell me.

"A few minutes later we all went down to the library and tried to attract Challoner's attention; but without result. I then suggested forcing an entry from the garden, which was done by breaking the glass, of one of the French–windows.

"We found Challoner seated at his table dead, shot through the head. He had an automatic pistol in his hand." Sir James paused; his voice had become husky with emotion. Presently he resumed.

"We telephoned for the police and a doctor, and I spent the time until they came in a thorough examination of the room. The French–windows had been securely bolted top and bottom from within, by means of a central handle. All the panes of glass were intact, with the exception of that we had broken. The door had been locked on the inside, and the key was in position. It was unlocked by Peters when he went into the hall to telephone. It has a strong mortice–lock and the key did not protrude through to the outer side, so that there was no chance of manipulating the lock from without. In the fireplace there was an electric stove, and from the shower of soot that fell when I raised the trap, it was clear that this had not been touched for some weeks at least.

"The doctor was the first to arrive. At my urgent request he refrained from touching the body. He said death had taken place from seven to ten hours previously as the result of the bullet wound in the temple. He had scarcely finished his examination when an inspector of police, who had motored over from Lewes, joined us.

"It took him very few minutes to decide that poor Challoner had shot himself. In this he was confirmed by the doctor. Still, I insisted that the body should not be removed."

"Why did you do that, Chief?" enquired Malcolm Sage, who had discarded the paper–knife and was now busy drawing geometrical figures with the thumb–nail of his right hand upon the blotting pad before him.

"Because I was not satisfied," was the reply. "There was absolutely no motive for suicide. Challoner was in good health and, if I know anything about men, determined to live as long as the gods give."

Again Malcolm Sage nodded his head meditatively.

"The jumping to hasty conclusions," he remarked, "has saved many a man his neck. Whom did you leave in charge?" he queried.

"The inspector. I locked the door; here is the key," he said, producing it from his jacket pocket. "I told him to allow no one into the room."

"Why were you there?" Malcolm Sage suddenly looked up, flashing that keen, steely look through his gold–rimmed spectacles that many men had found so disconcerting. "Ordinary visit?" he queried.

"No." Sir James paused, apparently deliberating something in his own mind. He was well acquainted with Malcolm Sage's habit of asking apparently irrelevant questions.

"There's been a little difficulty between Challoner and his nephew," he said slowly. "Some days back the boy announced his determination of marrying a girl he had met in London, a typist or secretary. Challoner was greatly upset, and threatened to cut him out of his will if he persisted. There was a scene, several scenes in fact, and eventually I was sent for as Challoner's oldest friend."

"To bring the nephew to reason," suggested Malcolm Sage.

"To give advice ostensibly; but in reality to talk things over," was the reply.

"You advised?" When keenly interested, Malcolm Sage's questions were like pistol–shots.

"That Challoner should wait and see the girl."

"Did he?" Malcolm Sage was intent upon outlining his hand with the point of the paper–knife upon the blotting pad.

Malcolm Sage, Detective

Again Sir James hesitated, only for a fraction of a second, however. "Yes; but unfortunately with the object of endeavouring to buy her off. Yesterday afternoon Dane brought her over. Challoner saw her alone. She didn't stay more than a quarter of an hour. Then she and Dane left the house together, he to see her to the station. An hour later he returned. I was in the hall at the time. He was in a very excited state. He pushed past me, burst into the library, banging the door behind him.

"That evening at dinner Challoner told me there had been a very unpleasant scene. He had warned the boy that unless he apologised to–day he would telephone to London for his lawyer, and make a fresh will entirely disinheriting him. Soon after the interview Dane went out of the house, and apparently did not return until late–as a matter of fact, after I had gone to bed. I was feeling tired and said 'good night' to Challoner about half–past ten in the library."

For some time Malcolm Sage gazed upon the outline he had completed, as if in it lay the solution of the mystery.

"It's a pity you let the butler unlock the door," he remarked regretfully.

Sir James looked across at his late chief–of–staff keenly. He detected something of reproach in his tone.

"Did you happen to notice if the electric light was on when you entered the library?"

"No," said Sir James, after a slight pause; "it was not."

Malcolm Sage reached across to the private telephone and gave the "three on the buzzer" that always galvanised Miss Gladys Norman into instant vitality.

"Miss Norman," said Sage as she entered, "can you lend me the small mirror I have seen you use occasionally?"

"Yes, Mr. Sage," and she disappeared, returning a moment later with the mirror from her handbag. She was accustomed to Malcolm Sage's strange requests.

"Feeling better?" he enquired as she turned to go.

"I'm all right now," she smiled, "and please don't send me home, Mr. Sage," she added, and she went out before he had time to reply.

A quarter of an hour later the two men entered Sir James's car, whilst Thompson and Dawkins, the official photographer to the Bureau, followed in that driven by Tims. Malcolm Sage would cheerfully have sacrificed anybody and anything to serve his late chief.

"And how am I to keep the shine off my nose without a looking-glass, Johnny?" asked Miss Norman of William Johnson, as she turned to resume her work.

"He won't mind if it shines," said the youth seriously; and Miss Norman gave him a look, which only his years prevented him from interpreting.

* * * * *

As the car drew up, the hall-door of "The Cedars" was thrown open by the butler, a fair-haired clean-shaven man of about forty-five, with grave, impassive face, and eyes that gave the impression of allowing little to escape them.

As he descended the flight of stone-steps to open the door of the car, a young man appeared behind him. A moment later Sir James was introducing him to Malcolm Sage as "Mr. Richard Dane."

Dark, with smoothly-brushed hair and a toothbrush moustache, he might easily have been passed over in a crowd without a second glance. He was obviously and acutely nervous. His fingers moved jerkily, and there were twitchings at the corners of his mouth that he seemed unable to control. It was not a good-tempered mouth. He appeared unconscious of the presence of Malcolm Sage. His eyes were fixed upon the second car, which had just drawn up, and from which Thompson and Dawkins were removing the photographic paraphernalia.

Peters conducted Sir James and Malcolm Sage to the dining-room, where luncheon was laid. "Shall I serve luncheon. Sir James?" he enquired, ignoring Dane, who was clearly unequal to the strain of the duties of host.

17

Malcolm Sage, Detective

Sir James looked across at Malcolm Sage, who shook his head.

"I'll see the library first," he said. "Sir James will show me. Fetch Dawkins," he said to Thompson, and he followed Sir James through the house out on to the lawn.

As they entered the library by the French–windows, a tall, sandy man rose from the arm–chair in which he was seated. He was Inspector Gorton of the Sussex County Constabulary. Malcolm Sage nodded a little absently. His eyes were keenly taking in every detail of the figure sprawling across the writing–table. The head rested on the left cheek, and there was an ugly wound in the right temple from which blood had dripped and congealed upon the table. In the right hand was clutched a small, automatic pistol. The arm was slightly curved, the weapon pointing to the left.

Having concluded his examination of the wound, Malcolm Sage drew a silk–handkerchief from his pocket, shook out its folds and spread it carefully over the blood–stained head of Mr. Challoner.

Sir James looked across at him, appreciation in his eyes. It was one of those little human touches, of which he had discovered so many in Malcolm Sage, and the heads of government departments in Whitehall so few.

Malcolm Sage next proceeded to regard the body from every angle, even going down on his knees to see the position of the legs beneath the table. He then walked round the room and examined everything with minute attention, particularly the key of the door, which Sir James had replaced in its position on the inside. The keyhole on both sides of the door came in for careful scrutiny.

He tried the door of a small safe at the far–end of the room; it was locked. He then examined the fastenings of the French windows.

Finally he returned to the table, where, dropping on one knee on the left–hand side of the body, he drew a penknife from his pocket, and proceeded with great care and deliberation to slit up the outer seam of the trousers so that the pocket lay exposed.

This in turn he cut open, taking care not to disturb the bunch of keys, which, attached to a chain, lay on the thigh, a little to the left.

Malcolm Sage, Detective

The others watched him with wide–eyed interest, the inspector breathing heavily.

Having assured himself that the keys would not slide off, Malcolm Sage rose and turned to Dawkins: "I want a plate from the right. the left, the front, and from behind and above. Also an exposure showing the position of the legs, and another of the keys."

Dawkins inclined his head. He was a grey, bald–headed little man who had only one thought in life, his profession. He seldom spoke, and when he did his lips seemed scarcely to part, the words slipping out as best they could.

Happy in the knowledge that his beloved camera was once more to be one of the principal witnesses in the detection of a crime, Dawkins set himself to his task.

"When Dawkins has finished," said Malcolm Sage, turning to the inspector, who had been watching the proceedings with ill–disguised impatience, "you can remove the body; but leave the pistol. Give Mr. Challoner's keys to Sir James. And now I think we might lunch," he said, turning to Sir James.

Malcolm Sage's attitude towards the official police was generally determined by their attitude towards him. In the Department Z days, he had been known at Scotland Yard as "Sage &Onions." What the phrase lacked in wit was compensated for by the feeling with which it was frequently uttered. The police officers made no effort to dissemble the contempt they felt for a department in which they saw a direct rebuke to themselves. Later, however, their attitude changed. and Malcolm Sage was brought into close personal touch with many of the best–known officers of the Criminal Investigation Department.

He had never been known to speak disparagingly, or patronisingly, of Scotland Yard. On the other hand, he lost no opportunity of emphasising the fact that it was the headquarters of the most efficient police force in the world. He did not always agree with its methods, which in many ways he regarded as out–of–date.

As Malcolm Sage left the room, the inspector shrugged his shoulders. The whole thing was so obvious that, but for the presence of Sir James Walton, he would have refused to delay the removal of the body. The doctor had pronounced the wound self–inflicted, and even if he had not done so, the circumstantial evidence was conclusive.

Malcolm Sage, Detective

Luncheon was eaten in silence, a constrained and uncomfortable meal. Malcolm Sage ate as he always ate when his mind was occupied, with entire indifference as to what was on the plate, from which his eyes never lifted.

Sir James made several ineffectual efforts to draw Dane into conversation; but at each remark the young man started violently, as if suddenly recalled to his surroundings. Finally Sir Iames desisted, and the meal concluded in abysmal silence.

Malcolm Sage then announced that he would examine the various members of the household, and Dane and Peters left the room.

One by one the servants entered, were interrogated, and departed. Even the gardener and his wife, who lived at the lodge by the main—gates, were cross—questioned.

Mrs. Trennett, the housekeeper, was incoherent in her voluble anxiety to give information. The maids were almost too frightened to speak, and from none was anything tangible extracted. No one had any reason for being near the library late at night. When Peters' turn came, he told his story with a clearness and economy of words that caused Malcolm Sage mentally to register him as a good witness. He was a superior kind of man, who had been in his present position only some six months; but during that time he had given every satisfaction, so much so that Mr. Challoner had remarked to Sir James that he believed he had found a treasure.

According to Peters' account, at a quarter—past eleven on the previous evening he had gone to the library, as was his custom, to see if there were anything else that Mr. Challoner required before he locked up for the night. On being told there was nothing, he had accordingly seen to the fastenings of doors and windows and gone to bed.

"What was Mr. Challoner doing when you entered the room?" enquired Malcolm Sage, intent upon a design he was drawing upon the surface of the salt.

"He was sitting at the table where I found him this morning."

"What was he actually doing?"

"I think he was checking his bankbook, sir."

"Did you notice anything strange about his manner?"

"No, sir."

"When you found that his bed had not been slept in were you surprised?"

"Not greatly, sir," was the response. "Once before a similar thing happened, and I heard from the other servants that on several occasions Mr. Challoner had spent the night in the library, having fallen asleep there."

"When you told Mr. Dane that his uncle had not slept in his room, and that the library door was locked on the inside, what did he say?"

"He said, 'Good Lord! Peters, something must have happened'."

"Mr. Dane knew that on previous occasions his uncle had spent the night in his study?" enquired Malcolm Sage, smoothing out the design upon which he had been engaged and beginning another.

"I think so, sir," was the response.

"The pistol was the one he used at target–practice?"

"Yes, sir."

"Where did he keep it?"

"In the third right–hand drawer of his table, sir."

"He was a good shot, I think you said?" Malcolm Sage turned to Sir James.

"Magnificent," he said warmly. "I have often shot with him."

"Do you know of any reason why Mr. Challoner should commit suicide?" Malcolm Sage enquired of Peters.

"None whatever, sir; he always seemed very happy."

"He had no domestic worries?"

Peters hesitated for a moment.

"He never mentioned any to me, sir."

"You have in mind certain events that occurred during the last few days, I take it?" said Malcolm Sage.

"That was in my mind, sir," was the response.

"You know of no way by which anyone could have got into the library and then out again, other than through the door or the window?"

Malcolm Sage had relinquished the salt–spoon and was now meditatively twirling a wineglass by its stem between his thumb and first finger.

"There is no other way, sir."

"Who has access to the library in the ordinary way? Tell the names of everybody who is likely to go in at any time."

"Outside Mr. Challoner and Mr. Dane, there is myself, Trennett the housekeeper, and Meston the housemaid."

"No one else."

"No one, sir, except, of course, the guests who might be staying in the house."

"I shall want the finger–prints of all those you have named, including yours, Sir James." Malcolm Sage looked across at Sir James Walton. "I can then identify those of any stranger that I may find." Sir James nodded.

Malcolm Sage, Detective

"It would be quite easy for Mr. Challoner to let anyone in through the French windows?" enquired Malcolm Sage, turning once more to Peters.

"Quite, sir."

"What time did Mr. Dane return last evening?"

"I think about a quarter to eleven, sir. He went straight to his room."

"That will be all now. Tell Mr. Dane I should like to see him."

Peters noiselessly withdrew.

A few minutes later Dane entered the room. Malcolm Sage gave him a keen, appraising look, then dropped his eyes. Dane was still acutely nervous. His fingers moved jerkily and the corners of his mouth twitched.

"Will you tell me what took place yesterday between you and your uncle?" said Malcolm Sage.

Dane looked about him nervously, as an animal might who has been trapped and seeks some means of escape. "We had a row," he began, then paused; "a terrible row," he added, as if to emphasise the nature of the quarrel.

"So I understand," said Malcolm Sage. "I know what it was about. Just tell me what actually took place. In as few words as possible, please."

"A week ago I told my uncle of my engagement, and he was very angry when he knew that my fiancee was–was—"

"A secretary," suggested Malcolm Sage, without looking up.

"Yes. He ordered me to break off the engagement at once, no matter what it might cost."

"He referred to his pocket rather than to your feelings, I take it?" said Malcolm Sage.

23

"Yes." There was a world of bitterness in the tone in which the word was uttered. "I refused. Four days ago Sir James came and, I think, talked things over with my uncle, who said he would see Enid, that is, my fiancee. She came yesterday afternoon. My uncle insisted on seeing her alone. She stayed only a few minutes."

His voice broke. He swallowed rapidly several times in succession, struggling to regain control of himself.

"You walked back to the station with her," remarked Malcolm Sage, "and she told you what had taken place. Your uncle had offered to buy her off. You were furious. You said many wild and extravagant things. Then you came back and went immediately into the library. What took place there?"

"I don't remember what I said. I think for the time I was insane. He had actually offered her money, notes. He had drawn them out of the bank on purpose." Again he stopped, as if the memory of the insult were too much for him.

"And you said?" suggested Malcolm Sage, twirling the wineglass slowly between his thumb and finger.

"I probably said what any other man would have said under similar circumstances." There was a quiet dignity about the way in which he uttered these words, although his fingers still continued to twitch.

"Did he threaten you, or you him?"

"I don't remember what I said; but my uncle told me that, unless I wrote to Enid to–day giving her up and apologised to him, he would telephone for his lawyer and make a fresh will, cutting me out of it entirely. I was to have until the next morning to decide, that is, to–day."

Malcolm Sage still kept his eyes averted. He contended that to look fixedly into the eyes of anyone undergoing interrogation was calculated to confuse him and render the replies less helpful.

"And what would your decision have been?" he asked.

"I told him that if he gave me ten years it would be the same."

"That you would not do as he wished?"

"Certainly not."

"Until this episode you were on good terms with each other?" Malcolm Sage had got a dessert spoon and fork to balance on the blade of a knife.

"Yes."

"You know of no reason why your uncle should take his life?"

"None whatever."

"This episode in itself would not be sufficient to cause him to commit suicide?"

"Certainly not. Sir James will tell you that he was a man of strong character."

"Do you believe he shot himself?" Malcolm Sage seemed absorbed in the rise and fall of the balancing silver.

"But for the locked door I should have said 'no'. "

"What were you proposing to do in the light of your refusal to break the engagement?"

"I had everything packed up ready. I meant to go away this morning."

"By the way, where did your uncle bank?" enquired Malcolm Sage casually.

"At the Southern Counties and Brown's Bank, Lewes," was the reply.

"Thank you. That will do, I think, for the present. You had better run round to your doctor and get him to give you something to steady your nerves," said Malcolm Sage, with eyes that had lost their professional glint. "They are all on edge."

25

Dane glanced at him in surprise; but there was only a cone of baldness visible.

"Thank you," he said. "I think I will," and he turned and left the room. He still seemed dazed and incapable of realising what was taking place.

Malcolm Sage rose and, walking over to the door, removed the key, examined the wards intently, then replaced it and, opening the door, walked across to the library.

CHAPTER III. MALCOLM SAGE'S MYSTERIOUS MOVEMENTS

MALCOLM SAGE found that Dawkins had completed his work, and the body of Mr. Challoner had been removed.

Seating himself at the table, he took the automatic pistol in his hand and deliberately removed the cartridges. Then placing the muzzle against his right temple he turned his eyes momentarily on Dawkins, who, having anticipated his wishes, had already adjusted the camera. He removed the cap, replaced it, and then quickly reversed the plate.

Pulling the trigger, Malcolm Sage allowed his head to fall forward, his right hand, which held the pistol, dropping on the table before him. Dawkins took another photograph.

"Now," said Malcolm Sage to Sir James. "You shoot me through the right temple, approaching from behind. Grip my head as if you expected me to resist."

Sir James did as he was requested, Dawkins making another exposure.

Malcolm Sage motioned Thompson to draw the curtains. Then dropping on to his knees by the library door, he took the small mirror he had borrowed from Miss Norman and, placing it partly beneath the door, carefully examined the reflection by the aid of an electric torch.

When he rose it was with the air of a man who had satisfied himself upon some important point. He then turned to Sir James.

Malcolm Sage, Detective

"You might get those finger–prints," he said casually. "Get everyone together in the dining–room. See that no one leaves it for at least a quarter of an hour. Thompson will go with you."

"Then you think it was murder?" questioned Sir James.

"I would sooner say nothing just at the moment," was the reply.

Whilst Sir James Walton and Thompson were occupied with a room–full of domestics, talking in whispers as if in the presence of death, Malcolm Sage was engaged in a careful examination of the bottoms of all the doors in the house by means of a mirror placed upwards beneath each. He also removed the keys and gave a swift look at the wards of each lock. He moved quickly; yet without haste, as if his brain had entire control of the situation. One door in particular appeared to interest him, so much that he entered the room and proceeded to examine it with great thoroughness, taking the utmost care to replace every–thing as he found it.

From the middle–drawer of the chest–of–drawers, he extracted from under a pile of clothes a thin steel object, some five or six inches in length, wound round with a fine, strong twine. This he slipped into his pocket and, going down into the hall, rang up the manager of the Lewes branch of the Southern Counties and Brown's Bank.

Passing into the library, he searched the drawers of the table at which Mr. Challoner had been found. In one of them he discovered the pass–book. Seating himself at the table, he proceeded to examine it carefully. Turning to the pockets at either end, where cancelled cheques are usually placed, he found both were empty.

When a few minutes later Sir James and Thompson entered with the finger–prints, Malcolm Sage was seated at the table smoking, his gaze concentrated upon the nail of the fourth finger of his right hand. With him a contemplation of his finger–nails in general indicated thoughtful attention; when, however, he raised the hand and began to subject some particular finger–nail to a thorough and elaborate examination, it generally meant the germination of some constructive thesis.

Taking the sheets of paper from Thompson, he went through them rapidly, then drawing a sheet of note–paper from the rack before him he scribbled a hasty note, enclosed it with one of the finger–prints in an envelope, which he sealed, addressed, and handed to Thompson with instructions to see that it was delivered without delay. He also told him to send Peters and Dane to the library.

Three minutes later Tims swung down the drive, his face beaming. He was to drive to Scotland Yard and "never mind the poultry on the road," as Thompson had phrased it.

Have you the key of the safe, Mr. Dane?" enquired Malcolm Sage as the young man entered, followed by Peters. Dane shook his head and looked at Peters.

"Mr. Challoner always wore it on his key–chain, sir," said the butler.

"Have you any objection to the safe being opened?" enquired Malcolm Sage of Dane.

"None whatever."

"Then perhaps you will open it?" said Malcolm Sage, turning to Sir James.

In the safe were found several bundles of letters and share–certificates, and an old cash–box containing some loose stamps; but nothing else.

Malcolm Sage dismissed Peters and Dane, saying that he would be returning to town after dinner. In the meantime he and Sir James strolled about the grounds, discussing the remarkable rise in the chess–world of Capablanca, whilst Dawkins was busily occupied in a darkened bath–room.

Dinner proved a far less sombre meal than luncheon. Malcolm Sage and Sir James between them succeeded in placing young Dane more at his ease. The haunted, shell–shock look left his eyes, and the twitching disappeared from the corners of his mouth.

It was nearly nine o'clock when the distant moan of a–hooter announced to Malcolm Sage's alert ears the return of Tims. He rose from the table and walked slowly to the door, where for some seconds he stood with his hand upon the knob.

As the car drew up he slipped into the hall, just as Peters opened the door.

28

Malcolm Sage, Detective

A moment later the butler started back, his right hand seemed to fly to his left breast pocket. At the same moment Malcolm Sage sprang forward. There was a flash, a report, and two bodies fell at the feet of Inspector Wensdale, of Scotland Yard, and another man standing beside him.

In a second, however, they had thrown themselves upon the struggling heap, and when Malcolm Sage rose to his feet it was to look down upon Peters pinned to the floor by the inspector, with the strange man sitting on his legs.

* * * * *

"There is no witness so sure as the camera," remarked Malcolm Sage as he gazed from one to the other of two photographs before him, one representing him holding an automatic to his own head, and the other in which Sir James was posing as a murderer. "It is strange that it should be so neglected at Scotland Yard." he added.

Silent and absorbed when engaged upon a problem, Malcolm Sage resented speech as a sick man resents arrowroot. At other times he seemed to find pleasure in lengthy monologues, invariably of a professional nature.

"But we use it a lot, Mr. Sage," protested Inspector Wensdale.

"For recording the features of criminals," was the retort. "No, Wensdale, you are obsessed by the finger–print heresy, quite regardless of the fact that none but an amateur ever leaves such a thing behind him, and the amateur is never difficult to trace."

He paused for a moment; but the inspector made no comment.

"The two greatest factors in the suppression of crime," continued Malcolm Sage, "are photography and finger–prints. Both are in use at Scotland Yard; but each in place of the other. Finger–prints are regarded as clues, and photography is a means of identification, whereas finger–prints are of little use except to identify past offenders, and photography is the greatest aid to the tracing of the criminal."

Malcolm Sage never failed to emphasise the importance of photography in the detection of crime. He probably used it more than all other investigators put together. He contended

29

that a photographic print established for all time what the eye could only dimly register for the moment, with the consequent danger of forgetfulness.

As the links in a chain multiplied, it was frequently necessary to refer to the scene of a crime, or tragedy, and then probably some important point would crop up, which the eye had not considered of sufficient importance to dwell upon. By then, in the case of a murder, the body would have been removed, and everything about it either re–ordered or obliterated.

Malcolm Sage proceeded to stuff his pipe with tobacco which he drew from the left–hand pocket of his jacket. He had discovered that a rubber–lined pocket was the best and safest pouch.

He picked up a third photograph and laid it beside the others. It was a print of Mr. Challoner's head, showing, marked in white, the course of the bullet towards the left of the frontal bone.

"A man shooting himself," began Malcolm Sage, "places the pistol in a position so that the muzzle is directed towards the back of the head. On the other hand, anyone approaching his victim from behind would have a tendency to direct the muzzle towards the front of the head. That is why I got Dawkins to take a photograph of me holding the pistol to my head and of you holding it from behind. These photographs will constitute the principal evidence at the trial."

Sir James nodded. He was too interested to interrupt.

"On this enlargement of the wound," continued Malcolm Sage, "you will see an abrasion on the side nearer the ear, as if the head had suddenly been jerked backwards between the time of the muzzle being placed against the temple and the actual firing of the shot."

Thompson leaned across to examine the photograph.

"If the eyes of some one sitting at a table are suddenly and unexpectedly covered from behind, the natural instinct is to jerk backwards so that the head may be turned to see who it is. That is exactly what occurred with Challoner. He jerked backwards, and the barrel of the pistol grazed the skin and was deflected still more towards the frontal bone."

Malcolm Sage, Detective

Sir James and Thompson exchanged glances. Dawkins stood by, a look of happiness in his eyes. His beloved camera was justifying itself once more. Inspector Wensdale breathed heavily.

"Apart from all this, the position of the head on the table, and the way in which the hand was holding the pistol, not to speak of the curve of the arm, were unnatural. You get some idea of this from the photograph that Dawkins took of me, although I could only simulate death by relaxing the muscles. Again, the head would hardly be likely to twist on to its side."

"The doctor ought to have seen that," said the inspector.

"Another thing against the theory of suicide was that the second joint of the first finger was pressing against the trigger. Mr. Challoner was an expert shot, and would instinctively have used the pad of the finger, not the second joint.

"The next step," continued Malcolm Sage, "was how could anyone get into the room and approach Challoner without being heard or sensed."

"He must have been very much absorbed in what he was doing," suggested Sir James.

Malcolm Sage shook his head, and for a few seconds gazed at the photographs before him.

"You will remember there was nothing on the table in front of him. I shall come to that presently. It is very unlikely that a man sitting at a table would not be conscious of me one approaching him from behind, no matter how quietly he stepped, unless that man's presence in the room were quite, a normal and natural thing. That gave me the clue to Peters. He is the only person who could be in the library without Challoner taking any notice of him. Consequently it was easy for him to approach his master and shoot him."

"But the locked door, sir," said Thompson.

"That is a very simple matter. An ordinary lead–pencil, with a piece of string tied to one end, put through the ring of the key to act as a lever, the cord being passed beneath the door, will lock any door in existence. The pencil can then be drawn under the door. This will show how it's done." Malcolm Sage reached across for a sheet of paper, and drew a rough sketch.

"That is why you examined the under–edge of the door." suggested Sir James.

Malcolm Sage nodded. "The marks of the cord were clearly defined and reflected in the mirror. Had the key been touched, it would have helped."

"How?" asked Inspector Wensdale.

"By means of the string the key is turned only just the point where the lever falls through the hole to the floor The fingers would turn beyond that point, not being delicate."

"Mr. Sage, you're a wonder," burst out the inspector.

"I then," proceeded Malcolm Sage, "examined all the other doors in the house, and I found that of one room, which I after discovered to be Peters', was heavily scored at the bottom. He had evidently practised fairly extensively before putting the plan into operation. He had also done the same thing with the library door, as there were marks of more than one operation. Furthermore, he was wiser than to take the risk of so clumsy a tool as a lead–pencil. He used this."

Malcolm Sage drew from his pocket the roll of twine with the thin steel instrument down the centre. It was a canvas–needle, to the eye of which the cord was attached.

"This was absolutely safe," he remarked. "Another thing I discovered was that one lock, and only one lock in the house, had recently been oiled–that of the library–door."

Sir James nodded his head several times. There was something of self–reproach in the motion.

"Now," continued Malcolm Sage, "we come back to why a man should be sitting at a table absorbed in gazing at nothing, and at a time when most of the household are either in bed or preparing for bed."

"Peters said that he was checking his pass–book," suggested Sir James.

"That is undoubtedly what he was doing," continued Malcolm Sage, "and Peters removed the pass–book, put it in a drawer, first destroying the cancelled cheques. He made a blunder in not replacing the pass–book with something else. That was the last link in the chain," he added.

"1 don't quite see—" began Sir James.

"Perhaps you did not read of a case that was reported from New York some eighteen months ago. It was very similar to that of Mr. Challoner. A man was found shot through the head, the door being locked on the inside, and a verdict of suicide was returned; but there was absolutely a reason why he should have taken his life. What actually happened was that Mr. Challoner went to the bank to draw five hundred pounds with which he hoped to bribe his nephew's fiancee. He trusted to the temptation of actual money rather than a cheque. When he was at the bank the manager once more asked him to return his pass–book, which had not been balanced for several months. He was very dilatory in such matters."

"That is true," said Dane, speaking for the first time.

"That evening he proceeded to compare it with his chequebook. I suspect that Peters had been forging cheques and he saw here what would lead to discovery. Furthermore, there was a considerable sum of money in the safe, and the quarrel between uncle and nephew to divert suspicion. This, however, was mere conjecture–that trouser–pocket photo. Dawkins," said Malcolm Sage, turning to the photographer, who handed it across to him.

"Now notice the position of these keys. They are put in head foremost, and do not reach the bottom of the pocket. They had obviously been taken away and replaced in the pocket as Challoner sat there. Had he gone to the safe himself and walked back to his chair, the position of the keys would have been quite different."

Instinctively each man felt in his trousers pocket, and found in his own bunch of keys a verification of the statement.

"The whole scheme was too calculated and deliberate for an amateur," said Malcolm Sage, knocking the ashes out of his pipe on to a brass ash–tray. "That is what prompted me to get the finger–prints of Peters, so that I might send them to Scotland Yard to see if anything was known of him there. The result you have seen."

"We've been on the look—out for him for more than a year," said Inspector Wensdale. "The New York police are rather interested in him about a forgery stunt that took place there some time ago."

"I am confident that when Challoner's affairs are gone into there will be certain cheques which it will be difficult to explain. Then again—there was the electric light," proceeded Malcolm Sage. "A man about to blow out his brains would certainly not walk across the room, switch off the light, and then find his way back to the table."

"That's true enough," said Inspector Wensdale. "On the other hand, a murderer, who has to stand at a door for at least some seconds, would not risk leaving on the light, which would attract the attention of anyone who might by chance be in the hall, or on the stairs."

Inspector Wensdale caught Thompson's left eye, which deliberately closed and then re—opened. There was a world of meaning in the movement.

"Well, I'm glad I didn't get you down on a fool's errand, Sage," said Sir James, rising. "I wonder what the local inspector will think."

"He won't," remarked Malcolm Sage; "that is why he assumed it was suicide."

"Did you suspect Peters was armed?" enquired Sir James.

"I saw the pistol under his left armpit," said Malcolm Sage. "It's well known with American gun—men as a most convenient place for quick drawing."

"If it hadn't been for you, Mr. Sage, he'd have got me," said Inspector Wensdale.

"There'll be a heavy car—full for Tims," remarked Malcolm Sage, as he walked towards the door.

CHAPTER IV. THE SURREY CATTLE–MAIMING MYSTERY

"DISGUISE," Malcolm Sage had once remarked, "is the chief characteristic of the detective of fiction. In actual practice it is rarely possible. I am a case in point. No one but a builder, or an engineer, could disguise the shape of a head like mine"; as he spoke he had stroked the top of his head, which rose above his strongly–marked brows like a down–covered cone.

He maintained that a disguise can always be identified, although not necessarily penetrated. This in itself would be sufficient to defeat the end of the disguised man by rendering him an object of suspicion. Few men can disguise their walk or stance, no matter how clever they might be with false beards, grease–paint and wigs.

In this Malcolm Sage was a bitter disappointment to William Thompson, the office junior. His conception of the sleuth had been tinctured by the vivid fiction with which he beguiled his spare time.

In the heart of William Johnson there were three great motions: his hero–worship of Malcolm Sage, his romantic devotion to Gladys Norman, and his wholesome fear of the robustious humour of Tims.

In his more imaginative moments he would create a world in which he was the recognised colleague of Malcolm Sage, the avowed admirer of Miss Norman, and the austere employer of Tims–chauffeurs never took liberties with the hair of their employers, no matter how knut–like it might be worn.

It was with the object of making sure of the first turret of his castle in Spain, that William Johnson devoted himself to the earnest study of what he conceived to be his future profession.

He read voraciously all the detective stories and police–reports he came across. Every moment he could snatch from his official duties he devoted to some scrap of paper, booklet or magazine. He strove to cultivate his reasoning powers. Never did a prospective client enter the Malcolm Sage Bureau without automatically setting into operation William Johnson's mental induction–coil. With eyes that were covertly keen, he would examine the visitor as he sat waiting for the two sharp buzzes on the private telephone which indicated that Malcolm Sage was at liberty.

It mattered little to William Johnson that error seemed to dog his footsteps; that he had "deduced" a famous pussyfoot admiral as a comedian addicted to drink; a lord, with a ten−century lineage, as a man selling something or other; a Cabinet Minister as a company promoter in the worst sense of the term; nothing could damp his zeal.

Malcolm Sage's "cases" he studied as intimately as he could from his position as junior; but they disappointed him. They seemed lacking in that element of drama he found so enthralling in the literature he read and the films he saw.

Malcolm Sage would enter the office as Malcolm Sage, and lrave it as Malcolm Sage, as obvious and as easily recognisable as St. Paul's Cathedral. He seemed indifferent to the dramatic possibilities of disguise.

William Johnson longed for some decrepit and dirty old man or woman to enter the Bureau, selling boot−laces or bananas and, on being peremptorily ordered out, to see the figure suddenly straighten itself, and hear his Chief's well−known voice remark, "So you don't recognise me, Johnson−good." There was romance.

He yearned for a "property−room," where executive members of the staff would disguise themselves beyond recognition. In his more imaginative moments he saw come out from that mysterious room a full−blooded Kaffir, whereas he knew that only Thompson had entered.

He would have liked to see Miss Norman shed her pretty brunetteness and reappear as an old apple−woman, who besought him to buy of her wares. He even saw himself being transformed into a hooligan, or a smart R.A.F. officer, complete with a tooth−brush moustache and "swish."

In his own mind he was convinced that, given the opportunity, he could achieve greatness as a master of disguise, rivalling the highly−coloured stories of Charles Peace. He had even put his theories to the test.

Malcolm Sage, Detective

One evening as Miss Norman, who had been working late, was on her way to Charing Cross Underground Station, she was accosted by a youth with upturned collar, wearing a shabby cap and a queer Charlie Chaplain moustache that was not on straight. In a husky voice he enquired his way to the Strand.

"Good gracious, Johnnie!" she cried involuntarily. "What on earth's the matter?"

A moment later, as she regarded the vanishing form of William Johnson, she wanted to kill herself for her lack of tact.

"Poor little Innocent!" she had murmured as she continued down Villiers Street, and there was in her eyes a reflection of the tears she had seen spring to those of William Johnson, whose first attempt at disguise had proved so tragic a failure.

Neither ever referred to the incident subsequently—although for days William Johnson experienced all the unenviable sensations of Damocles.

From that moment his devotion to Gladys Norman had become almost worship.

But William Johnson was not deterred, either by his own signal failure or his chief's opinion. He resolutely stuck to his own ideas, and continued to expend his pocket—money on tinted glasses, false—moustaches and grease paint; for hidden away in the inner recesses of his mind was the conviction that it was not quite playing the game, as the game should be played, to solve a mystery or bring a criminal to justice without having recourse to disguise.

It was to him as if Nelson had won the Battle of Trafalgar in a soft hat and a burberry, or Wellington had met Blucher in flannels and silk socks.

Somewhere in the future he saw himself the head of a "William Johnson Bureau," and in the illustrated papers a portrait of "Mr. William Johnson as he is," and beneath it a series of characters that would rival a Dickens novel, with another legend reading, "Mr. William Johnson as he appears."

With these day—dreams, the junior at the Malcolm Sage Bureau would occupy the time when not actually engaged either in the performance of his by no means arduous duties,

37

or in reading the highly–coloured detective stories from which he drew his inspiration.

From behind the glass–panelled door would come the tick–tack of Miss Norman's typewriter, whilst outside droned the great symphony of London, growing into a crescendo as the door was opened, dying away again as it fell to once more, guided by an automatic self–closer.

From these reveries William Johnson would be aroused either by peremptory blasts upon the buzzer of the private–telephone, or by the entry of a client.

One morning, as he was hesitating between assuming the disguise of a naval commander and a street–hawker, a florid little man with purple jowl and a white, bristling moustache hurtled through the swing–door, followed by a tall, spare man, whose clothing indicated his clerical calling.

"Mr. Sage in?" demanded the little man fiercely.

"Mr. Sage is engaged, sir," said the junior, his eyes upon the clergyman, in whose appearance there was something that caused William Johnson to like him on the spot. "Interrupt him," said the little, bristly man. "Tell him that General Sir John Hackblock wishes to see him immediately." The tone was suggestive of the parade–ground rather than a London office.

At that moment Gladys Norman appeared through the glass–panelled door. The clergyman immediately removed his hat, the general merely turned as if changing front receive a new foe.

"Mr. Sage will be engaged for about a quarter of an hour. I am his secretary," she explained. She, also, looked at the general's companion, wondering what sort of teeth were behind that gentle, yet firm mouth. "Perhaps you will take a seat," she added.

This time the clergyman smiled, and Gladys Norman knew that she too liked him. Sir John looked about him aggressively, blew out his cheeks several times, then flopped into a chair. His companion also seated himself, and appeared to become lost in a fit of abstraction.

Malcolm Sage, Detective

William Johnson returned to his table and became engrossed, ostensibly in the exploits of an indestructible trailer of men; but really in a surreptitious examination of the two callers.

He had just succeeded in deducing from their manner that they were father and son, and from the boots of the younger that he was low church and a bad walker, when two sharp blasts on the telephone–buzzer brought him to his feet and half–way across the office in what was practically one movement. With Malcolm Sage there were two things to be avoided, delay in answering a summons, and unnecessary words.

"This way, sir," he said, and led them through the glass–panelled door to Malcolm Sage's private room.

With a short, jerky movement of his head Malcolm Sage motioned his visitors to be seated. In that one movement his steel–coloured eyes had registered a mental photograph of the two men. That glance embraced all the details; the dark hair of the younger, greying at the temples, the dreamy grey eyes, the gentle curves of a mouth that was, nevertheless, capable of great sternness, and the spare, almost lean frame; then the self–important, over–bearing manner of the older man. "High Anglican, ascetic, out–of–doors," was Malcolm Sage's mental classification of the one, thus unconsciously reversing the William Johnson's verdict. The other he dismissed as a pompous ass.

"You Mr. Sage?" Sir John regarded the bald conical head and gold–rimmed spectacles as if they had been unpolished buttons on parade.

Malcolm Sage inclined his head slightly, and proceeded to look down at his fingers spread out on the table before him. After the first appraising glance he rarely looked at a client.

"I am Sir John Hackblock; this is my friend, the Rev. Geoffrey Callice." Again a slight inclination of the head indicated that Malcolm Sage had heard.

Mr Llewellyn John would have recognised in Sir John Hackblock the last man in the world who should have been brought into contact with Malcolm Sage. The Prime Minister's own policy had been to keep Malcolm Sage from contact with other Ministers, and thus reduce the number of his embarrassing resignations.

Malcolm Sage, Detective

"I want to consult you about a most damnable outrage," exploded the general. "It's inconceivable that in this—"

"Will you kindly be as brief as possible?" said Malcolm Sage, fondling the lobe of his left ear. "I can spare only a few minutes."

Sir John gasped, glared across at him angrily; then, seeming to take himself in hand, continued: "You've heard of the Surrey cattle–maiming outrages?" he enquired.

Malcolm Sage nodded.

"Well, this morning a brood–mare of mine was found hacked about in an unspeakable manner. Oh, the damn scoundrels!" he burst out as he jumped from his chair and began pacing up and down the room.

"I think it will be better if Mr. Callice tells me the details," said Malcolm Sage, evenly. "You seem a little over–wrought."

"Over–wrought!" cried Sir John. "Over–wrought! Dammit, so would you be if you had lost over a dozen beasts." In the army he was known as "Dammit Hackblock."

Mr. Callice looked across to the general, who, nodding acquiescence, proceeded to blow his nose violently, as if to bid Malcolm Sage defiance.

"This morning a favourite mare belonging to Sir John was found mutilated in a terrible manner—" Mr. Callice paused; there was something in his voice that caused Malcolm Sage to look up. The gentle look had gone from his face, his eyes flashed, and his mouth was set in a stern, severe line. A good preacher, Malcolm Sage decided as he dropped his eyes once more, and upon his blotting pad proceeded to develop the Pons Asinorum into a church.

In a voice that vibrated with feeling and suggested great self–restraint, Mr. Callice proceeded to tell the story of the latest outrage. How when found that morning the mare was still alive, of the terrible nature of her injuries, and that the perpetrator had disappeared leaving no trace.

"Her look, sir! Dammit!" the general broke in. "Her eyes have haunted me ever since. They—" His voice broke, and he proceeded once more to blow his nose violently

Mr. Callice went on to explain that after having seen the mare put out of her misery, Sir John had motored over to his lodgings and insisted that they should go together to Scotland Yard and demand that something be done.

"Callice is Chairman of the Watchers' Committee," broke in Sir John.

"I should explain," proceeded Mr. Callice. "that some time ago we formed ourselves into a committee to patrol the neighbourhood at night in the hope of tracing the criminal. On the way up Sir John remembered hearing of you in connection with Department Z and, as he was not satisfied with his call at Scotland Yard, he decided to come on here and place the matter in your hands."

"This is the twenty–ninth maiming?" Malcolm Sage remarked, as he proceeded to add a graveyard to the church.

"Yes, the first occurred some two years ago." Then, as if suddenly realising what Malcolm Sage's question implied, he added: "You have interested yourself in the affair?"

"Yes," was the reply. "Tell me what has been done."

"The police seem utterly at fault," continued Mr. Callice. "Locally we have organised watch–parties. My boys and I have been out night after night; but without result. I am a scoutmaster," he explained.

"The poor beasts' sufferings are terrible," he continued after a–slight pause. "It is a return to barbarism"; again there was the throb of indignation in his voice.

"You have discovered nothing?"

"Nothing," was the response, uttered in a tone of deep despondency. "We have even tried bloodhounds; but without result."

Malcolm Sage, Detective

"And now I want you to take up the matter, and don't care what the expense," burst out Sir John, unable to contain himself.

"I will consider the proposal and let you know," said Malcolm Sage, evenly. "As it is, my time is fully occupied at present; but later—" He never lost an opportunity of resenting aggression by emphasising the democratic tendency of the times. Mr. Llewellyn John had called it "incipient Bolshevism."

"Later!" cried Sir John in consternation. "Why, dammit, sir, there won't be an animal left in the county. This thing has been going on for two years now, and those damn fools at Scotland Yard—"

"If it were not for Scotland Yard," said Malcolm Sage quietly, as he proceeded to shingle the roof of the church, the graveyard having proved a failure, "we should probably have to sleep at night with pistols under our pillows."

"Eh!" Sir John looked across at him with a startled expression.

"Scotland Yard is the headquarters of the most efficient and highly−organised police force in the world," was the quiet reply.

"But, dammit! if they're so clever why don't they put a stop to this torturing of poor dumb beasts?" cried the general indignantly. "I've shown them the man. It's Hinds; I know it. I've just been to see that fellow Wensdale. Why, dammit! he ought to be cashiered, and I told him so."

"Who is Hinds?" Malcolm Sage addressed the question to Mr. Callice.

"He used to be Sir John's head gamekeeper——"

"And I discharged him," exploded the general. "I'll shoot a poacher or his dog; but, dammit! I won't set traps for them," and he purred out his cheeks aggressively.

"Hinds used to set traps to save himself the trouble of patrolling the preserves," explained Mr. Callice, "and one day Sir John discovered him actually watching the agonies of a dog caught across the hind−quarters in a man−trap." Again there−was a wave of feeling in the

42

voice, and a stern set about the mouth.

"It's Hinds right enough," cried the general with conviction. "The man's a brute. Now will you—?"

I will let you know as soon as possible whether or not I can take up the enquiry," said Malcolm Sage, rising. "That is the best I can promise."

"But—" began Sir John; then he–stopped and stared at Malcolm Sage as he moved towards the door.

"Dammit! I don't care what it costs," he spluttered explosively. "It'll be worth five hundred pounds to the man who catches the scoundrel. Poor Betty," he added in a softer tone.

"I will write to you shortly," said Malcolm Sage. There was dismissal in his tone.

With darkened jowl and bristling moustache Sir John strutted towards the door. Mr. Callice paused to shake hands with Malcolm Sage, and then followed the general, who, with a final glare at William Johnson, as he held open the swing–door, passed out into the street, convinced that now the country was no longer subject to conscription it would go rapidly to the devil.

For the next half–hour Malcolm Sage pored over a volume of press–cuttings containing accounts of previous cattle–maimings.

Following his usual custom in such matters, he had caused the newspaper accounts of the various mutilations to be collected and pasted in a press–cutting book. Sooner or later he had determined to devote time to the affair.

Without looking up from the book he pressed three times in rapid succession a button of the private–telephone. Instantly Gladys Norman appeared, notebook in hand. She had been heard to remark that if she were dead "three on the buzzer" would bring her to life again.

Malcolm Sage, Detective

"Whitaker and Inspector Wensdale," said Malcolm Sage, his eyes still on the book before him.

When deep in a problem Malcolm Sage's economy in words made it difficult for anyone but his own staff to understand his requirements.

Without a word the girl vanished and, a moment later, William Johnson placed Whitaker's Almanack on the table, then he in turn disappeared as silently as Gladys Norman.

Malcolm Sage turned to the calendar, and for some time studied the pages devoted to the current month (June) and July. As he closed the book there were three buzzes from the house–telephone, the signal that he was through to the number required. Drawing the pedestal–instrument towards him, he put the receiver to his ear.

"That Inspector Wensdale?–Yes! Mr. Sage speaking. It's about the cattle–maiming business.–I've just heard of it. I've not decided yet. I want a large–scale map of the district, with the exact spot of each outrage indicated, and the date.–To–morrow will do.–Yes, come round. Give me half an hour with the map first."

Malcolm Sage replaced the receiver as the buzzer sounded announcing another client.

* * * * *

"So there is nothing?" Malcolm Sage looked up enquiringly from the map before him.

"Nothing that even a stage detective could turn into a clue," said Inspector Wensdale, a big, clean–shaven man with hard, alert eyes.

Malcolm Sage continued his study of the map.

"Confound those magazine detectives!" the inspector burst out explosively. "They've always got a dust–pan full of clues ready made for 'em."

"To say nothing of finger–prints," said Malcolm Sage dryly. He never could resist a sly dig at Scotland Yard's faith in finger–prints as clues instead of means of identification.

Malcolm Sage, Detective

"It's a bit awkward for me, too, Mr. Sage," continued the inspector, confidentially. "Last time The Daily Telegram went for us because—"

"You haven't found a dust—pan full of clues?" suggested Malcolm Sage, who was engaged in forming geometrical designs with spent matches.

"They're getting a bit restive, too, at the Yard," he continued. He was too disturbed in mind for flippancy. "It was this cattle—maiming business that sent poor old Scott's number up," he added, referring to Detective Inspector Scott's failure to solve the mystery. "Now the general's making a terrible row. Threatens me with the Commissioner."

For some seconds Malcolm Sage devoted himself to his designs. "Any theory?" he enquired at length, without looking up.

"I've given up theorising," was the dour reply.

In response to a further question as to what had been done, the inspector proceeded to detail how the whole neighbourhood had been scoured after each maiming, and how, night after night, watchers had been posted throughout the district but without result.

"I have had men out night and day," continued the inspector gloomily. "He's a clever devil, whoever he is. It's my opinion the man's a lunatic," he added.

Malcolm Sage looked up slowly.

"What makes you think that?" he asked.

"His cunning, for one thing," was the reply. "Then it's so senseless. No," he added with conviction, "he's no more an ordinary man than Jack—the—Ripper was."

He went on to give details of his enquiries among those living in the district. There was absolutely nothing to attach even the remotest suspicion to any particular person. Rewards had been offered for information; but all without producing the slightest evidence or clue.

Malcolm Sage, Detective

"This man Hinds?" enquired Malcolm Sage, looking about for more matches.

"Oh! the general's got him on the brain. Absolutely nothing in it. I've turned him inside out. Why, even the Deputy Commissioner had a go at him, and if he can get nothing out of a man, there's nothing to get out."

"Well," said Malcolm Sage rising, "keep the fact to yourself that I am interested. I suppose, if necessary, you could arrange for twenty or thirty men to run down there?" he queried.

"The whole blessed Yard if you like, Mr. Sage," was the feeling reply.

"We'll leave it at that for the present then. By the way, if you happen to think you see me in the neighbourhood you needn't remember that we are acquainted."

The inspector nodded comprehendingly and, with a heart lightened somewhat of its burden, he departed. He had an almost child–like faith in Malcolm Sage.

For half an hour Malcolm Sage sat engrossed in the map of the scene of the maimings. On it were a number of red–ink crosses with figures beneath. In the left–hand bottom corner was a list of the various outrages, with the date and the time, as near as could be approximated, against each.

The numbers in the bottom corner corresponded with those beneath the crosses. From time to time he referred to the two copies of Whitaker's Almanack open before him, and made notes upon the writing–pad at his side. Finally he ruled a square upon the map and then drew two lines diagonally from corner to corner. Then–without looking up from the map, he pressed the buttons of the private–telephone. "Tims," he said through the mouthpiece.

Five minutes later Malcolm Sage's chauffeur was standing opposite his Chief's table, ready to go anywhere and do anything.

"To–morrow will be Sunday, Tims."

"Yessir."

Malcolm Sage, Detective

"A day of rest."

"Yessir!"

"We are going out to Hempdon, near Selford," Malcolm Sage continued, pointing to the map. Tims stepped forward and bent over to identify the spot. "The car will break down. It will take you or any other mechanic two hours to put it right."

"Yessir," said Tims, straightening himself.

"You understand," said Malcolm Sage, looking at him sharply, "you or any other mechanic?"

"Yessir," repeated Tims, his face sphinx–like in its lack of expression.

He was a clean–shaven, fleshless little man who, had he not been a chauffeur, would probably have spent his life with a straw between his teeth, hissing lullabies to horses.

"I shall be ready at nine," said Malcolm Sage, and with another "Yessir" Tims turned to go.

"And Tims."

"Yessir." He about–faced smartly on his right heel. "You might apologise for me to Mrs. Tims for depriving her of you on Sunday. Take her out to dinner on Monday and charge it to me."

"Thank you, sir, very much, sir," said Tims, his face expressionless.

"That is all, Tims, thank you."

Tims turned once more and left the room. As he walked towards the outer door he winked at Gladys Norman and, with a sudden dive, made a frightful riot of William Johnson's taut–like hair. Then, without change of expression, he passed out to tune up the car for its run on the morrow.

Malcolm Sage, Detective

Malcolm Sage's staff knew that when "the Chief" was what Tims called "chatty" he was beginning to see light, so Tims whistled loudly at his work: for he, like all his colleagues, was pleased when "the Chief" saw reason to be pleased.

The following morning, as they trooped out of church, the inhabitants of Hempdon were greatly interested in the breakdown of a large car, which seemed to defy the best efforts of the chauffeur to coax into movement. The owner drank cider at the Spotted Woodpigeon and talked pleasantly with the villagers, who, on learning that he had never even heard of the Surrey cattle–maimings, were at great pains to pour information and theories into his receptive ear.

The episode quite dwarfed the remarkable sermon preached by Mr. Callice, in which he exhorted his congregation to band themselves together to track down him who was maiming and torturing God's creatures, and defying the Master's merciful teaching.

It was Tom Hinds, assisted by a boy scout, who conducted Malcolm Sage to the scene of the latest outrage. It was Hinds who described the position of the mare when she was discovered, and it was he who pocketed two half–crowns as the car moved off Londonwards.

That evening Malcolm Sage sat long and late at his table, engrossed in the map that Inspector Wensdale had sent him.

Finally he subjected to a thorough and exhaustive examination the thumb–nail of his right hand. It was as if he saw in its polished surface the tablets of destiny.

The next morning he wrote a letter that subsequently caused Sir John Hackblock to explode into a torrent of abuse of detectives in general, and one investigator in particular. It stated in a few words that, owing to circumstances over which he had no control, Malcolm Sage would not be able to undertake the enquiry with which Sir John Hackblock had honoured him until the end of the month following. He hoped, however, to communicate further with his client soon after the 23rd of that month.

CHAPTER V. INSPECTOR WENSDALE IS SURPRISED

NEARLY a month had elapsed, and the cattle—maiming mystery seemed as far off solution as ever. The neighbourhood in which the crimes had been committed had once more settled down to its usual occupations, and Scotland Yard had followed suit.

Sir John Hackblock had written to the Chief Commissioner and a question had been asked in the House.

Inspector Wensdale's colleagues had learned that it was dangerous to mention in his presence the words "cattle" or "maiming." The inspector knew that the affair was referred to as "Wensdale's Waterloo," and his failure to throw light on the mystery was beginning to tell upon his nerves.

For three weeks he had received no word from Malcolm Sage. One morning on his arrival at Scotland Yard he was given a telephone message asking him to call round at the Bureau during the day.

"Nothing new?" queried Malcolm Sage ten minutes later, as the inspector was shown into his room by Thompson.

The inspector shook a gloomy head and dropped his heavy frame into a chair.

Malcolm Sage indicated with a nod that Thompson was to remain.

"Can you borrow a couple of covered government lorries?" queried Malcolm Sage.

"A couple of hundred if necessary," said the inspector dully.

"Two will be enough," was the dry rejoinder. "Now listen carefully, Wensdale. I want you to have fifty men housed some ten miles away from Hempdon on the afternoon of the 22nd. Select men who have done scouting, ex—boy scouts, for preference. Don't choose any with bald heads or with very light hair. See that they are wearing dark clothes and dark shirts and, above all, no white collars. Take with you a good supply of burnt cork such as is used by nigger minstrels."

49

Malcolm Sage, Detective

Malcolm Sage paused, and for the fraction of a second there was a curious fluttering at the corners of his mouth.

Inspector Wensdale was sitting bolt upright in his chair gazing at Malcolm Sage as if he had been requested to supply two lorry–loads of arch–angels.

"It will be moonlight, and caps might fall off," explained Malcolm Sage. "You cannot very well ask a man to black his head. Above all," he continued evenly, "be sure you give no indication to anyone why you want the men, and tell them not to talk. You follow me?" he queried.

"Yes," said the inspector, "I–I follow."

"Don't go down Hempdon way again, and tell no one in the neighbourhood; no one, you understand, is to know anything about it. Don't tell the general, for instance."

"Him!" There was a world of hatred and contempt in the inspector's voice. Then he glanced a little oddly at Malcolm Sage.

Malcolm Sage went on to elaborate his instructions. The men were to be divided into two parties, one to form a line north of the scene of the last outrage, and the other to be spread over a particular zone some three miles the other side of Hempdon. They were to blacken their faces and hands, and observe great care to show no light colouring in connection with their clothing. Thus they would be indistinguishable from their surroundings.

"You will go with one lot," said Malcolm Sage to the inspector, "and my man Finlay with the other. Thompson and I will be somewhere in the neighbourhood. You will be given a password for purposes of identification. You understand?"

"I think so," said the inspector in a tone which was suggestive that he was very far from understanding.

"I'll have everything typed out for you, and scale–plans of where you are to post your men. Above all, don't take anyone into your confidence."

Malcolm Sage, Detective

Inspector Wensdale nodded and looked across at Thompson, as if to assure himself that after all it really was not some huge joke.

"If nothing happens on the 22nd, we shall carry on on the second, third, and fourth nights. In all probability we shall catch our man on the 23rd."

"Then you know who it is?" spluttered the inspector in surprise.

"We shall know on the 23rd," said Malcolm Sage dryly, as he rose and walked towards the door. Taking the hint, Inspector Wensdale rose also and, with the air of a man not yet quite awake, passed out.

"You had better see him to—morrow, Thompson," said Malcolm Sage, "and explain exactly how the men are to be disposed. Make it clear that none must show themselves. If we actually see anyone in the act, they must track him, not try to take him." Thompson nodded his head comprehendingly. "Make it clear that they are there to watch; but I doubt if they'll see anything," he added.

At eleven o'clock on the night of July the 23rd, two motor lorries glided slowly along some three miles distant from one another. From their interiors silent forms dropped noiselessly on to the moon—white road. A moment later, slipping into the shadow of the hedge, they disappeared. All the previous night men had watched and waited; but nothing had happened. Now they were to try again.

Overhead the moon was climbing the sky, struggling against masses of cloud that from time to time swung themselves across her disc.

In the village of Hempdon all was quiet. The last light had been extinguished, the last dog had sent forth a final challenging bark, hoping that some neighbouring rival would answer and justify a volume of canine protest.

On the western side of the highway, and well behind the houses, two figures were standing in the shadow cast by a large oak. Their faces and hands were blackened, rendering them indistinguishable from their surroundings.

51

One wore a shade over a pair of gold–rimmed spectacles, a precaution against the moonlight being reflected on the lenses.

Half an hour, an hour, an hour and a half passed. They waited. Presently one gripped the arm of the other and pointed. At the back of the house immediately opposite there was a slight movement in the shade cast by a hedge. Then the line readjusted itself and the shadow vanished. A moment later it reappeared in a patch of moonlight, looking like a large dog.

Stooping low, Malcolm Sage and Thompson followed the dog–like form, themselves taking advantage of every patch of shadow and cover that offered.

The mysterious form moved along deliberately and without haste, now disappearing in the shadow cast by some tree or bush, now reappearing once more on the other side.

It was obviously taking advantage of everything that tended to conceal its movements.

Once it disappeared altogether, and for five minutes the two trackers lay on their faces and waited.

"Making sure he's not being followed," whispered Thompson, and Malcolm Sage nodded.

Presently the figure appeared once more and, as if reassured continued its slow and deliberate way.

Once a dog barked, a short, sharp bark of uncertainty. Again there was no sign of the figure for some minutes. Then it moved out from the surrounding shadows and continued its stealthy progress.

Having reached the outskirts of the village, it continued its crouching course along the western side of the hedge flanking the roadside.

Malcolm Sage and Thompson followed under the shadow of a hedge running parallel.

Malcolm Sage, Detective

For a mile the slow and laborious tracking continued. Suddenly Malcolm Sage stopped. In the field on their right two horses were grazing in the moonlight. It was the scene of the tragedy of the month previous!

For some minutes they waited expectantly. Suddenly Malcolm Sage gripped Thompson's arm and pointed. From under the hedge a dark patch was moving slowly towards the nearer of the two animals. It was apparently the form of a man, face downwards, wriggling along inch by inch without bending a limb.

"Get across. Cut off his retreat," whispered Sage. "Look out for the knife."

Thompson nodded and slid away under cover of the hedge separating the field in which the horses were from that along which the watchers had just passed.

Slowly the form approached its quarry. Once the horse lifted its head as though scenting danger; but the figure was approaching up–wind.

Suddenly it raised itself, appearing once more like a large dog. Then with a swift, panther–like movement it momentarily disappeared in the shadow cast by the horse.

There was a muffled scream and a gurgle, as the animal collapsed, then silence.

A minute later the form seemed to detach itself from the carcase and wriggled along towards the hedge, a dark patch upon the grass.

Malcolm Sage was already half–way through the second field, keeping well under the shelter of the hedge. He reached a spot where the intersecting hedge joined that running parallel with the high–road. There was a hole sufficiently large for a man to crawl through from one field to the other. By this Malcolm Sage waited, a life–preserver in his hand.

At the sound of the snapping of a twig, he gripped his weapon; a moment later a round, dark shape appeared through the hole in the hedge. Without hesitating Malcolm Sage struck.

Malcolm Sage, Detective

There was a sound, half grunt, half sob, and Malcolm Sage was on his feet gazing down at the strangest creature he had ever encountered.

Clothed in green, its face and hands smeared with some pigment of the same colour, lay the figure of a tall man. Round the waist was a belt from which was suspended in its case a Gurkha's kukri.

Malcolm Sage bent down to unbuckle the belt. He turned the man on his back. As he did so he saw that in his hand was a small, collapsible tin cup covered with blood, which also stained his lips and chin, and dripped from his hands, whilst the front of his clothing was stained in dark patches.

"I wonder who he is," muttered Thompson, as he gazed down at the strange figure.

"Locally he is known as the Rev. Geoffrey Callice," remarked Malcolm Sage quietly.

And Thompson whistled.

"And that damned scoundrel has been fooling us for years." Sir John Hackblock glared at Inspector Wensdale as if it were he who was responsible for the deception.

They were seated smoking in Sir John's library after a particularly early breakfast.

"I always said it was the work of a madman," said the inspector in self–defence.

"Callice is no more mad than I am," snapped Sir John. "I wish I were going to try him," he added grimly. "The scoundrel! To think—" His indignation choked him.

"He is not mad in the accepted sense," said Malcolm Sage as he sucked meditatively at his pipe. "I should say that it is a case of race–memory."

"Race–memory! Dammit! what's that?" Sir John Hackblock snapped out the words in his best parade–ground manner. He was more purple than ever about the jowl, and it was obvious that he was prepared to disagree with everyone and everything. As Lady Hackblock and her domestics would have recognised without difficulty, Sir John was angry.

"How the devil did you spot the brute?" he demanded, as Malcolm Sage did not reply immediately.

"Race–memory," he remarked, ignoring the question, "is to man what instinct is to animals; it defies analysis or explanation." Sir John stared; but it was Inspector Wensdale who spoke. "But how did you manage to fix the date, Mr. Sage?" he enquired.

"By the previous outrages," was the reply.

"The previous outrages!" cried Sir John. "Dammit! how did they help you?"

"They all took place about the time the moon was at full. There were twenty–eight in all." Malcolm Sage felt in his pocket and drew out a paper. "These are the figures."

In his eagerness Sir John snatched the paper from his hand, and with Inspector Wensdale looking over his shoulder, read:

Day before full moon —4 Full moon —15 Day after full moon —7 Second day after —2 Total–28

"Well, I'll damned!" exclaimed Sir John, looking up from the paper at Malcolm Sage, as if he had solved the riddle of the universe. The inspector's only comment was a quick indrawing of breath.

Sir John continued to stare at Malcolm Sage, the paper stiffly held in his hand.

"That made matters comparatively easy," continued Malcolm Sage. "The outrages were clearly not acts of revenge on any particular person; for they involved nine different owners. They were obviously the work of someone subject to a mania, or obsession, which gripped him when the moon was at the full."

"But how did you fix the actual spot?" burst out Inspector Wensdale excitedly.

"Each of the previous acts had been either in a diametrically opposite direction from that immediately preceding it, or practically on the same spot. For instance, the first three were north, east, and south of Hempdon, in the order named. Then the cunning of the

55

perpetrator prompted him to commit a fourth, not to the west; but to the south, within a few yards of the previous act. The criminal argued, probably subconsciously, that he would be expected to complete the square."

"But what made you fix on Hempdon as the headquarters of the blackguard?" enquired Sir John.

"That was easy," remarked Malcolm Sage, polishing the thumb—nail of his left hand upon the palm of his right.

"Easy!" The exclamation burst. involuntarily from the inspector.

"You supplied me with a large—scale map showing the exact spot where each of the previous maimings had taken place. I drew a square to embrace the whole. Lines drawn diagonally from corner to corner gave me the centre of gravity."

"But—" began the inspector.

Ignoring the interruption Malcolm Sage continued. "A man committing a series of crimes from a given spot was bound to spread his operations over a fairly wide area in order to minimise the chance of discovery. The longer the period and the larger the number of crimes, the greater the chance of his being located somewhere near the centre of his activities."

"Well, I'm damned!" remarked Sir John for the second time. Then suddenly turning to Inspector Wensdale, "Dammit!" he exploded, "why didn't you think of that?"

"There was, of course, the chance of his striking in another direction," continued Malcolm Sage, digging into the bowl of his pipe with a penknife, "so I placed the men in such a way that if he did so he was bound to be seen."

Inspector Wensdale continued to gaze at him, eager to hear more.

"But what was that you said about race—memory?" Sir John had quietened down considerably since Malcolm Sage had begun his explanation.

Malcolm Sage, Detective

"I should describe it as a harking back to an earlier phase. It is to the mind what atavism is to the body. In breeding, for instance"–Malcolm Sage looked across to Sir John–"you find that an offspring will manifest characteristics, or a taint, that is not to be found in either sire or dam."

Sir John nodded.

"Well, race–memory is the same thing in regard to the mental plane, a sort of subconscious wave of reminiscence. In Callice's case it was in all probability the memory of some sacrificial rite of his ancestors centuries ago."

"A case of heredity."

"Broadly speaking, yes. At the full moon this particular tribe, whose act Callice has reproduced, was in the habit of slaughtering some beast, or beasts, and drinking the blood, probably with the idea of absorbing their strength or their courage. Possibly the surroundings at Hempdon were similar to those where the act of sacrifice was committed in the past."

"It must be remembered that Callice was an ascetic, and consequently highly subjective. Therefore when the wave of reminiscence is taken in conjunction with the surroundings, the full moon and his high state of subjectivity, it is easy to see that material considerations might easily be obliterated. That is why I watched the back entrance to his lodgings."

"And all the time we were telling him our plans," murmured the inspector half to himself.

"Yes, and he would go out hunting himself," said Sir John. "Damn funny, I call it. Anyway, he'll get seven years at least."

"When he awakens he will remember nothing about it. You cannot punish a man for a subconscious crime." Sir John snorted indignantly; but Inspector Wensdale nodded his head slowly and regretfully.

D "Anyway, I owe you five' hundred pounds," said Sir John to Malcolm Sage; "and, dammit! it's worth it," he added.

Malcolm Sage shrugged his shoulders as he rose to go. "I was sorry to have to hit him," he said regretfully, "but I was afraid of that knife. A man can do a lot of damage with a thing like that. That's why I told you not to let your men attempt to take him, Wensdale."

"How did you know what sort of knife it was?" asked the inspector.

"Oh! I motored down here, and the car broke down. Incidentally I made a lot of acquaintances, including Callice's patrol-leader, a bright lad. He told me a lot of things about Callice and his ways. A remarkable product the boy scout," he added. "Kipling calls him 'the friend of all the world.'"

Sir John looked across at Inspector Wensdale, who was strongly tempted to wink.

"Don't think too harshly of Callice," said Malcolm Sage as he shook hands with' Sir John. "It might easily have been you or I, had we been a little purer in mind and thought."

And with that he passed out of the room with Inspector Wensdale followed by Sir John Hackblock, who was endeavouring to interpret the exact meaning of the remark.

"They said he was a clever devil," he muttered as he returned to the library after seeing his guests off, "and, dammit! they were right."

CHAPTER VI. THE STOLEN ADMIRALTY MEMORANDUM

WELL," cried Tims, one Saturday night, as he pushed open the kitchen door of the little flat he occupied over the garage. "How's the cook, the stove, and the supper?"

"I'm busy," said Mrs. Tims, a little, fair woman, with blue eyes, an impertinent nose, and the inspiration of neatness in her dress, as she altered the position of a saucepan on the stove and put two plates in the oven to warm.

This was the invariable greeting between husband and wife. Tims went up behind her, gripped her elbows to her side, and kissed her noisily.

"I told you I was busy," she said.

"You did, Emmelina," he responded. "I heard you say so, and how's his Nibs?"

The last remark was addressed to an object that was crawling towards him with incoherent cries and gurgles of delight. Stooping down, Tims picked up his eighteen–months–old–son and held him aloft, chuckling and mouthing his glee.

"You'll drop him one of these days," said Mrs. Tims, "and then there'll be a pretty hullaballoo."

"Well, he's fat enough to bounce," was the retort. "Ain't you, Jimmy?"

Neither Tims nor Mrs. Tims seemed to be conscious that without variations these same remarks had been made night after night, week after week, month after month.

"How's Mr. Sage?" was the question with which Mrs. Tims always followed the reference to the bouncing of Jimmy.

"Like Johnny Walker, still going strong," glibly came me reply, just as it came every other night. "He was asking about you to–day," added Tims.

"About me?" Mrs. Tims turned, all attention, her cooking for the time forgotten.

"Yes, wanted to know when I was going to divorce you."

"Don't be silly, Jim," she cried. "What did he say, really?" she added, as she turned once more to the stove.

"Oh! He asked if you were well," replied Tims, more interested in demonstrating with the person of his son how an aeroplane left the ground than in his wife's question.

"Anything else?" enquired Mrs. Tims, prodding a potato with a fork to see if it were done.

Tims was not deceived by the casual tone in which the question was asked. He was wont to say that, if his wife wanted his back teeth, she would get them.

Malcolm Sage, Detective

"Nothing, my dear, only to ask if his Nibs was flourishin'," and with a gurgle of delight the aeroplane soared towards the ceiling. Mrs. Tims had not forgotten the time when Malcolm Sage visited her several times when she was ill with pneumonia. She never tired of telling her friends of his wonderful knowledge of household affairs. He had talked to her of cooking, of childish ailments, of shopping, in a way that had amazed her. His knowledge seemed universal. He had explained to her among other things how cracknel biscuits were made and why croup was so swift in its action.

Tims vowed that the Chief had done her more good than the doctor, and from that day Malcolm Sage had occupied chief place in Mrs. Tims's valhalla.

"Quaint sort o' chap, the Chief," Tims would remark sometimes in connection with some professional episode.

"Pity you're not as quaint," would flash back the retort from Mrs. Tims, whose conception of loyalty was more literal than that of her husband.

Supper finished and his Nibs put to bed, Tims proceeded to enjoy his pipe and evening paper, whilst Mrs. Tims got out her sewing. From time to time Tims's eyes would wander over towards the telephone in the corner.

Finally he folded up the paper, and proceeded to knock out the ashes from his pipe preparatory to going to bed. His eyes took a last look at the telephone just as Mrs. Tims glanced up.

"Don't sit there watching that telephone!" she cried, "anyone would think you were wanting—"

'Brrrrrrr–brrrrrrrr–brrrrr," went the bell. "Now perhaps you're happy," cried Mrs. Tims as he rose to answer the call, whilst she put on the kettle to make hot coffee to fill the thermos flasks without which she never allowed the car to go out at night. It was her tribute to "the Chief".

In his more expansive moments Malcolm Sage would liken himself to a general practitioner in a disease–infected district It is true that there was no speaking–tube, with its terrifying whistle, a few feet from his head; but the telephone by his bedside was

60

always liable to arouse him from sleep at any hour of the night.

As Tims had folded up his newspaper with a view to bed Malcolm Sage was removing his collar before the mirror on his dressing–table, when his telephone bell rang. Rogers, his man, looked interrogatingly at his master, who, shaking his head, passed over to the instrument and took up the receiver.

"Yes, this is Malcolm Sage–Speaking–Yes." Then for a few minutes he listened with an impassive face. "I'll be off within ten minutes–The Towers, Holdingham, near Guildford—I understand."

While he was speaking, Rogers, a little sallow–faced man with fish–like eyes and expressionless face, had moved over to the other telephone and was droning in a monotonous, un–inflected voice, "Chief wants car in five minutes."

It was part of Malcolm Sage's method to train his subordinates to realise the importance of intelligent and logical inference.

Returning to the dressing–table, Malcolm Sage took up another collar, slipped a tie between the fold, and proceeded to put it on. As he did so he gave instructions to Rogers, who, note–book in hand, and with an expression of indifference that seemed to say "Kismet," silently recorded his instructions.

"My address will be The Towers, Holdingham, near Guildford. Be on the look–out for messages,"

Without a word Rogers closed the book and, picking up a suit–case, which was always ready for emergencies, he left the room. Two minutes later Malcolm Sage followed and, without a word, entered the closed car that had just drawn up before his flat in the Adelphi.

Rogers returned to the flat, switched the telephone on to his own room, and prepared himself for the night, whilst Malcolm Sage, having eaten a biscuit and drunk some of Mrs. Tims's hot coffee, lay back to sleep as the car rushed along the Portsmouth road.

Malcolm Sage, Detective

In the library at The Towers three men were seated, their faces lined and drawn as if some great misfortune had suddenly descended upon them; yet their senses were alert.

"He ought to be here any minute now," said Mr. Llewellyn John, the Prime Minister, taking out his watch for the hundredth time.

Sir Lyster Grayne, First Lord of the Admiralty, shook his head. "He should do it in an hour," said Lord Beamdale, the Secretary of War, "if he's got a man who knows the road."

"Sage is sure—" began Sir Lyster; then he stopped abruptly, and turned in the direction of the further window.

A soft tapping as of a finger–nail upon a pane of glass was clearly distinguishable. It ceased for a few seconds, recommenced, then ceased again.

Mr. Llewellyn John looked first at Sir Lyster and then on towards where Lord Beamdale sat, heavy of frame and impassive of feature.

Sir Lyster rose and walked quickly over to the window. As he approached the tapping recommenced. Swinging back the curtain he disappeared into the embrasure.

The others heard the sound of the window being raised and then closed again. A moment later Malcolm Sage appeared, followed by Sir Lyster, who once more drew the curtain.

At the sight of Malcolm Sage, Mr. Llewellyn John's features relaxed from their drawn, tense expression. A look of relief flashed momentarily into Lord Beamdale's fish–like eyes.

"Thank God you've come, Sage!" cried Mr. Llewellyn John, with a sigh of relief as he grasped Malcolm Sage's hand as if it had been a lifebelt and he a drowning man. "I think you have met Lord Beamdale," he added.

Malcolm Sage bowed to the War Minister, then with great deliberation removed his overcoat, carefully folded it, and placed it upon a chair, laying his cap on top. He then selected a chair at the table that gave him a dear view of the faces of the three Ministers, and sat down.

"Why did you come to the window?" enquired Sir Lyster as he resumed his own seat. "Did you know this was the library?"

"I saw a crack of light between the curtains," replied Malcolm Sage. "It may be desirable that no one should know I have been," he added.

"Something terrible has happened, Sage," broke in the Prime Minister, his voice shaking with excitement. He had with difficulty contained himself whilst Malcolm Sage was taking off his overcoat and explaining his reason for entering by the window. "It's–it's—" His voice broke.

"Perhaps Sir Lyster will tell me, or Lord Beamdale," suggested Malcolm Sage, looking from one to the other. Lord Beamdale shook his head.

"Just a bare outline, Sir Lyster," said Malcolm Sage, spreading out his fingers before him.

Slowly, deliberately, and with perfect self —possession, Sir Lyster explained what had happened.

"The Prime Minister and Lord Beamdale came down with me on Thursday night to spend the week–end," he said. "Incidentally we were to discuss a very important matter connected with this country's–er–foreign policy." The hesitation was only momentary. "Lord Beamdale brought with him a document of an extremely private nature. This I had sent to him earlier in the week for consideration and comment.

"If that document were to get to a certain Embassy in London no one can foretell the calamitous results. It might even result in another war, if not now certainly later. It was, I should explain, of a private and confidential nature, and consequently quite frankly expressed."

"And you must remember—" began Mr. Llewellyn John excitedly.

"One moment, sir," said Malcolm Sage quietly, without looking up from an absorbed contemplation of a bronze letter–weight fashioned in the form of a sphinx.

63

Malcolm Sage, Detective

Mr. Llewellyn John sank back into his chair and Sir Lyster resumed.

"Just over an hour and a half ago, that is to say soon after eleven o'clock, it was discovered that the document in question was missing and in its place had been substituted a packet of sheets of blank paper."

"Unless it's found, Sage," cried Mr. Llewellyn John, jumping from his chair in his excitement, "the consequences are too awful to contemplate."

For a few seconds he strode up and down the room, then turning to his chair, sank back into its comfortable depths. "Where was the document kept?" enquired Malcolm Sage, his long, sensitive fingers stroking the back of the sphinx.

"In the safe," replied Sir Lyster, indicating with a nod a small safe let into the wall.

"You are in the habit of using it for valuable documents?" queried Malcolm Sage.

"As a matter of fact very seldom. It is mostly empty." was the reply.

"Why?"

"I have a larger safe in my dressing–room, in which I keep my papers. During the day I occasionally use this to save going up and down stairs."

"Where do you keep the key?"

"When there is anything in the safe I always carry it about with me."

"And at other times?"

"Sometimes in a drawer in my writing–table," said Sir Lyster; "but generally I have it on me."

"When was the document put into the safe?"

"At a quarter to eight to–night, just as the second dressing–gong was sounding."

"And you yourself put it in, locked the door, and have retained the key ever since?" Malcolm Sage had exhausted the interest of the sphinx and was now drawing diagrams with his forefinger upon the morocco surface of the table.

Sir Lyster nodded. "I put the key in the pocket of my evening vest when I changed," he said. "After the other guests had retired, the Prune Minister raised a point that necessitated reference to the document itself. It was then I discovered the substitution."

But for that circumstance the safe would not have been opened until when?" queried Malcolm Sage.

Late to—night, when I should have transferred the packet to the safe in my dressing—room."

"Would you have examined the contents?"

"No. It is my rule to cut adrift from official matters from dinner—time on Saturday until after breakfast on Monday It was only in deference to the Prime Minister's particular wish that we referred to the document to—night."

"I take it that the rule you mention is known to your guests and servants?"

"Certainly."

"There is no doubt that it was the document itself that you put in the safe?"

"None; the Prime Minister and Lord Beamdale saw me do it."

"No doubt whatever," corroborated Mr. Llewellyn John, whilst Lord Beamdale wagged his head like a mandarin.

"Does anyone else know that it is missing?" asked Malcolm Sage after a short pause.

Sir Lyster shook his head.

"Only we three; and, of course, the thief," he added.

Malcolm Sage nodded. He had tired of the diagrams, and now sat stroking the back of his head.

"Has anyone left the house since the discovery; that is, as far as you know?" he queried at length.

"No one," said Sir Lyster.

"The servants, of course, have access to this room?"

"Yes; but only Walters, my butler, is likely to come here in the evening, except, of course, my secretary."

"Where does he dine?"

"'Miss Blair,'" corrected Sir Lyster, "always takes her meals in her own sitting–room, where she works. It is situated at the back of the house on the ground floor."

Again Malcolm Sage was silent, this time for a longer period.

"So far as you know, then," he said at length, addressing Sir Lyster, "only three people in the house were acquainted with the existence of the document; you, the Prime Minister, and Lord Beamdale."

Sir Lyster inclined his head.

"You are certain of that?" Malcolm Sage looked up swiftly and keenly. "Your secretary and Lady Grayne, for instance, they knew nothing about it?"

"Nothing; of that I am absolutely certain," replied Sir Lyster coldly.

"And the nature of the document?" enquired Malcolm Sage.

Sir Lyster looked across at Mr. Llewellyn John, who turned interrogatingly to Lord Beamdale. "I am afraid it is of too private a nature to—" he hesitated.

Malcolm Sage, Detective

"If you require me to trace something," said Malcolm Sage evenly, "you must at least tell me what that something is."

"It is a document which—" began Lord Beamdale, then he, too, paused.

"But, surely, Sage," broke in Mr. Llewellyn John, "it is not necessary to know the actual contents?"

"If you had lost something and would not tell me whether it was a dog or a diamond, would you expect me to find it?"

"But—" began Mr. Llewellyn John.

"I'm afraid we are wasting time, gentlemen," said Malcolm Sage, rising. "I would suggest Scotland Yard. The official police must work under any handicap imposed. I regret that I am unable to do so."

He walked across to the chair where lay his cap and coat.

"Now, Sage," said Mr. Llewellyn John tactfully, "you mustn't let us down, you really mustn't." Then turning to Sir Lyster, he said, "I can see his point. If he doesn't know the nature of the document, he cannot form a theory as to who is likely to have taken it. Perhaps under the circumstances, Grayne, we might take Sage into our confidence; at least to such extent as he thinks necessary."

Sir Lyster made ho response, whilst Lord Beamdale, whose economy in words had earned for him the sobriquet of "Lord Dumbeam," sat with impassive face.

"Perhaps I can help you," said Malcolm Sage, still standing by the chair on which lay his cap and coat. "At the end of every great war the Plans Departments of the Admiralty and the War Office are busy preparing for the next war. I suggest that this document was the Admiralty draft of a plan of operations to be put into force in the event of war occurring between this country and an extremely friendly power. It was submitted to the War Office for criticism and comment as far as land–operations were concerned. Another Power, unfriendly to the friendly power, would find in this document a very valuable red–herring to draw across the path of its own perplexities,"

Good heavens!" cried Mr. Llewellyn John, starting upright in his chair. "How on earth did you know?"

"It seems fairly obvious," said Malcolm Sage, as he returned to his chair and resumed his stroking of the sphinx's back. "Who else knew of the existence of the document?" he enquired.

"No one outside the Admiralty and the War—" Lyster stopped suddenly. From the corridor, apparently just outside the library door came the sound of a suppressed scream, followed by a bump against the woodwork.

Rising and moving swiftly across the room, Sir Lyster threw open the door, revealing a gap of darkness into which a moment later slid two figures, a pretty, fair–haired girl and a wizened little Japanese with large round spectacles and an automatic smile.

"I'm so sorry. Sir Lyster," faltered the girl, as she stepped timidly into the room, "but I was frightened. Some one had switched off the lights and I ran into—" She turned to the Japanese, who stood deprecating and nervous on the threshold. "I lose my passage," he said, baring his teeth still further; "I go to find cigarette–case of my master. He leave it in beelyard–room. I go—"

With a motion of his hand Sir Lyster dismissed the man, who slipped away as if relieved at getting off so lightly.

"You are up late. Miss Blair," he said coldly, turning to the girl.

"I'm so sorry," she said; "but Lady Grayne gave me some letters, and there was so much copying for–you that—" She paused, then added nervously, "I didn't know it was so late."

"You had better go to bed, now," said Sir Lyster. With a charming smile she passed out, Sir Lyster closing the door behind her. As he turned into the room his eye caught sight of the chair in which Malcolm Sage had been sitting.

"Where is Mr. Sage?" He looked from Mr. Llewellyn John to Lord Beamdale.

As he spoke Malcolm Sage appeared from the embrasure of the window through which he had entered, and where he had taken cover as Sir Lyster rose to open the door.

"You see. Sage is not supposed to be here." explained Mr. Llewellyn John.

"Your secretary has an expensive taste in perfume." remarked Malcolm Sage casually, as he resumed his seat. "It often characterises an intensely emotional nature," he added musingly.

"Emotional nature!" repeated Sir Lyster. "As a matter of fact she is extremely practical and self–possessed. You were saying—" he concluded with the air of a man who misses a trifling subject in favour of one of some importance.

"Diplomatists should be trained physiognomists," murmured Malcolm Sage. "A man's mouth rarely lies, a woman's never."

Sir Lyster stared. "Now," continued Malcolm Sage, "I should like to know who is staying here."

Sir Lyster proceeded to give some details of the guests and servants. The domestic staff comprised twenty–one, and none had been in Sir Lyster's employ for less than three years. They were all excellent servants, of irreproachable character, who had come to him with good references. Seventeen of the twenty–one lived in the house. There were also four lady's–maids and five men–servants attached to the guests. Among the men–servants was Sir Jeffrey Trawler's Japanese valet.

There was something in Sir Lyster's voice as he mentioned this fact that caused Malcolm Sage to look up at him sharply.

"The man you have just seen," Sir Lyster explained. "He has been the cause of some little difficulty in the servants'–hall. They object to sitting down to meals with a Chinaman, as they call him."

"He seems intelligent?" remarked Malcolm Sage casually.

Malcolm Sage, Detective

"On the contrary, he is an extremely stupid creature," was the reply. "He is continually losing himself. Only yesterday morning I myself found him wandering about the corridor leading to my bedroom. Walters has also mentioned the matter to me."

Sir Lyster then passed on to the guests. They comprised Mrs. Selton, an aunt of Sir Lyster; Sir Jeffrey and Lady Trawlor, old friends of their hostess; Lady Whyndale and her two daughters. There were also Mr. Gerald Nash, M.P., and Mr. and Mrs. Richard Winnington, old friends of Sir Lyster and Lady Grayne.

Later I may require a list of the guests," said Malcolm Sage, when Sir Lyster had completed his account. "You said, I think, that the key of the safe was sometimes left in an accessible place?"

"Yes, in a drawer."

"So that anyone having access to the room could easily have taken a wax impression."

Sir Lyster flushed slightly. "There is no one—" he began.

"There is always a potential someone," corrected Malcolm Sage, raising his eyes suddenly and fixing them full upon Sir Lyster.

"The question is, Sage," broke in Mr. Llewellyn John tactfully, "what are we to do?"

"I should first like to see the inside of the safe and the dummy packet," said Malcolm Sage, rising. "No, I will open it myself if you will give me the key," he added, as Sir Lyster rose and moved over to the safe.

Taking the key, Malcolm Sage kneeled before the safe door and, by the light of an electric torch, surveyed the whole of the surface with keen–sighted eyes. Then placing the key in the lock he turned it, and swung back the door, revealing a long official envelope as the sole contents. This he examined carefully without touching it, his head thrust inside the safe.

"Is this the same envelope as that in which the document was enclosed?" he enquired, without looking round.

The three men had risen and were grouped behind Malcolm Sage, watching him with keen interest.

"It's the same kind of envelope, but—" began Sir Lyster, when Lord Beamdale interrupted.

"It's the envelope itself," he said. "I noticed that the right–hand top corner was bent in rather a peculiar manner."

Malcolm Sage rose and, taking out the envelope, carefully examined the damaged corner, which was bent and slightly torn.

"Yes, it's the same," cried Mr. Llewellyn John. "I remember tearing it myself when putting in the document."

"How many leaves of paper were there?" enquired Malcolm Sage.

"Eight, I think," replied Sir Lyster.

"Nine," corrected Lord Beamdale. "There was a leaf in front blank but for the words, 'Plans Department.'"

"Have you another document from the same Department?" enquired Malcolm Sage of Sir Lyster.

"Several."

"I should like to see one." Sir Lyster left the room, and Malcolm Sage removed the contents of the envelope. Carefully counting nine leaves of white foolscap, he bent down over the paper, with his face almost touching it.

When Sir Lyster re–entered with another document in his hand Malcolm Sage took it from him and proceeded to subject it to an equally close scrutiny, holding up to the light each sheet in succession.

"I suppose. Sir Lyster, you don't by any chance use scent?" enquired Malcolm Sage without looking up.

"Mr. Sage!" Sir Lyster was on his dignity.

"I see you don't," was Malcolm Sage's calm comment as he resumed his examination of the dummy document. Replacing it in the envelope, he returned it to the safe, closed the door, locked it, and put the key in his pocket.

"Well! what do you make of it?" cried Mr. Llewellyn John eagerly.

"We shall have to take the Postmaster–General into our confidence."

"Woldington!" cried Mr. Llewellyn John in astonishment. "Why?"

Sir Lyster looked surprised, whilst Lord Beamdale appeared almost interested.

"Because we shall probably require his help."

"How?" enquired Sir Lyster.

"Well, it's rather dangerous to tamper with His Majesty's mails without the connivance of St. Martins–le–Grand," was the dry retort. .

"But—" began Mr. Llewellyn John, when suddenly he stopped short.

Malcolm Sage had walked over to where his overcoat lay, and was deliberately getting into it.

"You're not going, Mr. Sage?" Sir Lyster's granite–like control seemed momentarily to forsake him. "What do you advise us to do?"

"Get some sleep," was the quiet reply.

"But aren't you going to search for—?" He paused as Malcolm Sage turned and looked full at him.

A search would involve the very publicity you are anxious to avoid," was the reply.

"But—" began Mr. Llewellyn John, when Malcolm Sage interrupted him.

"The only effective search would be to surround the house with police, and allow each occupant to pass through the cordon after having been stripped. The house would then have to be gone through; carpets and boards pulled up; mattresses ripped open; chairs—"

"I agree with Mr. Sage," said Sir Lyster, looking across at the Prime Minister coldly.

"Had I been a magazine detective I should have known exactly where to find the missing document," said Malcolm Sage. "As I am not"—he turned to Sir Lyster—"it will be necessary for you to leave a note for your butler telling him that you have dropped somewhere about the house the key of this safe, and instructing him to have a thorough search made for it. You might casually mention the loss at breakfast, and refer to an important document inside the safe which you must have on Monday morning. Perhaps the Prime Minister will suggest telephoning to town for a man to come down to force the safe should the key not be found."

Malcolm Sage paused. The others were gazing at him with keen interest.

"Leave the note unfolded in a conspicuous place where anyone can see it," he continued.

"I'll put it on the hall-table," said Sir Lyster.

Malcolm Sage nodded. "It is desirable that you should all appear to be in the best of spirits." There was a fluttering at the corners of Malcolm Sage's mouth, as he lifted his eyes for a second to the almost lugubrious countenance of Lord Beamdale. "Under no circumstances refer to the robbery, even amongst yourselves. Try to forget it."

"But how will that help?" enquired Mr. Llewellyn John, whose nature rendered him singularly ill-adapted to a walking-on part.

"I will ask you, sir," said Malcolm Sage, turning to him, "to give me a letter to Mr. Woldington, asking him to do as I request. I will give him the details."

73

Malcolm Sage, Detective

"But why is it necessary to tell him?" demanded Lyster.

"That I will explain to you to-morrow. That will need to be ready by Monday," explained Malcolm Sage, "earlier if possible. A few lines will do," he added, turning to Mr. Llewellyn John.

"I suppose we must," said the Prime Minister, looking from Sir Lyster to Lord Beamdale.

"I hope to call before lunch," said Malcolm Sage, "but as Mr. Le Sage from the Foreign Office. You will refuse to discuss official matters until Monday. I shall probably ask you to introduce me to everyone you can. It may happen that I shall disappear suddenly."

"But cannot you be a little less mysterious?" said Sir Lyster, with a touch of asperity in his voice.

"There is nothing mysterious," replied Malcolm Sage. "It seems quite obvious. Everything depends upon how clever the thief is." He looked up suddenly, his gaze passing from one to another of the bewildered Ministers.

"It's by no means obvious to me," cried Mr. Llewellyn John, complainingly.

"By the way, Sir Lyster, how many cars have you in the garage?" enquired Malcolm Sage. "In case we want them," he added.

"I have two, and there are"–he paused for a moment–"five others," he added; "seven in all."

"Any carriages, or dog-carts?"

"No. We have no horses."

"Bicycles?"

"A few of the servants have them," replied Sir Lyster, a little impatiently.

"The bicycles are also kept in the garage, I take it?"

"They are." This time there was no mistaking the note of irritation in Sir Lyster's voice.

"There may be several messengers from Whitehall tomorrow," said Malcolm Sage, after a pause. "Please keep them waiting until they show signs of impatience. It is important. Whatever happens here, it would be better not to acquaint the police—whatever happens," he added with emphasis. "And now, sir"—he turned to Mr. Llewellyn John—"I should like that note to the Postmaster—General."

Mr. Llewellyn John sat down reluctantly at a table and wrote a note.

But suppose the thief hands the document to an accomplice?" said Sir Lyster presently, with something like emotion in his voice.

'That's exactly what I am supposing," was Malcolm Sage's reply and, taking the note that Mr. Llewellyn John held out to him, he placed it in his breast pocket, buttoned up his overcoat, and walked across to the window through which he had entered. With one hand upon the curtain he turned.

"If I call you may notice that I have acquired a slight foreign accent," he said, and with that he slipped behind the curtain. A moment later the sound was heard of the window being quietly opened and then shut again.

"Well, I'm damned!" cried Lord Beamdale, and for the moment Mr. Llewellyn John and Sir Lyster forgot their surprise at Malcolm Sage's actions in their astonishment at their colleague's remark.

CHAPTER VII. THE OUTRAGE AT THE GARAGE

WHEN Mr. Walters descended the broad staircase of The Towers on the Sunday morning he found two things to disturb him—Sir Lyster's note on the hall—table, and the Japanese valet "lost" in the conservatory.

He read the one with attention, and rebuked the other with acrimony. Having failed to find the missing key himself, he proceeded to the housekeeper's room, and poured into the large and receptive ear of Mrs. Eames the story of his woes.

"And this a Sunday too," the housekeeper was just remarking, in a fat, comfortable voice, when Richards, the chauffeur, burst unceremoniously into the room.

"Someone's taken the pencils from all the magnetos," he shouted angrily, his face moist with heat and lubricant.

"Is that your only excuse for bursting into a lady's room without knocking?" enquired Mr. Walters, with an austere dignity he had copied directly from Sir Lyster. "If you apply to me presently I will lend you a pencil. In the meantime—"

"But it's burglars. They've broken into the garage and taken the pencils from every magneto, every blinkin' one," he added by way of emphasis.

At the mention of the word "burglars," Mr. Walters's professional composure of feature momentarily forsook him; his jaw dropped. Recovering himself instantly, however, he hastened out of the room, closely followed by Richards, leaving Mrs. Eames speechless, the oval cameo locket heaving and down upon her indignant black–silk bosom. A man had sworn in her presence and had departed unrebuked.

On reaching the garage Mr. Walters gazed vaguely about him He was entirely unversed in mechanics, and Richards persisted in pouring forth technicalities that bewildered him. The chauffeur also cursed loudly and with inspiration, until reminded that it was Sunday, when he lowered his voice, at the same time increasing the density of his language.

Mr. Walters was frankly disappointed. There was no outward sign of burglars. At length he turned interrogatingly to Richards.

"Just a–goin' to tune 'em up I was," explained Richards for the twentieth time, "when I found the bloomin' engines had gone whonky, then—"

"Found the engines had gone what?" enquired Mr. Walters.

"Whonky, dud, na–poo," explained Richards illuminatingly, whilst Mr. Walters gazed at him icily. "Then in comes Davies," he continued, nodding in the direction of a little round–faced man, with "chauffeur" written on every inch of him, "and 'e couldn't get 'is blinkin' 'arp to 'um neither. Then we starts a–lookin' round, when lo and be'old! what do

76

we find? Some streamin', saturated son of sin an' whiskers 'as pinched the ruddy pencils out of the scarlet 'magnetos."

"The float's gone from my carburettor."

The voice came from a long, lean man who appeared suddenly out of the shadows at the far–end of the garage.

Without a word Richards and Davies dashed each to a car. A minute later two yells announced that the floats from their carburettors also had disappeared.

Later Richards told how that morning he had found the door of the garage unfastened, although he was certain that he had locked it the night before.

This was sufficient for Mr. Walters. Fleeing from the bewildering flood of technicalities and profanity of the three chauffeurs, he made his way direct to Sir Lyster's room. Here he told his tale, and was instructed instantly to telephone to the police.

At the telephone further trouble awaited him. He could get no reply from the exchange. He tried the private wire to the Admiralty; but with no better result.

He accordingly reported the matter to Sir Lyster, who was by then with Lord Beamdale in the library. It was the Minister of War who reminded his host of Malcolm Sage's strange request that whatever happened the police were not to be communicated with.

"But Sage could not have anticipated this–this monstrous outrage," protested Sir Lyster, white with anger. He had already imperiously put aside Lord Beamdale's suggestion that the whole affair might be a joke.

"Still, better do as he said," was the rejoinder and, as later Mr. Llewellyn John concurred, Sir Lyster decided to await the arrival of Malcolm Sage before taking further steps.

One by one the guests drifted down to breakfast, went out to the garage to see for themselves, and then returned to discuss the affair over coffee and kidneys, tea and toast.

Malcolm Sage, Detective

It subsequently transpired that without exception the cars had been entirely put out of commission. From each the pencil had been removed from the magneto, and the float from the carburettor. From the bicycles the pedals had been taken away, with the exception of those belonging to Miss Blair and one of the housemaids, the only two ladies' machines in the place.

"A veritable Claude Duval," someone remarked; but this brought little consolation to the owners of the wrecked cars. It was a fine day, too, which added to their sense of hardship.

As Sir Lyster left the breakfast–room he encountered Miss Blair crossing the hall. She looked very fresh and pretty, with a demure, almost childlike expression of feature. Her cheeks were flushed with health and exercise.

"Would you like me to cycle over to Odford to the police?" she enquired. "My machine is quite all right. I have just been for a spin."

"No–er–not at present, thank you. Miss Blair," said Sir Lyster, a little embarrassed at having to refuse to do the obvious thing. He passed across the hall into the library, and Miss Blair, having almost fallen over the Japanese valet, "lost" in a corridor leading to the billiard–room, went out to condole with Richards and tell him of a strange epidemic of mishaps that seemed to have descended upon the neighbourhood. She herself had passed a motor–cycle, two push–bicycles, and a Ford car, all disabled by the roadside.

All that morning the Prime Minister, Sir Lyster, and Lord Beamdale waited and wondered. Finding the strain of trying to look cheerful too much for them, they shut themselves up in the library on the plea of pressing official business; this, in spite of Sir Lyster's well–known week–end rule.

Hour after hour passed; yet not only did Malcolm Sage fail to put in an appearance, but nothing was heard or seen of the promised bogus official messengers.

At luncheon more than one guest remarked upon the distrait and absent–minded appearance of the three Ministers, and deduced from the circumstance a grave political crisis.

Malcolm Sage, Detective

The afternoon dragged its leaden course. Throughout the house there was an atmosphere of unrest. Among themselves the guests complained because no action had been taken to track down the despoiler of their cars. Walters had rendered the lives of the domestic staff intolerable by insisting upon search for the missing key being made in the most unlikely and inaccessible places, although in his own mind he was convinced that it had been stolen by the errant Japanese.

In the library sat the three Ministers, for the most part gazing either at one another or at nothing in particular. They were waiting for something to happen: none knew quite what.

Dinner passed, a dreary meal; the ladies withdrew to the drawing—room; but still the heavy atmosphere of foreboding remained. It was nearly half—past nine when Walters entered and murmured something in Sir Lyster's ear.

An eager light sprang into Mr. Llewellyn John's eyes as the First Lord rose, made his apologies, and left the room. It was only by the exercise of great self—control that the Prime Minister refrained from jumping up and bolting after him.

Two minutes later Walters again entered the dining—room, with a request that Mr. Llewellyn John and Lord Beamdale would join Sir Lyster in the library.

As Walters threw open the library—door, they found Malcolm Sage seated at the table, his fingers spread out before him, whilst Sir Lyster stood by the fireplace.

"Ask Miss Blair if she will come here to take down an important letter, Walters," said Sir Lyster.

"Well?" cried Mr. Llewellyn John, as soon as Walters had closed the door behind him. "Have you got it?"

"The document is now in a strong—room at the General Post Office," said Malcolm Sage without looking up. "I thought it would be safer there."

"Thank God!" cried Mr. Llewellyn John, collapsing into a chair.

Malcolm Sage glanced across at him and half rose.

"I'm all right, Sage," said Mr. Llewellyn John; "but coming after this awful day of anxiety, the news was almost too much for me."

"Who took it from the safe then?" enquired Sir Lyster. "I—" he stopped short as the door opened, and Miss Blair entered, notebook in hand, looking very dainty in a simple grey frock, relieved by a bunch of clove carnations at the waist. Closing the door behind her, she hesitated for a moment, a smile upon her moist, slightly–parted lips.

"I'm sorry to disturb you, Miss Blair," began Sir Lyster, "but Mr. Sage—" he paused.

"It was Miss Blair who removed the document from the safe," said Malcolm Sage quietly, his eyes bent upon the finger–tips of his right hand.

"Miss Blair!" cried Sir Lyster, his hand dropping from the mantelpiece to his side.

For the fraction of a second the girl stood just inside the door; then as the significance of Malcolm Sage's words dawned upon her, the smile froze upon her lips, the blood ebbed from her face, leaving it drawn and grey, and the notebook dropped from her fingers. She staggered forward a few steps, then, clutching wildly at the edge of the table, she swayed from side to side. With an obvious effort she steadied herself, her gaze fixed upon her accuser.

Slowly Malcolm Sage raised his eyes, cold, grey, inflexible, and fixed them upon the terrified girl.

The three Ministers appeared not yet to have realised the true nature of the drama being enacted before them.

"Miss Blair," said Malcolm Sage quietly, "what are your relations with Paul Cressit?"

Twice she essayed to speak, but no sound came. "I–I–er–know him," she faltered at length.

"I wondered," said Malcolm Sage slowly.

"What does this mean, Mr. Sage?" enquired Sir Lyster.

Malcolm Sage, Detective

"I will tell you," said Malcolm Sage, whilst Lord Beamdale placed a chair into which Miss Blair collapsed. "Last night whilst you were at dinner Miss Blair opened your safe with a duplicate key made from a wax impression. She abstracted a valuable document, putting in its place some sheets of blank paper." He paused.

"Go on," almost gasped Mr. Llewellyn John.

"She took the document to her room and hid it, a little uncertain as to how she should get it to her accomplice. This morning she saw Sir Lyster's note on the hall–table, and emboldened by the thought that the theft had not been discovered, she cycled out to Odford and posted the document to Paul Cressit at his chambers in Jermyn Street." Again Malcolm Sage paused and drew from his pocket a note.

"In the envelope was enclosed this note." He handed to Mr. Llewellyn John a half sheet of paper on which was typed:

"Paul, dearest, I have done it. I will ring you up tomorrow. I shall ask for Tuesday off. You will keep your promise, dear, and save me, won't you? If you don't I shall kill myself. G."

"Miss Blair," said Sir Lyster coldly, "what have you to say?"

"N–nothing," she faltered, striving to moisten her grey lips.

"If you will tell the truth," said Malcolm Sage, "you still have a chance. If not—" he paused significantly. She gulped noisily, striving to regain her power of speech.

"You–you promise?" She looked across at Mr. Llewellyn John.

"Whatever Mr. Sage says we endorse," he replied gravely.

"Both of us?" she repeated.

"Both," said Malcolm Sage.

"I–I love him," she moaned; then after a pause she added: "It was to save the disgrace. He promised, he swore he would if I did it."

"Swore he would do what?" said Malcolm Sage.

"Marry me."

Malcolm Sage raised his eyes to Sir Lyster, who was standing implacable and merciless.

The girl's head had fallen forward upon the table, and her shoulders were heaving convulsively.

Rising, Malcolm Sage walked across and placed his hand upon her arm.

"It will be better for everybody if you will try and control yourself," he said gently, "and above all tell us the truth."

As if surprised at the gentleness of his tone, she slowly raised her drawn face and looked at him in wonder.

"Now listen to me," continued Malcolm Sage, drawing up a chair and seating himself beside her, "and tell me if I am wrong. Whilst you were acting as Sir Lyster's secretary you met Paul Cressit at the Admiralty, and you were attracted to him."

She nodded, with a quick indrawing of her breath.

"He made violent love to you and you succumbed. Later you took him into your confidence in regard to a certain matter and he promised to marry you. He put you off from time to time by various excuses. You were almost distracted at the thought of the disgrace. He persuaded you to take a wax impression of Sir Lyster's key, on the chance of it one day being useful."

Again she nodded, whilst the three men listened as if hypnotised.

"Finally he swore that he would marry you if you would steal this document, and he showed you a special licence. Am I right?"

She nodded again, and then buried her head in her arms.

"I suppose," said Malcolm Sage quietly, "he did not happen to mention that he was already married?"

"Married!" She started up, her eyes blazing. "It isn't true, oh! it isn't true," she cried.

"I'm afraid it is," said Malcolm Sage, with feeling in his voice.

With a moan of despair her head fell forward upon the table, and hard dry sobs shook her frail body.

"Miss Blair," said Malcolm Sage presently, when she had somewhat regained her self–control, "my advice to you is to write out a full confession and bring it to me at my office to–morrow morning. It is your only chance: and now you must go to your room." He rose, assisted her to her feet, and led her to the door which he closed behind her. "That I think concludes the enquiry," he said, as he walked over to the fireplace and, leaning against the mantel–piece, he began to fill his pipe. "Unless," he added, turning to Mr. Llewellyn John, "you would like to see Cressit."

The Prime Minister looked across at Sir Lyster and then at Lord Beamdale. Both shook their heads.

"What we should like, Sage," said Mr. Llewellyn John, "is a little information as to what has been happening."

With great deliberation Malcolm Sage proceeded to light his pipe. When it was drawing to his entire satisfaction, he turned to Mr. Llewellyn John and, with the suspicion of a fluttering at the corners of his mouth, remarked:

"I hope you have not been inconvenienced about the telephone."

"We could get no reply from the exchange," said Sir Lyster, "and the wire to the Admiralty is out of order."

"I had to disconnect you after I left this morning," said Malcolm Sage quietly. "My chauffeur swarmed up one of the standards. Incidentally he wrecked an almost new pair of breeches."

"They'll have to go in the Naval Estimates," cried Mr. Llewellyn John, who was feeling almost jovial now the tension of the past twenty–four hours had been removed.

"From the first," proceeded Malcolm Sage, "it was obvious that this theft was planned either at the Admiralty or at the War Office."

"That is absurd!" cried Sir Lyster with heat, whilst Lord Beamdale leaned forward, his usually apathetic expression of indifference giving place to one of keen interest.

"I accepted the assurance that only three people in this house knew of the existence of the document," Malcolm Sage proceeded, as if there had been no interruption. "There was no object in any of those three persons stealing that to which they had ready access."

Lord Beamdale nodded his agreement with the reasoning.

"Therefore," continued Malcolm Sage, "the theft must have been planned by someone who knew about the document before it came here, and furthermore knew that it was to be here at a certain time. To confirm this hypothesis we have the remarkable circumstances that the blank paper substituted for the original document was, in quality and the number of sheets, identical with that of the document itself."

"Good," ejaculated Lord Beamdale, himself a keen mathematician. Mr. Llewellyn John and Sir Lyster exchanged glances.

"It was almost, but not quite, obvious that the exchange had been effected by a woman."

"How obvious?" enquired Mr. Llewellyn John.

"'Few women pass unperfumed to the grave,'" quoted Malcolm Sage. "I think it was Craddock who said that," he added, and Mr. Llewellyn John made a mental note of the phrase.

"The handle of the safe door was corrugated, and the lacquer had worn off, leaving it rough to the touch. When I kneeled down before the safe it was not to examine the metal work, but to see if the thief had left a scent."

"A scent?" repeated Sir Lyster.

"On the handle of the door there was a distinct trace of perfume, very slight, but I have a keen sense of smell, although a great smoker. On the document itself there was also evidence of a rather expensive perfume, not unlike that used by Miss Blair. Furthermore, it was bent in a rather peculiar manner, which might have resulted from its being carried in the belt of a woman's frock. It might, of course, have been mere chance," he added; "but the envelope did not show a corresponding bend."

Again Lord Beamdale nodded appreciatively.

"Although several people have had an opportunity of taking a wax impression of the key, the most likely were Miss Blair and Walters–that, however, was a side issue."

"How?" enquired Sir Lyster.

"Because primarily we were concerned with making the criminal himself, or herself, divulge the secret."

"That's why you would not allow the loss to be made known," broke in Mr. Llewellyn John.

"The thief," continued Malcolm Sage, with a slight inclination of his head, "would in all probability seize the first safe opportunity of getting rid of the plunder."

"But did you not suspect the Japanese?" broke in Lord Beamdale.

"For the moment I ruled him out," said Malcolm Sage, "as I could not see how it was possible for him to know about the existence of the document in question, and furthermore, as he had been in the house less than two days, there was no time for him to get a duplicate key."

"What did you do then?" queried Sir Lyster.

"I motored back to town, broke in upon the Postmaster–General's first sleep, set on foot enquiries at the Admiralty and War Office, in the meantime arranging for The Towers to be carefully watched." Malcolm Sage paused for a moment; then as none of his hearers spoke he continued:

"I had a number of people in the neighbourhood–motorists, cyclists, and pedestrians. No one could have left the house and grounds without being seen.

"Miss Blair found the morning irresistible, and took an early spin on her bicycle to Odford, where she posted a packet in a pillar–box situated in a street that was apparently quite empty."

"And you secured it?" enquired Mr. Llewellyn John, leaning forward eagerly.

"I'm afraid I quite spoilt the local postmaster's Sunday by requesting that a pillar–box should be specially cleared, and producing an authority from the Postmaster–General. After he had telegraphed to headquarters and received a reply confirming the letter, he reluctantly acquiesced."

"And it was addressed to this man Cressit?" enquired Sir Lyster.

"Yes. He is a temporary staff–clerk in the Plans Department. Incidentally he is something of a Don Juan, and the cost of living has increased considerably, as you know, sir," he added, turning to the Prime Minister.

Mr. Llewellyn John smiled wanly. It was his political "cross," this cost–of–living problem.

"And what shall we do with him?" enquired Sir Lyster. "The scoundrel," he added.

"I have almost done with him as a matter of fact," said Malcolm Sage.

"Done with him?" exclaimed Lord Beamdale.

"I sent him a telegram in Miss Blair's name to be at Odford Station to—night at seven: then I kidnapped him."

"Good heavens, Sage! What do you mean?" cried Mr. Llewellyn John, with visions of the Habeas Corpus Act and possible questions in the House, which he hated.

"We managed to get him to enter my car, and then we went through him—that is a phrase from the crook—world. We found upon him the marriage certificate, and later I induced him to confess. I am now going to take him back to my office, secure his finger—prints and physical measurements, which will be of interest at Scotland Yard."

"But we are not going to prosecute," said Mr. Llewellyn John anxiously.

"Mr. Paul Cressit will have forty—eight hours in which to leave the country," said Malcolm Sage evenly. "He will not return, because Scotland Yard will see that he does not do so. There will probably be an application to you, sir," Malcolm Sage continued, turning to Mr. Llewellyn John, "to confirm what I tell them."

"Excellent!" cried Mr. Llewellyn John. "I congratulate you. Sage. You have done wonders."

"But I fail to understand your saying that you would be here this morning," said Sir Lyster, "and under an assumed name with—"

"A foreign accent," suggested Malcolm Sage. "The thief might have been an old hand at the game, and too clever to fall into a rather obvious trap. In that case I might have been forced, as a foreigner, to salute the hands of all the ladies in the house. I learnt to click my heels years ago in Germany." Again there was a suspicious movement at the corners of Malcolm Sage's mouth.

"But—" began Sir Lyster.

"To identify the scent?" broke in Mr. Llewellyn John. Malcolm Sage inclined his head slightly.

"The Foreign Office messengers?" queried Lord Beamdale.

"I decided that pedestrians and cyclists would do as well. I merely wanted the house watched. There were quite a number of casualties to cars and bicycles in the neighbourhood," he added dryly.

"But why did you cut us off from the telephone?" enquired Mr. Llewellyn John.

"The accomplice might have got through, and I could afford to take no risks."

"Well, you have done splendidly, Sage," said Mr. Llewellyn John heartily, "and we are all greatly obliged. By the way, there's another little problem awaiting you. Someone broke into the garage last night and wrecked all the cars and bicycles—"

"Except two," said Malcolm Sage.

"Then you've heard." Mr. Llewellyn John looked at hint in surprise.

"The man who did it is in my car outside with Cressit."

"You've got him as well?" cried Mr. Llewellyn John excitedly. "Sage, you're a miracle of sagacity," he added, again mentally noting the phrase.

"The missing pencils, floats, and pedals you will find on the left–hand side of the drive about half–way down, under a laurel bush," said Malcolm Sage quietly.

"And who is this fellow who did this scandalous thing?" demanded Sir Lyster.

"My chauffeur."

"Your chauffeur!"

"I could not risk the thief having access to a fast car."

"But what if this fellow Cressit refuses to go?" enquired Lord Beamdale.

"He won't," said Malcolm Sage grimly. "D.O.R.A. is still in operation. I had to remind him of the fact."

88

Malcolm Sage picked up his hat and coat and walked towards the door. "I must be going," he said. "I have still several things to attend to. You won't forget about the plunder from the garage?" he added.

"But what am I to do about Miss Blair?" asked Sir Lyster.

"That's a question I think you will find answered in the Gospel of St. Luke—the seventh chapter and I think the forty—seventh verse"; and with that he was gone, leaving three Ministers gazing at one another in dumb astonishment.

Had a cynic been peeping into the library of The Towers a few minutes later, he would have discovered three Cabinet Ministers bending over a New Testament, which Sir Lyster had fetched from his wife's boudoir, and the words they read were: "Wherefore I say unto thee. Her sins, which are many, are forgiven; for she loved much."

"Strange," murmured Lord Beamdale, "very strange," and the others knew that he was referring, not to the text, or to the unhappy girl—but to Malcolm Sage.

"We are always surprised when we find Saul among the prophets," remarked Mr. Llewellyn John, and he made a mental note of the phrase. It might do for the "Wee Frees."

CHAPTER VIII. GLADYS NORMAN DINES WITH THOMPSON

"TOMMY," remarked Miss Gladys Norman one day as Thompson entered her room through the glass—panelled door, "have you ever thought what I shall do fifty years hence?"

"Darn my socks," replied the practical Thompson.

"I mean," she proceeded with withering deliberation, "what will happen when I can't do the hundred in ten seconds?"

Thompson looked at her with a puzzled expression.

Malcolm Sage, Detective

"My cousin Will says that if you can't do the hundred yards in ten seconds you haven't an earthly," she explained. "It's been worrying me. What am I to do when I'm old and rheumaticky and the Chief does three on the buzzer? He's bound to notice it and he'll look."

Malcolm Sage's "look" was a slight widening of the eyes as he gazed at a delinquent. It was his method of conveying rebuke. That "look" would cause Thompson to swear earnestly under his breath for the rest of the day, whilst on Gladys Norman it had several distinct effects, the biting of her lower lip, the snubbing of Thompson, the merciless banging of her typewriter, and a self–administered rebuke of "Gladys Norman, you're a silly little ass," being the most noticeable.

For a moment Thompson thought deeply, then with sudden inspiration he said, "Why not move your table nearer his door?"

"What a brain!" she cried, regarding him with mock admiration. "You must have been waving it with Hindes' curlers. Yes," she added, "you may take me out to dinner to —night, Tommy."

Thompson was in the act of waving his hat wildly over his head when Malcolm Sage came out of his room. For the fraction of a second he paused and regarded his subordinates. "It's not another war, I hope," he remarked, and, without waiting for a reply, he turned, re–entered his room and closed the door. Gladys Norman collapsed over her typewriter, where with heaving shoulders she strove to mute her mirth with a ridiculous dab of pink cambric.

Thompson looked crestfallen. He had turned just in time to see Malcolm Sage re–enter his room.

Three sharp bursts on the buzzer brought Gladys Norman to her feet. There was a flurry of skirt, the flash of a pair of shapely ankles, and she disappeared into Malcolm Sage's room.

"It's a funny old world," remarked Gladys Norman that evening, as she and Thompson sat at a sheltered table in a little Soho restaurant.

"It's a jolly nice old world," remarked Thompson, looking up from his plate, "and this chicken is It."

"Chicken first; Gladys Norman also ran," she remarked scathingly.

Thompson grinned and returned to his plate.

"Why do you like the Chief, Tommy?" she demanded.

Thompson paused in his eating, resting his hands, still holding knife and fork, upon the edge of the table. The suddenness of the question had startled him.

"If you must sit like that, at least close your mouth," she said severely.

Thompson replaced his knife and fork upon the plate.

"Well, why do you?" she queried.

"Why do I what?" he asked.

She made a movement of impatience. "Like the Chief, of course." Then as he did not reply she continued: "Why does Tims like him, and the Innocent, and Sir James, and Sir John Dene, and the whole blessed lot of us. Why is it, Tommy, why?"

Thompson merely gaped, as if she had propounded some unanswerable riddle.

"Why is it?" she repeated. Then as he still remained silent she added, "There's no hurry, Tommy dear; just go on listening with your mouth. I quite realise the compliment."

"I'm blessed if I know," he burst out at last. "I suppose it's because he's 'M.S.'" and he returned to his plate.

"Yes, but why is it?" she persisted, as she continued mechanically to crumble her bread. "That's what I want to know; why is it?"

Malcolm Sage, Detective

Thompson looked at her a little anxiously. By nature he was inclined to take things for granted, things outside his profession that is.

"It's a funny old world, Tommikins," she repeated at length, picking up her knife and fork, "funnier for some than for others."

Thompson looked up with a puzzled expression on his face. There were times when he found Gladys Norman difficult to understand.

"For a girl, I mean," she added, as if that explained it. Thompson still stared. The remark did not strike him as illuminating.

"It may be," she continued meditatively, "that I like doing things for the Chief because he was my haven of refuge from a wicked world; but that doesn't explain why you and Tims——"

"Your haven of refuge!" repeated Thompson, making a gulp of a mouthful, and once more laying down his knife and fork, as he looked across at her curiously.

"Before I went to the Ministry I had one or two rather beastly experiences." She paused as if mentally reviewing some unpleasant incident.

"Tell me, Gladys." Thompson was now all attention.

"Well, I once went to see a man in Shaftesbury Avenue who had advertised for a secretary. He was a funny old bean," she added reminiscently, "all eyes and no waist, and more curious as to whether I lived alone, or with my people, than about my speeds. So I told him my brother was a prizefighter, and——"

"But you haven't got a brother," broke in Thompson.

"I told him that for the good of his soul, Tommy, and of the girls who came after me," she added a little grimly.

"It was funny," she continued after a pause. "He didn't seem a bit eager to engage me after that. Said my speeds (which I hadn't told him) were not good enough; but to show

92

there was no ill—feeling he tried to kiss me at parting. So I boxed his ears, slung his own inkpot at him and came away. Oh! it's a great game, Tommy, played slow," she added as an after—thought, and she hummed a snatch of a popular fox—trot.

"The swine!"

Thompson had just realised the significance of what he had heard. There was an ugly look in his eyes.

"I then got a job at the Ministry of Economy and later at the Ministry of Supply, and the Chief lifted me out by my bobbed hair and put me into Department Z. That's why I call him my haven of refuge. See, dearest?"

"What's the name of the fellow in Shaftesbury Avenue?" demanded Thompson, his thoughts centring round the incident she had just narrated.

"Naughty Tommy," she cried, making a face at him. "Mustn't get angry and vicious. Besides," she added, "the Chief did for him."

"You told him?" cried Thompson incredulously, his interest still keener than his appetite.

"I did," she replied airily, "and he dropped a hint at Scotland Yard. I believe the gallant gentleman in Shaftesbury Avenue has something more than a smack and an inky face to remember little Gladys by. He doesn't advertise for secretaries now."

Thompson gazed at her, admiration in his eyes.

"But that doesn't explain why I always want to please the Chief, does it?" she demanded. "In romance, the knight kills the villain for making love to the heroine, and then gets down to the same dirty work himself. Now the Chief ought to have been bursting with volcanic fires of passion for me. He should have crushed me to his breast with merciless force, I beating against his chest—protector with my clenched fists. Finally I should have lain passive and unresisting in his arms, whilst he covered my eyes, ears, nose and 'transformation' with fevered, passionate kisses; not pecks like yours, Tommy; but the real thing with a punch in them."

93

"What on earth—" began Thompson, when she continued.

"There should have been a fearful tempest on the other side of his ribs. I should—"

"Don't talk rot, Gladys," broke in Thompson.

"I'm not talking rot," she protested. "I read it all in a novel that sells by the million." Then after a moment's pause she continued: "He saved me from the dragon; yet he doesn't even give me a box of chocolates, and everybody in Whitehall knows that chocolates and kisses won the war. When I fainted for him and he carried me into his room, he didn't kiss me even then."

"You wouldn't have known it if he had," was Thompson's comment.

"Oh! wouldn't I?" she retorted. "That's all you know about girls, Mr. Funny Thompson."

He stared across at her, blinking his eyes in bewilderment.

"He doesn't take me out to dinner as other chiefs do," she continued; "yet I hop about like a linnet when he buzzes for me. Why is it?"

She gazed across at Thompson challengingly.

A look of anxiety began to manifest itself upon his good−natured features. Psycho−analysis was not his strong point. In a vague way he began to suspect that Gladys Norman's devotion to Malcolm Sage was not strictly in accordance with Trade Union principles.

"There, get on with your chicken, you poor dear," she laughed, and Thompson, picking up his knife and fork, proceeded to eat mechanically. From time to time he glanced covertly across at Gladys.

"As to the Chief's looks," she continued, "his face is keen and taut, and he's a strong, silent man; yet can you see his eyes hungry and tempestuous, Tommy? I can't. Why is it," she demanded, "that when a woman writes a novel she always stunts the strong, silent man?"

Malcolm Sage, Detective

Thompson shook his head, with the air of a man who has given up guessing.

"Imagine getting married to a strong, silent man," she continued, "with only his strength and his silence, and perhaps a cheap gramophone, to keep you amused in the evenings." She shuddered. "No," she said with decision, "give me a regular old rattle–box without a chin, like you, Tommy."

Mechanically Thompson's hand sought his chin, and Gladys laughed.

"Anyway, I'm not going to marry, in spite of the tube furniture posters. Uncle Jake says it's all nonsense to talk about marriages being made in heaven; they're made in the Tottenham Court Road."

Thompson had, however, returned to his plate. In her present mood, Gladys Norman was beyond him. Realising the state of his mind, she continued: "He's got a head like a pierrot's cap and it's as bald as a fivepenny egg, when it ought to be beautifully rounded and covered with crisp curly hair. He wears glasses in front of eyes like bits of slate, when they ought to be full of slumbrous passion. His jaw is all right, only he doesn't use it enough, in books the strong, silent man is a regular old chin–wag, and yet I fall over myself to answer his buzzer. Why is it, I repeat?" She looked across at him mischievously, enjoying the state of depression to which she had reduced him.

Thompson merely shook his head.

"For all that," she continued, picking up her own knife and fork, which in the excitement of describing Malcolm Sage she had laid down, "for all that he would make a wonderful lover–once you could get him started," and she laughed gleefully as if at some hidden joke.

Thompson gazed at her over a fork piled with food, which her remark had arrested half–way to his mouth.

"He's chivalrous," she continued. "Look at the way he always tries to help up the very people he has downed. It's just a game with him—"

"No, it's not," burst out Thompson, through a mouthful of chicken and saute potato.

She gave him a look of disapproval that caused him to swallow rapidly.

"The Chief doesn't look on it as a game," he persisted. "He's out to stop crime and—"

"But that's not the point," she interrupted. "What I want to know is why do I bounce off my chair like an india–rubber ball when he buzzes?" she demanded relentlessly. "Why do I want to please him? Why do I want to kick myself when I make mistakes? Why–Oh! Tommy," she broke off, "if only you had a brain as well as a stomach," and she looked across at him reproachfully.

"Perhaps it's because he never complains," suggested Thompson, as he placed his knife and fork at the "all clear" angle, and leaned back in his chair with a sigh of contentment.

"You don't complain. Tommy," she retorted; "but you could buzz yourself to blazes without getting me even to look up."

For fully a minute there was silence; Gladys Norman continued to gaze down at the debris to which she had reduced her roll.

"No," she continued presently, "there is something else. I've noticed the others; they're just the same." She paused, then suddenly looking across at him she enquired, "What is loyalty, Tommy?"

"Standing up and taking off your hat when they play 'God Save the King,' " he replied glibly.

She laughed, and deftly nicked a bread pill she had inst manufactured, catching Thompson beneath the left eye and causing him to blink violently.

"You're a funny old thing," she laughed. "You know quite well what I mean, only you're too stupid to realise it Look at the Innocent–for him the Chief is the only man in all the world. Then there's Tims. He'd get up in the middle of the night and drive the Chief to blazes, and hang the petrol. Then there's you and me."

Thompson drew a cigarette case from his pocket.

"I think I know why it is," she said, nodding her pretty head wisely. She paused, and as Thompson made no comment she continued: "It's because he's human, warm flesh and blood."

"But when I'm warm flesh and blood," objected Thompson, with corrugated brow, "you tell me not to be silly."

"Your idea of warmth, my dear man, was learnt on the upper reaches of the Thames after dark," was the scathing retort.

"Yes, but—" he began, when she interrupted him.

"Look what he did for Miss Blair. Had her at the office and then—then—looked after her."

"And afterwards got her a job," remarked Thompson. "But that's just like the Chief," he added.

"Where did you meet him first, Tommy?" she enquired, as she leaned forward slightly to light her cigarette at the match he held out to her.

"In a bath," was the reply, as Thompson proceeded to light his own cigarette.

"You're not a bit funny," she retorted.

"But it was," he persisted.

"Was what?"

"In a bath. He hadn't had one before and—"

"Not had a bath!" she cried. "If you try to pull my leg like that. Tommy, you'll ladder my stockings."

"But I'm not," protested Thompson. "I met the Chief in a Turkish bath, and he went into the hottest room and crumpled, so I looked after him, and that's how I got to know him."

"Of course, you couldn't have happened to mention that it was a Turkish bath. Tommy, could you?" she said. "That wouldn't be you at all. But what makes him do things like he did for Miss Blair?"

"I suppose because he's the Chief," was Thompson's reply.

Gladys Norman sighed elaborately. "There are moments, James Thompson," she said, "when your conversation is almost inspiring," and she relapsed into silence.

For the last half–hour Thompson had been conscious of a feeling of uneasiness. It had first manifested itself when he was engaged upon a lightly grilled cutlet; had developed as he tackled the lower joint of a leg of chicken; and become an alarming certainty when he was half–way through a plate of apple tart and custard. Gladys Norman's interest in Malcolm Sage had become more than a secretarial one.

Mentally he debated the appalling prospect. By the time coffee was finished he had reached an acute stage of mental misery. Suddenly life had become, not only tinged, but absolutely impregnated with wretchedness.

It was not until they had left the restaurant and were walking along Shaftesbury Avenue that he summoned up courage to speak.

"Gladys," he said miserably, "you're not—" then he paused, not daring to put into words his thought.

"He's so magnetic, so compelling," she murmured dreamily. "He knows so much. Any girl might—"

She did not finish the sentence; but stole a glance at Thompson's tragic face.

They walked in silence as far as Piccadilly Circus, then in the glare of the light she saw the misery of his expression.

"You silly old thing," she laughed, as she slipped her arm through his. "You funny old thing," and she laughed again.

That laugh was a Boddy lifebelt to the sinking heart of Thompson.

CHAPTER IX. THE HOLDING UP OF LADY GLANEDALE

MORE trouble. Tommy," remarked Gladys Norman one morning as James Thompson entered her room. He looked across at her quickly, a keen flash of interest in his somnolent brown eyes.

"Somebody's pinched Lady Glanedale's jewels. Just had a telephone message. What a happy place the world would be without drink and crime——"

"And women," added Thompson, alert of eye, and prepared to dodge anything that was coming.

"Tommy, you're a beast. Get thee hence!" and bending over her typewriter, she became absorbed in rattling words on to paper.

Thompson had just reached the third line of "I'm Sorry I Made You Cry," when his quick eye detected Malcolm Sage as he entered the outer office.

With a brief "Good morning," Malcolm Sage passed into his room, and a minute later Gladys Norman was reading from her note–book the message that had come over the telephone to the effect that early that morning a burglar had entered Lady Glanedale's bedroom at the Home Park, Hyston, the country house of Sir Roger Glanedale, and, under threat from a pistol, had demanded her jewel–case, which she had accordingly handed to him.

As the jewels were insured with the Twentieth Century Insurance Corporation, Ltd., Malcolm Sage had been immediately communicated with, that he might take up the enquiry with a view to tracing the missing property.

One of Malcolm Sage's first cases had been undertaken for this company in connection with a burglary. He had been successful in restoring the whole of the missing property. In consequence he had been personally thanked by the Chairman at a fully attended Board Meeting, and at the same time presented with a gold–mounted walking–stick, which, as he remarked to Sir John Dene, no one but a drum—major in full dress would dare to carry.

Having listened carefully as she read her notes, Malcolm Sage dismissed Gladys Norman with a nod, and for some minutes sat at his table drawing the inevitable diagrams upon his blotting pad. Presently he rose, and walked over to a row of shelves filled with red—backed volumes, lettered on the back "Records," with a number and a date.

Every crime or curious occurrence that came under Malcolm Sage's notice was duly chronicled in the pages of these volumes, which contained miles of press—cuttings. They were rendered additionally valuable by an elaborate system of cross—reference indexing.

After referring to an index—volume, Malcolm Sage selected one of the folios, and returned with it to his table. Rapidly turning over the pages he came to a newspaper—cutting, which was dated some five weeks previously. This he read and pondered over for some time. It ran:

'DARING BURGLARY. COUNTRY MANSION ENTERED

'BURGLAR'S SANG—FROID

'In the early hours of yesterday morning a daring burglary was committed at the Dower House, near Hyston, the residence of Mr. Gerald Comminge, who was away from home at the time, by which the burglar was able to make a rich haul of jewels.

'In the early hours of the morning Mrs. Comminge was awakened by the presence of a man in her room. As she sat up in bed, the man turned an electric torch upon her and, pointing a revolver in her direction, warned her that if she cried out he would shoot. He then demanded to know where she kept her jewels, and Mrs. Comminge, too terrified to do anything else, indicated a drawer in which lay her jewel—case.

'Taking the jewel—case and putting it under his arm, the man threatened that if she moved or called out within a quarter of an hour he would return and shoot her. He then got out of the window on to a small balcony and disappeared.

'It seems that he gained admittance by clambering up some ivy and thus on to the narrow balcony that runs the length of one side of the house. Immediately on the man's disappearance, Mrs. Comminge fainted. On coming to she gave the alarm, and the police were immediately telephoned for. Although the man's footprints are easily discernible upon the mould and the soft turf, the culprit seems to have left no other clue.

'The description that Mrs. Comminge is able to give of her assailant is rather lacking in detail, owing to the shock she experienced at his sudden appearance. It would appear that the man is of medium height and slight of build. He wore a cap and a black handkerchief tied across his face just beneath his eyes, which entirely masked his features. With this very inadequate description of the ruffian the police have perforce to set to work on the very difficult task of tracing him.'

For some time Malcolm Sage pondered over the cutting, then rising he replaced the volume and rang for Thompson.

An hour later Tims was carrying him along in the direction of Sir Roger Glanedale's house at a good thirty–five miles an hour.

The Home Park was an Elizabethan mansion that had been acquired by Sir Roger Glanedale out of enormous profits made upon the sale of margarine. As Tims brought the car up before the front entrance with an impressive sweep, the hall–door was thrown open by the butler, who habitually strove by an excessive dignity of demeanour to remove from his mental palate the humiliating flavour of margarine.

Malcolm Sage's card considerably mitigated the impression made upon Mr. Hibb's mind by the swing with which Tims had brought the car up to the door.

Malcolm Sage was shown into the morning–room and told that her ladyship would see him in a few minutes. He was busy in the contemplation of the garden when the door opened and Lady Glanedale entered.

He bowed and then, as Lady Glanedale seated herself at a small table, he took the nearest chair.

She was a little woman, some eight inches too short for the air she assumed, fair, good–looking; but with a hard, set mouth. No one had ever permitted her to forget that she had married margarine.

101

Malcolm Sage, Detective

"You have called about the burglary?" she enquired, in a tone she might have adopted to a plumber who had come to see to a leak in the bath.

Malcolm Sage bowed. "Perhaps you will give me the details," he said. "Kindly be as brief as possible," his "incipient Bolshevism" manifesting itself in his manner.

Lady Glanedale elevated her eyebrows; but, as Malcolm Sage's eyes were not upon her, she proceeded to tell her story.

"About one o'clock this morning I was awakened to find a man in my bedroom," she began. "He was standing between the bedstead and the farther window, his face masked. He had a pistol in one hand, which he pointed towards me, and an electric torch in the other. I sat up in bed and stared at him. 'If you call out I shall kill you,' he said. I asked him what he wanted. He replied that if I gave him my jewel–case and did not call for help, he would not do me any harm.

"Realising that I was helpless, I got out of bed, put on a wrapper, opened a small safe I have set in the wall, and handed him one of the two jewel–cases I possess.

"He then made me promise that I would not ring or call out for a quarter of an hour, and he disappeared out of the window.–

"At the end of a quarter of an hour I summoned help, and my stepson, the butler, and several other servants came to my room. We telephoned for the police, and after breakfast we telephoned to the insurance company."

For fully a minute there was silence. Malcolm Sage decided that Lady Glanedale certainly possessed the faculty of telling a story with all the events in their proper sequence. He found himself with very few questions to put to her.

"Can you describe the man?" he asked as he mechanically turned over the leaves of a book on a table beside him.

"Not very well," she replied. "I saw little more than a silhouette against the window. He was of medium height, slight of build and I should say young."

"That seems to agree with the description of the man who robbed Mrs. Comminge," he said as if to himself.

"That is what the inspector said," remarked Lady Glanedale.

"His voice?"

'Was rather husky, as if he were trying to disguise it."

"Was it the voice of a man of refinement or otherwise?"

"I should describe it as middle–class," was the snobbish response.

"The mask?"

"It looked like a silk handkerchief tied across his nose. It was dark in tone; but I could get only a dim impression."

Malcolm Sage inclined his head comprehendingly. "You know Mrs. Comminge?"

"Intimately."

"You mentioned two jewel–cases," he said.

"The one stolen contained those I mostly wear," replied Lady Glanedale, "in the other I keep some very valuable family jewels."

"What was the value of those stolen?"

"About 8,000 pounds," she replied, "possibly more. I should explain, perhaps, that Sir Roger was staying in town last night, and so far I have not been able to get him on the telephone. He was to have stayed at the Ritzton; but apparently he found them full and went elsewhere."

"You have no suspicion as to who it was that entered your room?"

"None whatever," said Lady Glanedale.

"The police have already been?" he enquired, as he examined with great intentness a rose he had taken from a bowl beside him.

"Yes, they came shortly after we telephoned. They gave instructions that nothing was to be touched in the room, and no one was to go near the ground beneath the windows."

Malcolm Sage nodded approvingly, and returned the rose to the bowl.

"And now," he said, "I think I should like to see the room. By the way, I take it that you keep your safe locked?"

"Always," said Lady Glanedale.

"Where do you keep the key?"

"In the bottom right–hand drawer of my dressing–table, under a pile of handkerchiefs."

"As soon as you can I should like to see a list of the jewels," said Malcolm Sage, as he followed Lady Glanedale towards the door.

"My maid is copying it out now," she replied, and led the way up the staircase, along a heavily–carpeted corridor, at the end of which she threw open a door giving access to a bedroom.

Malcolm Sage entered and gave a swift look about him, seeming to note and catalogue every detail. It was a large room, with two windows looking out on to a lawn. On the right was a door, which. Lady Glanedale explained, led to Sir Roger's dressing–room.

He walked over to the window near the dressing–room and looked out.

"That is the window he must have entered by; he went out that way," explained Lady Glanedale.

"You spoke of a stepson," said Malcolm Sage. "He is a man, I presume?"

104

"He is twenty–three." Lady Glanedale elevated her eyebrows as if surprised at the question.

"Can you send for him?"

"Certainly, if you wish it." She rang the bell, and a moment later requested the maid who answered it to ask Mr. Robert to come immediately.

"Do you sleep with lowered blinds?" enquired Malcolm Sage.

"The one nearest my bed I always keep down; the other I pull up after putting out my light."

"Did you awaken suddenly, or gradually–as if it were your usual time to awaken?"

"It was gradual," said Lady Glanedale, after a pause for thought. "I remember having the feeling that someone was looking at me." ,,>

"Was the light from the torch shining on your face?"

"No, it was turned to the opposite side of the room, on my right as I lay in bed."

At that moment a young man in tweeds entered. "You want me. Mater?" he enquired; then, looking across at Malcolm Sage with a slightly troubled shadow in his eyes, he bowed.

"This is Mr. Sage from the insurance company," said Lady Glanedale coldly. "He wishes to see you."

Again there was the slightly troubled look in young Glanedale's eyes.

"Perhaps you will place Mr. Glanedale in the exact position in which the man was standing when you first saw him," said Malcolm Sage.

Without a word Lady Glanedale walked over to the spot she had indicated, young Glanedale following. When she had got him into the desired position she turned interrogatingly to Malcolm Sage.

"Now," he said, "will you be so kind as to lie on your bed in the same position in which you were when you awakened."

For a moment Lady Glanedale's eyebrows indicated surprise. She used her eyebrows more than any other feature for the purpose of expressing emotion. Without comment, however, she lay down upon the bed on her right side, closed her eyes, then a moment later sat up and gazed in the direction where Glanedale stood looking awkward and self–conscious.

"Perhaps you will repeat every movement you made," said Malcolm Sage. "Try to open the safe–door exactly as you did then, and leave it at the same angle. Every detail is important."

Lady Glanedale rose, picked up a wrapper that was lying over a chair–back, put it on and, walking over to the safe, turned the key that was in the lock, and opened it. Then, standing between the safe and Glanedale, she took out a jewel–case and closed the door. Finally she walked over to where her stepson stood, and handed him the jewel–case.

"Thank you," said Malcolm Sage. "I wanted to see whether or not the man had the opportunity of seeing into the safe."

"I took care to stand in front of it," she said.

"So I observed. You allowed the quarter of an hour to elapse before you raised the alarm?"

"Certainly, I had promised," was the response.

"But a promise extorted by threats of violence is not binding," he suggested as he pulled meditatively at his right ear.

"It is with me," was the cold retort.

He inclined his head slightly.

"I notice that the ground beneath the windows has been roped off."

"The inspector thought it had better be done, as there were footprints."

"I will not trouble you further for the present. Lady Glanedale," said Malcolm Sage, moving towards the door. "I should like to spend a little time in the grounds. Later I may require to interrogate the servants."

Young Glanedale opened the door and his step–mother, followed by Malcolm Sage, passed out. They descended the stairs together.

"Please don't trouble to come out," said Malcolm Sage. "I shall probably be some little time," this as Lady Glanedale moved towards the hall–door. "By the way," he said, as she turned towards the morning–room where she had received him, "did you happen to notice if the man was wearing boots, or was he in stockinged feet?"

"I think he wore boots," she said, after a momentary pause.

"Thank you," and Malcolm Sage turned towards the door, which was held open by the butler.

Passing down the steps and to the left, he walked round to the side of the house, where the space immediately beneath Lady Glanedale's windows had been roped off.

Stepping over the protecting rope, he examined the ground beneath the window through which the burglar had entered.

Running along the side of the house was a flower–bed some two feet six inches wide, and on its surface was clearly indicated a series of footprints. On the side of the painted water–pipe were scratches such as might have been made by someone climbing up to the window above.

Drawing a spring metal–rule from his pocket, he proceeded to take a series of measurements, which he jotted down in a notebook.

He next examined the water-pipe up which the man presumably had climbed, and presently passed on to a similar pipe farther to the left. Every inch of ground he subjected to a careful and elaborate examination, lifting the lower branches of some evergreens and gazing beneath them.

Finally, closing his notebook with a snap, Malcolm Sage seated himself upon a garden-seat and, carefully filling and lighting his pipe, he became absorbed in the polished pinkness of the third finger-nail of his left hand.

A quarter of an hour later he was joined by young Glanedale.

"Found anything?" he enquired.

"There are some footprints," said–Malcolm Sage looking at him keenly. "By the way, what did you do when you heard of the robbery?"

"I went to the Mater's room."

"And after that?"

"I rushed downstairs and started looking about."

'You didn't happen to come anywhere near this spot, or walk upon the mould there?" He nodded at the place he had just been examining.

"No; as a matter of fact, I avoided it. The Mater warned me to be careful."

Malcolm Sage nodded his head.

"Did the butler join you in your search?" he enquired.

"About five minutes later he did. He had to go back and put on some things; he was rather sketchy when he turned up in the Mater's room." Glanedale grinned at the recollection.

"And you?" Malcolm Sage flashed on him that steel grey look of interrogation. For a moment the young man seemed embarrassed, and he hesitated before replying.

"As a matter of fact, I hadn't turned in," he said at length.

"I see," said Malcolm Sage, and there was something in his tone that caused Glanedale to look at him quickly.

"It was such a rippin' night that I sat at my bedroom window smoking," he explained a little nervously.

"Which is your bedroom window?"

Glanedale nodded in the direction of the farther end of the house.

"That's the governor's dressing–room," he said, indicating the window on the left of that through which the burglar had escaped, "and the next is mine."

"Did you see anything?" enquired Malcolm Sage, who, having unscrewed the mouthpiece of his pipe, proceeded to clean it with a blade of grass.

Again there was the slightest suggestion of hesitation before Glanedale replied.

"No, nothing. You see," he added hastily, "I was not looking out of the window, merely sitting at it. As a matter of fact, I was facing the other way."

"You heard no noise?"

Glanedale shook his head.

"So that the first intimation you had of anything being wrong was what?" he asked.

"I heard the Mater at her door calling for assistance, and I went immediately."

Malcolm Sage turned and regarded the water–pipe speculatively.

"I wonder if anyone really could climb up that," he said. "I'm sure I couldn't."

"Nothing easier," said Glanedale. "I could shin up in two ticks," and he made a movement towards the pipe.

"No," said Malcolm Sage, putting a detaining hand upon his arm. "If you want to demonstrate your agility, try the other. There are marks on this I want to preserve."

"Right–o," cried Glanedale with a laugh, and a moment later he was shinning up the further pipe with the agility of a South Sea islander after coconuts.

Malcolm Sage walked towards the pipe, glanced at it, and then at the footprints beneath.

"You were quite right," he remarked casually. Then a moment later he enquired: "Do you usually sit up late?"

"We're not exactly early birds," Glanedale replied a little irrelevantly. "The Mater plays a lot of bridge, you know," he added.

"And that keeps you out of bed?"

"Yes and no," was the reply. "I can't afford to play with the Mater's crowd; but I have to hang about until after they've gone. The governor hates it. You see," he added confidentially, "when a man's had to make his money, he knows the value of it."

"True," said Malcolm Sage, but from the look in his eyes his thoughts seemed elsewhere.

"By the way, what time was it that you had a shower here last night?"

"A shower?" repeated Glanedale. "Oh! yes, I remember, it was just about twelve o'clock; it only lasted about ten minutes."

"I'll think things over," said Malcolm Sage, and Glanedale, taking the hint, strolled off towards the house.

Malcolm Sage, Detective

Malcolm Sage walked over to where an old man was trimming a hedge. "Could you lend me a trowel for half an hour?" he enquired.

"No, dang it, I can't," growled the old fellow. "I ain't a–going to lend no more trowels or anythink else."

"Why?" enquired Malcolm Sage.

"There's my best trowel gone out of the tool–house," he grumbled, "and I ain't a–going to lend no others."

"How did it go?"

"How should I know?" he complained. "Walked out, I suppose, same as trowels is always doin'."

"When did you miss it?"

"It was there day 'fore yesterday I'll swear, and I ain't a–going to lend no more."

"Do you think the man who took the jewels stole it?" enquired Malcolm Sage.

"Dang the jools," he retorted, "I want my trowel," and, grumbling to himself, the old fellow shuffled off to the other end of the hedge.

Half an hour later Malcolm Sage was in Hyston, interviewing the inspector of police, who was incoherent with excitement. He learned that Scotland Yard was sending down a man that afternoon, furthermore that elaborate enquiries were being made in the neighbourhood as to any suspicious characters having recently been seen.

Malcolm Sage asked a number of questions, to which he received more or less impatient replies. The inspector was convinced that the robbery was the work of the same man who had got away with Mrs. Comminge's jewels, and he was impatient with anyone who did not share this view.

From the police station Malcolm Sage went to The Painted Flag, where, having ordered lunch, he got through to the Twentieth Century Insurance Corporation, and made an appointment to meet one of the assessors at Home Park at three o'clock.

CHAPTER X. A LESSON IN DEDUCTION

MR. GRIMWOOD, of the firm of Grimwood, Gallon and Davy, insurance assessors, looked up from the list in his hand. He was a shrewd little man, with side–whiskers, pince–nez that would never sit straight upon his aquiline nose, and an impressive cough.

He glanced from Malcolm Sage to young Glanedale, then back again to Malcolm Sage; finally he coughed.

The three men were seated in Sir Roger Glanedale's library awaiting the coming of Lady Glanedale.

"And yet Mr. Glanedale heard nothing," remarked Mr. Grimwood musingly. "Strange, very strange."

"Are you in the habit of sitting smoking at your bedroom window?" enquired Malcolm Sage of Glanedale, his eyes averted.

"Er_no, not exactly," was the hesitating response.

"Can you remember when last you did such a thing?" was the next question.

"I'm afraid I can't," said Glanedale, with an uneasy laugh.

"Perhaps you had seen something that puzzled you," continued Malcolm Sage, his restless fingers tracing an imaginary design upon the polished surface of the table before him.

Glanedale was silent. He fingered his moustache with a nervous hand. Mr. Grimwood looked across at Malcolm Sage curiously.

"And you were watching in the hope of seeing something more," continued Malcolm Sage.

"I–" began Glanedale, starting violently, then he stopped.

"Don't you think you had better tell us exactly what it was you saw," said Malcolm Sage, raising a pair of gold–rimmed eyes that mercilessly beat down the uneasy gaze of the young man.

"I–I didn't say I saw anything."

"It is for you to decide, Mr. Glanedale," said Malcolm Sage, with an almost imperceptible shrug of his shoulders, "whether it is better to tell your story now, or under cross–examination in the witness–box. There you will be under oath, and the proceedings will be public."

At that moment Lady Glanedale entered, and the three men rose. "I am sorry to interrupt you," she said coldly, "but Sir Roger has just telephoned and wishes to speak to Mr. Glanedale."

"I fear we shall have to keep Sir Roger waiting," said Malcolm Sage, walking over to the door and closing it.

Lady Glanedale looked at him in surprise. "I do not understand," she began.

"You will immediately," said Malcolm Sage quietly. "We were just discussing the robbery." He slightly stressed the word "robbery."

"Really—" began Lady Glanedale.

"Mr. Glanedale was sitting at his window smoking," continued Malcolm Sage evenly. "He cannot remember ever having done such a thing before. I suggested that something unusual had attracted his attention, and that he was waiting to see what would follow. I was just about to tell him what had attracted his attention when you entered. Lady Glanedale."

Glanedale looked across at his step–mother and then at Malcolm Sage. His misery was obvious.

"Last night, soon after twelve," continued Malcolm Sage, "Mr. Glanedale happened to look out of his window and was surprised to see a figure moving along towards the left. It was not the figure of a man with a handkerchief tied across his face as a mask; but a woman. He watched. He saw it pause beneath the second window of your bedroom, Lady Glanedale, not the one by which the burglar entered. Then it stooped down."

Malcolm Sage's fingers seemed to be tracing each movement of the mysterious figure upon the surface of the table. Lady Glanedale gazed at his long, shapely hands as if hypnotised.

"Presently," he continued, "it returned to the first window, where it was occupied for some minutes. Mr. Glanedale could not see this; but the figure was engaged in making footprints and marking the sides of the water–pipe with a shoe or boot as high up as it could reach. It—"

"How dare you make such an accusation!" cried Lady Glanedale, making an effort to rise; but she sank back again in her chair, her face plaster–white.

"I have made no accusation," said Malcolm Sage quietly. "I am telling what Mr. Glanedale saw."

A hunted look sprang to Lady Glanedale's eyes. She tore her eyes from those magnetic fingers and gazed about her wildly as if meditating flight. Her throat seemed as if made of leather.

"Would you be prepared to deny all this in the witness–box under oath, Mr. Glanedale?" enquired Malcolm Sage.

Glanedale looked at him with unseeing eyes, then across at his step–mother.

"The woman had put on a pair of men's boots that the footprints might be masculine. They were so much too large for her that she had to drag her feet along the ground. The boots were those of a man weighing, say, about eleven and a half stone; the weight inside

114

those boots shown by the impression in the mould was little more than seven stone."

Lady Glanedale put out her hand as if to ward off a blow; but Malcolm Sage continued mercilessly, addressing Glanedale. "The length of a man's stride is thirty inches; between these steps the space was less than fifteen inches. Skirts are worn very narrow."

He paused, then, as Lady Glanedale made no reply, he turned to Glanedale.

"I asked you this morning," he said, "to climb the other pipe for the double purpose of examining the impress of your boots on the mould as you left the ground and when you dropped back again on to the mould. Also to see what sort of marks a pair of leather boots would make upon the weatherworn paint of the pipe.

"As you sprang from the ground and clutched the pipe, there was a deep impress on the mould of the soles of both boots, deep at the toes and tapering off towards the heel. On your return you made distinct heel–marks as well."

Lady Glanedale had buried her face in her hands. She must blot out the sight of those terrible hands! Glanedale sat with his eyes upon Malcolm Sage as if hypnotised.

"There was a shower of rain last night about twelve, an hour before the alleged burglar arrived; yet the footprints were made before the rain fell. In two cases leaves had been trodden into the footprints; yet on these leaves were drops of rain just as they had fallen."

The hands seemed to draw the leaves and indicated the spots of water as if they had been blood. Glanedale shuddered involuntarily.

"In the centre–part of the pipe there were no marks, although there were light scratches for as high up as the arm of a short person could reach, and as far down from the bedroom window as a similar arm could stretch. These scratches were quite dissimilar from those made on the other pipe."

Lady Glanedale moaned something unintelligible.

"Although there had been a shower and the mould was wet," proceeded Malcolm Sage, "there were no marks of mud or mould on the pipe, on the window–sill, or in Lady

Glanedale's bedroom, which, I understand, had purposely not been swept. A man had slid down that water–pipe; yet he had done so without so much as removing the surface dust from the paint.

"He had reached the ground as lightly as a fairy, without making any mark upon the mould; the footprints were merely those of someone approaching and walking from the pipe."

Glanedale drew a cigarette case from his pocket; opened it, took out a cigarette, then, hesitating a moment, replaced it, and returned the case to his pocket, his eyes all the time on Malcolm Sage.

"I think," continued Malcolm Sage, "we shall find that the burglar has buried the jewel–case a few yards to the right of the pipe he is supposed to have climbed." His forefinger touched a spot on the extreme right of the table. "There are indications that the mould has been disturbed. Incidentally a trowel is missing—"

Glanedale suddenly sprang to his feet, just as Lady Glanedale fell forward in her chair–she had fainted.

"It's a very unpleasant business," remarked Mr. Goodge, the General Manager of the Twentieth Century Insurance Company, as he looked up from reading a paper that Malcolm Sage had just handed to him. In it Lady Glanedale confessed the fraud she had sought to practise upon the Corporation. "A very unpleasant business," he repeated.

Malcolm Sage gazed down at his finger–nails, as if the matter had no further interest for him. When his brain was inactive, his hands were at rest.

"I don't know what view the Board will take," continued Mr. Goodge, as Malcolm Sage made no comment.

"They will probably present me with another walking–stick," he remarked indifferently.

Mr. Goodge laughed. Malcolm Sage's walking–stick had been a standing joke between them.

"What made you first suspect Lady Glanedale?" he enquired.

"She had omitted to rehearse the episode of the burglary, and consequently when it came to reconstructing the incident, she failed in a very important particular." Malcolm Sage paused.

"What was that?" enquired Mr. Goodge with interest, as he pushed a box of cigars towards Malcolm Sage, who, however, shaking his head, proceeded to fill his pipe.

"She had already told me that the key of the safe was always kept beneath a pile of handkerchiefs in one of the drawers of her dressing–table; yet when I asked her to go through exactly the same movements and actions as when the burglar entered her room, she rose direct from the bed and went to the safe. The dressing–table was at the other end of the room, and to get to it she would have had to pass the spot where she said the man was standing."

Mr. Goodge nodded his head appreciatively.

"The next point was that I discovered it was Lady Glanedale who suggested to the police inspector that means should be taken to prevent anyone approaching the water–pipe by which the man was supposed to have climbed. She was anxious that the footprints should be preserved.

"Another point was that young Glanedale happened to remark that his step–mother was much addicted to bridge, and that the stakes were too high to admit of his joining in. Also that men who have themselves accumulated their wealth know the value of money. Sir Roger disliked bridge and probably kept his lady short."

"Most likely," agreed Mr. Goodge. "He has the reputation of being a bit shrewd in money matters. When did you begin to suspect Lady Glanedale?"

"From the first," was the reply. "Everything rang false. Lady Glanedale's story suggested that it had been rehearsed until she had it by heart," continued Malcolm Sage. "It was too straightforward, too clearly expressed for the story of a woman who had just lost eight thousand pounds' worth of jewels. When I put questions to her she hesitated before replying, as if mentally comparing her intended answer with what she had already told.

117

"Then she was so practical in preparing a list of the lost jewels at once, and in warning her stepson not to go near the spot beneath her window, as there might be footprints; this at a time when she was supposed to be in a state of great excitement."

"Did you suspect young Glanedale at all?" queried Mr. Goodge.

"No," said Malcolm Sage, "but to make quite sure I cast doubt upon the possibility of anyone climbing the pipe. If he had been concerned he would not have volunteered to prove I was wrong."

"True," said Mr. Goodge as he examined critically the glowing end of his cigar. "Lady Glanedale seems to have done the job very clumsily, now that you have explained everything."

"Even the professional criminal frequently underrates the intelligence of those whose business it is to frustrate him; but Lady Glanedale's efforts in marking the water–pipe would not have deceived a child. A powerful magnifying–glass will show that on all such exterior pipes there is an accumulation of dust, which would be removed from a large portion of the surface by anyone climbing either up or down. Lady Glanedale had thought marks made by a boot or a shoe would be sufficient confirmation of her story. She is rather a stupid woman," he added, as he rose to go.

"I suppose she got the idea from the Comminge affair?"

"Undoubtedly," was the response; "but as I say, she is a stupid woman. Vanity in crime is fatal; it leads the criminal to underrate the intelligence of others. Lady Glanedale is intensely vain."

"The Board will probably want to thank you personally," said Mr. Goodge as he shook hands; "but I'll try and prevent them from giving you another walking–stick," he laughed as he opened the door.

CHAPTER XI. THE MCMURRAY MYSTERY

OF the many problems upon which Malcolm Sage was engaged during the early days of the Malcolm Sage Bureau, that concerning the death of Professor James McMurray, the eminent physiologist, was perhaps the most extraordinary. It was possessed of several remarkable features; for one thing the murderer had disappeared leaving no clue; for another the body when found seemed to have undergone a strange change, many of the professor's sixty—five years appearing to have dropped from him in death as leaves from an autumn tree.

It was one of those strange crimes for which there is no apparent explanation, consequently the strongest weapon the investigator has, that of motive, was absent. As far as could be gathered the dead professor had not an enemy in the world. He was a semi—recluse, with nothing about him to tempt the burglar; yet he had been brutally done to death in his own laboratory, and the murderer had made good his escape without leaving anything likely to prove helpful to the police.

One day as Gladys Norman, like "panting Time," toiled after her work in vain, striving to tap herself up to date with an accumulation of correspondence, the telephone—bell rang for what seemed to her the umpteenth time that morning. She seized the receiver as a dog seizes a rat, listened, murmured a few words in reply, then banged it back upon its rest.

"Oh dear!" she sighed. "I wish they'd let him alone. The poor dear looks tired out." She turned to William Johnson, who had just entered. "Why don't you hurry up and become a man, Innocent," she demanded, "so that you can help the Chief?"

William Johnson looked vague and shuffled his feet. His .admiration of Malcolm Sage's secretary rendered him self—conscious in her presence.

"Sir John Dene and Sir Jasper Chambers to see the Chief," he announced, obviously impressed by the social importance of the callers.

"Sure it's not the Shah of Persia and Charlie Chaplin?" she asked wearily as she rose from her table and, walking over to the door marked "Private," passed into Malcolm Sage's room.

Reappearing a moment later she instructed William Johnson to show the visitors in at once.

Malcolm Sage, Detective

As the two men passed through Miss Norman's room, they formed a striking contrast. Sir John Dene short, thick–set, alert, with the stamp of the West–End upon all he wore; Sir Jasper Chambers tall, gaunt and dingy, with a forehead like the bulging eaves of an Elizabethan house, and the lower portion of his face a riot of short grizzled grey hair that seemed to know neither coercion nor restraint. His neck appeared intent on thrusting itself as far as possible out of the shabby frock–coat that hung despairingly from his narrow shoulders.

"I wonder," murmured Gladys Norman, as she returned to her typing, "how many geraniums he had to give for those clothes."

"Mornin', Mr. Sage," cried Sir John Dene.

Malcolm Sage rose. There was an unwonted cordiality in the way in which he extended his hand.

"This is Sir Jasper Chambers." Sir John Dene turned to his companion. "You'll be able to place him," and he twirled the unlit cheroot between his lips with bewildering rapidity.

Sir Jasper bowed with an old–world courtliness and grace that seemed strangely out of keeping with his lank and un–picturesque bearing. Malcolm Sage, however, held out his hand with the air of one wishing to convey that a friend of Sir John Dene merited special consideration.

He motioned the two men to seats and resumed his own. Both declined the box of cigars he proffered. Sir John Dene preferring the well–chewed cheroot between his lips, whilst Sir Jasper drew a pipe from the tail–pocket of his frock–coat, which with long fleshless fingers he proceeded to fill from a chamois–leather tobacco–pouch.

"I've brought Sir Jasper along," said Sir John Dene. "You've heard about the murder of his friend Professor McMurray. He didn't want to come; but I told him you'd, be tickled to death, and that you'd get it all figured out for him in two wags of a chipmunk's tail."

Malcolm Sage looked across at the eminent philanthropist, whose whole attention seemed absorbed in the filling of his well–worn briar.

120

Malcolm Sage, Detective

Sir Jasper's wise charities and great humanitarianism were world–famous. It was Will Blink, the Labour demagogue, who had said that of all the honours conferred during the century, Sir Jasper Chambers' O.M. had alone been earned, the others had been either bought or wangled.

The McMurray Murder was the sensation of the hour. The newspapers had "stunted" it, and the public, always eager for gruesome sensation, had welcomed it as if it had been a Mary Pickford film.

Four days previously. Professor James McMurray of Gorling, in Essex, had been found dead in his laboratory, his head fearfully battered in by some blunt instrument.

It was the professor's custom, when engaged upon important research work, to retire, sometimes for days at a time, to a laboratory he had built in his own grounds.

Meals were passed through a small wicket, specially constructed for that purpose in the laboratory wall, and the professor's servants had the most explicit instructions on no account to disturb him.

A fortnight previously Professor McMurray had retired to his laboratory to carry out an important series of experiments. He informed his butler that Sir Jasper Chambers, his lifelong friend, would visit him on the third day, and that dinner for two was to be supplied in the usual way, through the wicket.

On the evening in question, Sir Jasper Chambers had arrived and stayed until a little past nine. He then left the laboratory and proceeded to the house, where he told the butler that his master was quite well, and that in all probability his researches would occupy him another week.

Eight days later, when the butler took the professor's luncheon down to the laboratory, he noticed that the breakfast–tray had not been removed from the shelf just inside the wicket. Convinced that the professor had been so absorbed in his researches that he had forgotten the meal, the butler placed the luncheon–tray beside that containing the breakfast, thinking it better to leave the earlier meal as a reminder to the professor of his forgetfulness.

Malcolm Sage, Detective

At dinner–time the butler was greatly surprised to find that both breakfast and luncheon had remained as he had left them; still, remembering how definite and insistent the professor had been that he was not to be disturbed, the butler had, after consulting with the housekeeper, decided to do nothing for the moment, and contented himself with ringing several times the electric–bell that was the signal of another meal.

An hour later he went once more to the wicket, only to discover that nothing had been touched. Hurrying back to the house with all speed he had conferred with Mrs. Graham, the housekeeper, and, on her insistence, he had telephoned to the police.

Sergeant Crudden of the Essex County Constabulary immediately bicycled over to "The Hollows," Professor McMurray's residence, and, after hearing the butler's story, he had decided to force the door; there are no windows, the laboratory being lighted from above, in order to secure entire privacy.

To the officer's surprise the door yielded readily, having apparently been previously forced. Entering the laboratory he was horrified to discover the body of the professor lying in the centre of the floor, his head literally smashed by a terrible blow that had obviously been delivered from behind.

Acting on the instructions of the police–sergeant, the butler had telephoned the news to the police–station at Strinton with the result that shortly afterwards Inspector Brewitt arrived with a doctor.

The police had made no statement; but there were some extraordinary rumours current in the neighbourhood. One was to the effect that it was not Professor McMurray's body that had been discovered; but that of a much younger man who bore a striking resemblance to him.

"You have seen the accounts of my friend's terrible end?" enquired Sir Jasper, as he took the box of matches Malcolm Sage handed him and proceeded to light his pipe.

Malcolm Sage nodded. His gaze was fixed upon Sir Jasper's grey worsted socks, which concertinaed up his legs above a pair of strangely–fashioned black shoes.

Malcolm Sage, Detective

"He was about to enter upon a series of experiments with a serum he had discovered, his object being to lengthen human life."

Sir Jasper spoke in a gentle, well–modulated voice, in which was a deep note of sadness. He and Professor McMurray had been life–long friends, their intimacy appearing to become strengthened by the passage of years.

"You were the last to see him alive, I understand." Malcolm Sage picked up his fountain–pen and began an elaborate stipple design of a serpent upon the blotting–pad.

"Eight days before he was found I dined with him," said Sir Jasper, his voice a little unsteady.

"What happened?" Malcolm Sage enquired without looking up.

"I arrived at seven o'clock," continued Sir Jasper. "From then until half–past we talked upon things of general interest after which we dined. Later he told me he was about to enter upon a final series of experiments, the result of which would, in all probability, either be fatal to himself, or mean the lengthening of human life."

He paused, gazing straight in front of him, ejecting smoke from his lips in staccatoed puffs. Then he continued: "He said that he had recently made a will, which was lying with his solicitor, and he gave me certain additional instructions as to the disposal of his property."

"Did he seem quite normal?" enquired Malcolm Sage, adding a pair of formidable fangs to his reptile.

"He was calm and confident. At parting he told me I should be the first to know the result."

"Have you any reason to believe that Professor McMurray had enemies?" Malcolm Sage enquired.

"None," was the reply, uttered in a tone of deep conviction, accompanied by a deliberate wagging of the head.

"He was confident of the success of his experiments?"

"Absolutely."

"And you?"

"I had no means of knowing," was the reply.

"You were his greatest friend and his only confidant?" suggested Malcolm Sage, adding the sixth pair of legs to his creation.

"Yes."

"And you were to be the first to be told of the result of the experiments?"

"Those were his last words to me." There was a suggestion of emotion in Sir Jasper's otherwise even voice.

"Can you remember his actual words?"

"Yes; I remember them," he replied sadly. "As we shook hands he said, 'Well, Chambers, you will be the first to know the result.'"

Again there was silence, broken at length by Malcolm Sage, who stroked the back of his head with his left hand. His eyes had returned to Sir Jasper's socks.

"Do you think the professor had been successful in his experiments?" he enquired.

"I cannot say." Again Sir Jasper shook his head slowly and deliberately.

"Did you see the body?"

"I did."

"Is there any truth in the rumours that he looked much younger?"

Malcolm Sage, Detective

"There was certainly a marked change, a startling change," was the reply.

"But death plays odd tricks with years," suggested Malcolm Sage, who was now feeling the lobe of his left ear as if to assure himself of its presence.

"True," said Sir Jasper, nodding his head as if pondering the matter deeply. "True."

"There was an article in last month's The Present Century by Sir Kelper Jevons entitled 'The Dangers of Longevity'. Did you read it.?" enquired Malcolm Sage.

"I did."

"I read it too," broke in Sir John Dene, who had hitherto remained an interested listener, as he sat twirling round between his lips the still unlit cheroot. "A pretty dangerous business it seems to me, this monkeying about with people's glands."

"It called attention to the danger of any interference with Nature's carefully-adjusted balances between life and death," continued Malcolm Sage, who had returned to the serpent which now sported a pair of horns, "and was insistent that the lengthening of human life could result only in harm to the community. Do you happen to know if Professor McMurray had seen this?"

"He had." Sir Jasper leaned forward to knock the ashes from his pipe into the copper tray on Malcolm Sage's table. "We talked of it during dinner that evening. His contention was that science could not be constricted by utilitarianism, and that Nature would adjust her balances to the new conditions."

"But," grumbled Sir John Dene, "it wouldn't be until there had been about the tallest kind of financial panic this little globe of misery has ever seen."

"The article maintained that there would be an intervening period of chaos," remarked Malcolm Sage meditatively, as he opened a drawer and took from it a copy of The Present Century. "I was particularly struck with this passage," he remarked:

"'It is impossible to exaggerate the extreme delicacy of the machinery of modern civilization,' he read. 'Industrialism, the food-supply, existence itself are dependent upon

125

the death–rate. Reduce this materially and it will inevitably lead to an upheaval of a very grave nature. For instance, it would mean an addition of something like a million to the population of the United Kingdom each year, over and above those provided for by the normal excess of births over deaths, and it would be years before Nature could readjust her balances.'"

Malcolm Sage looked across at Sir Jasper, who for some seconds remained silent, apparently deep in thought. "I think," he said presently, with the air of a man carefully weighing his words, "that McMurray was inclined to underestimate the extreme delicacy of the machinery of modem civilisation. I recall his saying that the arguments in that article would apply only in the very unlikely event of someone meeting with unqualified success. That is to say, by the discovery of a serum that would achieve what the Spaniards hoped of the Fountain of Eternal Youth, an instantaneous transformation from age to youth."

"A sort of Faust stunt," murmured Sir John Dene.

Sir Jasper nodded his head gravely.

For some minutes the three men sat silent. Sir Jasper gazing straight in front of him, Sir John Dene twirling his cheroot between his lips, his eyes fixed upon the bald dome–like head of Malcolm Sage, whose eyes were still intent upon his horned reptile, which he had adorned with wings. He appeared to be thinking deeply.

"It's up to you, Mr. Sage, to get on the murderer's trail," said Sir John Dene at length, with the air of a man who has no doubt as to the result.

"You wish me to take up the case, Sir John?" enquired Malcolm Sage, looking up suddenly.

"Sure," said Sir John Dene as he rose. "I'll take it as a particular favour if you will. Now I must vamoose. I've got a date in the city." He jerked himself to his feet and extended a hand to Malcolm Sage. Then turning to Sir Jasper, who had also risen, he added, "You leave it to Mr. Sage, Sir Jasper. Before long you won't see him for dust. He's about the livest wire this side of the St. Lawrence," and with this enigmatical assurance, he walked to the door, whilst Malcolm Sage shook hands with Sir Jasper.

Malcolm Sage, Detective

"Johnnie," said Miss Norman, as William Johnson entered her room in response to a peremptory call on the private-telephone, "Inspector Carfon is to honour us with a call during me next few minutes. Give him a chair and a copy of The Sunday at Home, and watch the clues as they peep out of his pockets. Now buzz off."

William Johnson returned to his table in the outer office and the lurid detective story from which Miss Norman's summons had torn him. He was always gratified when an officer from Scotland Yard called; it seemed to bring him a step nearer to the great crook-world of his dreams. William Johnson possessed imagination; but it was the imagination of the films.

A quarter of an hour later he held open the door of Malcolm Sage's private room to admit Inspector Carfon, a tall man with small features and a large forehead, above which the fair hair had been sadly thinned by the persistent wearing of a helmet in the early days of his career.

"I got your message, Mr. Sage," he began, as he flopped into a chair on the opposite side of Malcolm Sage's table. "This McMurray case is a teaser. I shall be glad to talk it over with you."

"I am acting on behalf of Sir Jasper Chambers," said Malcolm Sage. "It's very kind of you to come round so promptly, Carfon," he added, pushing a box of cigars towards the inspector.

"Not at all, Mr. Sage," said Inspector Carfon as he selected a cigar. "Always glad to do what we can, although we are supposed to be a bit old-fashioned," and he laughed the laugh of a man who can afford to be tolerant.

"I've seen all there is in the papers," said Malcolm Sage. "Are there any additional particulars?"

"There's one thing we haven't told the papers, and it wasn't emphasised at the inquest." The inspector leaned forward impressively.

Malcolm Sage remained immobile, his eyes on his fingernails.

"The doctor," continued the inspector, "says that the professor had been dead for about forty–eight hours, whereas we know he'd eaten a dinner about twenty–six hours before he was found."

Malcolm Sage looked up slowly. In his eyes there was an alert look that told of keen interest.

"You challenged him?" he queried.

"Rather!" was the response, "but he got quite ratty. Said he'd stake his professional reputation and all that sort of thing."

Malcolm Sage meditatively inclined his head several times in succession; his hand felt mechanically for his fountain–pen.

"Then there was another thing that struck me as odd," continued Inspector Carfon, intently examining the end of his cigar. "The professor had evidently been destroying a lot of old correspondence. The paper–basket was full of torn–up letters and envelopes, and the grate was choc–a–bloc with charred paper. That also we kept to ourselves."

"That all?"

"I think so," was the reply. "There's not the vestige of a clue that I can find."

"I see," said Malcolm Sage, looking at a press–cutting lying before him, "that it says there was a remarkable change in the professor's appearance. He seemed to have become rejuvenated."

"The doctor said that sometimes 'death smites with a velvet hand.' He was rather a poetic sort of chap," the inspector added by way of explanation.

"He saw nothing extraordinary in the circumstance?"

"No," was the response. "He seemed to think he was the only one who had ever seen a dead man before. I wouldn't mind betting I've seen as many stiffs as he has, although perhaps he's caused more."

Then as Malcolm Sage made no comment, the inspector proceeded.

"What I want to know is what was the professor doing while the door was being broken open?"

"There were no signs of a struggle?" enquired Malcolm Sage, drawing a cottage upon his thumb–nail.

"None. He seems to have been attacked unexpectedly from behind."

"Was there anything missing?"

"We're not absolutely sure. The professor's gold watch can't be found; but the butler is not certain that he had it on him."

For some time there was silence. Malcolm Sage appeared to be pondering over the additional facts he had just heard.

"What do you want me to do, Mr. Sage?" enquired the inspector at length.

"I was wondering whether you would run down with me this afternoon to Gorling."

"I'd be delighted," was the hearty response. "Somehow or other I feel it's not an ordinary murder. There's something behind it all."

"What makes you think that?" Malcolm Sage looked up sharply.

"Frankly, I can't say, Mr. Sage," he confessed a little shamefacedly, "it's just a feeling I have."

"The laboratory has been locked up?"

"Yes; and I've sealed the door. Nothing has been touched."

Malcolm Sage nodded his head approvingly and, for fully five minutes, continued to gaze down at his hands spread–out on the table before him.

Malcolm Sage, Detective

"Thank you, Carfon. Be here at half–past two."

"The funeral's to–day, by the way," said the inspector as he rose and, with a genial "good morning," left the room.

For the next hour Malcolm Sage was engaged in reading the newspaper accounts of the McMurray Mystery, which he had already caused to be pasted up in the current press–cutting book; he gathered little more from them, however, than he already knew.

That afternoon, accompanied by Inspector Carfon, Malcolm Sage motored down to "The Hollows," which lies at the easternmost end of the village of Gorling.

The inspector stopped the car just as it entered the drive. The two men alighted and, turning sharply to the right, walked across the lawn towards an ugly red–brick building, screened from the house by a belt of trees. Malcolm Sage had expressed a wish to see the laboratory first.

It was a strange–looking structure, some fifty feet long by about twenty feet wide, with a door on the further side. In the red–brick wall nearer the house there was nothing to break the monotony except the small wicket through which the professor's meals were passed.

Malcolm Sage twice walked deliberately round the building. In the meantime the inspector had removed the seal from the padlock and opened the door.

"Did you photograph the position of the body?" enquired Malcolm Sage, as they entered.

"I hadn't a photographer handy," said the inspector apologetically, as he closed the door behind him; "but I managed to get a man to photograph the wound."

"Put yourself in the position of the body," said Malcolm Sage.

The inspector walked to the centre of the room, near a highly–polished table, dropped on to the floor and, after a moment's pause, turned and lay on his left side, with right arm outstretched.

Malcolm Sage, Detective

From just inside the door Malcolm Sage looked about him. At the left extremity a second door gave access to another apartment, which the professor used as a bedroom.

A little to the right of the door, on the opposite side, stood the fireplace. This was full of ashes, apparently the charred remains of a quantity of paper that had been burnt. On the hearth were several partially−charred envelopes, and the paper−basket contained a number of torn−up letters.

"That will do, Carfon," said Malcolm Sage, as he walked over to the fireplace and, dropping on one knee, carefully examined the ashes, touching them here and there with the poker.

He picked up something that glittered and held it out to the inspector who scrambled to his feet, and stood looking down with keen professional interest.

"Piece of a test tube," remarked Malcolm Sage, as he placed the small piece of glass upon the table.

"Moses' aunt!" gasped the inspector. "I missed that, though I saw a lot of bits of glass. I thought it was an electric bulb."

"Somebody had ground it to powder with his heel, all except this piece. Looks as if there might have been more than one," he added more to himself than to the inspector.

"These are not letters," he continued without looking up.

"Not letters?"

"The paper is all of the same quality. By the way, has anyone disturbed it?" He indicated the grate.

"No one," was the reply.

Malcolm Sage rose to his feet. For some minutes he stood looking down at the fireplace, stroking the back of his head, deep in thought.

Presently he picked up the poker, a massive steel affair, and proceeded to examine the fire–end with great minuteness.

"It was done with the other end," said the inspector. "He must have wiped it afterwards. There was no sign of blood or hair."

Malcolm Sage ignored the remark, and continued to regard the business–end of the poker. Walking over to the door he examined the fastenings. Having taken a general survey he next proceeded to a detailed scrutiny of everything the place contained. From the fireplace he picked up what looked like a cinder and placed it in a small box, which he put in his pocket.

The polished surface of the table he subjected to a careful examination, borrowing the inspector's magnifying–glass for the purpose. On hands and knees he crawled round the table, still using the magnifying–glass upon the linoleum, with which the floor was covered. From time to time he would pick up some apparently minute object and transfer it to another small box. At length he rose to his feet as if satisfied.

"The professor did not smoke?" he queried.

"No; but the murderer did," was the rather brusque reply. Inspector Carfon was finding the role of audience trying, alike to his nerves and to his temper.

"Obviously," was Malcolm Sage's dry retort. "He also left his pipe behind and had to return for it. It was rather a foul pipe, too," he added.

"Left his pipe behind!" cried the inspector, his irritation dropping from him like a garment. "How on earth—!" In his surprise he left the sentence unfinished.

"Here," Malcolm Sage indicated a dark stain on the highly–polished table, "and here," he pointed to a few flecks of ash some four or five inches distant, "are indications that a pipe has remained for some considerable time, long enough for the nicotine to drain through the stem; it was a very foul pipe, Carfon."

"But mightn't that have trickled out in a few minutes, or while the man was here?" objected Inspector Carfon.

"With a wet smoker the saliva might have drained back," said Malcolm Sage, his eyes upon the stain, "but this is nicotine from higher up the stem, which would take time to flow out. As to leaving it on the table, what inveterate smoker would allow a pipe to lie on a table for any length of time unless he left it behind him? The man smoked like a chimney, look at the tobacco ash in the fireplace."

The inspector stared at Malcolm Sage, chagrin in his look.

"Now that photograph, Carfon," said Malcolm Sage. Taking a letter–case from his breast–pocket. Inspector Carfon drew out a photograph folded in half. This he handed to Malcolm Sage, who, after a keen glance at the grim and gruesome picture, put it in his pocket.

"I thought so," he murmured.

"Thought what, Mr. Sage?" enquired the inspector eagerly.

"Left–handed." When keenly interested Malcolm Sage was more than usually economical in words. "Clean through the left side of the occipital bone," Malcolm Sage continued. "No right–handed man could have delivered such a blow. That confirms the poker."

The inspector stared.

"The sockets of the bolts, and that of the lock, have been loosened from the inside with the poker," explained Malcolm Sage in a matter–of–fact tone. "The marks upon the poker suggest a left–handed man. The wound in the head proves it."

"Then the forced door was a blind?" gasped the inspector.

"The murderer was let in by the professor himself, who was subsequently attacked from behind as he stood with his back to the fireplace. You are sure the grate has not been touched?" He suddenly raised his eyes in keen interrogation.

Inspector Carfon shook his head. He had not yet recovered from his surprise.

"Someone has stirred the ashes about so as to break up the charred leaves into small pieces to make identification impossible. This man has a brain," he added.

The inspector gave vent to a prolonged whistle. "I knew there was something funny about the whole business," he said as if in self–defence.

Malcolm Sage had seated himself at the table, his long thin fingers outspread before him. Suddenly he gave utterance to an exclamation of annoyance.

The inspector bent eagerly forward.

"The pipe," he murmured. "I was wrong. He put it down because he was absorbed in something, probably the papers he burnt."

"Then you think the murderer burnt the papers?" enquired the inspector in surprise.

"Who else?" asked Malcolm Sage, rising. "Now we'll see the butler."

Whilst the inspector was locking and re–sealing the door, Malcolm Sage walked round the building several times in widening circles, examining the ground carefully; but there had been no rain for several weeks, and nothing upon its surface suggested a footprint.

CHAPTER XII. THE MARMALADE CLUE

A Malcolm Sage and Inspector Carfon crossed the lawn from the laboratory, Sir Jasper Chambers was seen coming down the drive towards them.

"There's Sir Jasper," cried the inspector.

When they reached the point where the lawn joined the drive they paused, waiting for Sir Jasper to approach. He walked with long, loose strides, his head thrust forward, his mind evidently absorbed and far away from where he was. His coat flapped behind him, and at each step his trousers jerked upwards, displaying several inches of grey worsted sock.

"Good afternoon, Sir Jasper," said Inspector Carfon, stepping forward and lifting his hat.

Malcolm Sage, Detective

Sir Jasper stopped dead, with the air of one who has suddenly been brought to a realisation of his whereabouts. For a moment he stared blankly, then apparently recognition came to his aid.

"Good afternoon, inspector," he responded, lifting his black felt hat with a graceful motion that seemed strangely out–of–keeping with his grotesque appearance. In the salutation he managed to include Malcolm Sage, who acknowledged it with his customary jerky nod.

"We have just been looking at the laboratory," said the inspector.

"Ah!" Sir Jasper nodded his head several times. "The laboratory!"

"Will you oblige me with your pouch, Carfon," said Malcolm Sage, drawing his pipe from his pocket. "I've lost mine."

Inspector Carfon thrust his hand into his left–hand pocket, then began to go hurriedly through his other pockets with the air of a man who has lost something.

"I had it a quarter of an hour ago," he said. "I must have dropped it in the—"

"Allow me, sir," said Sir Jasper, extending to Malcolm Sage his own pouch, which he had extracted from his tail–pocket whilst the inspector was still engaged in his search. Malcolm Sage took it and with a nod proceeded to fill his.

'Looks like Craven Mixture," he remarked without looking up from the pipe which he was cramming from Sir Jasper's pouch. Malcolm Sage was an epicure in tobacco.

"No; it's Ormonde Mixture," was the reply. "I always smoke it. It is singularly mellow," he added, "singularly mellow." He continued to look straight in front of him, whilst the inspector appeared anxious to get on to the house.

Having completed his task, Malcolm Sage folded the tobacco–pouch and handed it back to Sir Jasper. "Thank you," he said, and proceeded to light his pipe.

135

Apparently seeing nothing to detain him further, Sir Jasper lifted his hat, bowed and passed on.

"Regular old cove, isn't he?" remarked the inspector as they watched the ungainly figure disappear round the bend of the drive.

"A great man, Carfon," murmured Malcolm Sage, "a very great man," and he turned and walked towards the house.

The front door of "The Hollows" was opened by the butler, a gentle–faced old man, in appearance rather like a mid–Victorian lawyer. At the sight of the inspector, a troubled look came into his eyes.

"I want to have a few words with you," said Malcolm Sage quietly.

The old man led the way to the library. Throwing open the door for them to pass in, he followed and closed it behind him. Malcolm Sage seated himself at the table and Inspector Carfon also dropped into a chair. The butler stood, his hands half–closed before him, the palm of one resting upon the knuckles of the other. His whole attitude was half–nervous, half–fearful, and wholly deprecating.

"I'm afraid this has been a great shock to you," said Malcolm Sage.

Inspector Carfon glanced across at him. There was an unaccustomed note of gentleness in his tone.

"It has indeed, sir," said the butler, and two tears gathered upon his lower lids, hung pendulous for a second, then raced one another down either side of his nose. It was the first sympathetic word the old man had heard since the police had arrived, insatiable for facts.

"Sit down," said Malcolm Sage, without looking up, "I shall not keep you many minutes." His tone was that one might adopt to a child.

The old man obeyed, seating himself upon the edge of the chair, one hand still placed upon the other.

"You mustn't think because the police ask a lot of questions that they mean to be unkind," said Malcolm Sage.

"I–I believe they think I did it," the old man quavered, "and–and I'd have done anything—"His voice broke, the tears coursing down his colourless cheeks.

"I want you to try to help me find out who did kill your master," continued Malcolm Sage, in the same tone, "and you can do that by answering my questions."

There was no restless movement of fingers now. The hard, keen look had left his eyes, and his whole attention seemed to be concentrated upon soothing the old man before him.

With an obvious effort the butler strove to control himself.

"Did the professor ever have visitors at his laboratory?"

"Only Sir Jasper, sir. He was—"

"Just answer my questions," said Malcolm Sage gently. "He told you, I think, never on any account to disturb him?"

"Yes, sir."

"Did you ever do so?"

"Only once, sir."

"That was?"

"When Mrs. Graham, that's the housekeeper, sir, set fire to the curtains of her room. I was afraid for the house, sir, and I ran down and knocked at the laboratory door."

"Did the professor open it?"

"No, sir."

"Perhaps he did not hear you?"

"Yes, he did, sir. I knocked and kicked for a long time, then I ran back to the house and found the fire had been put out."

"Did Professor McMurray ever refer to the matter?"

"He was very angry when I next saw him, sir, three days later."

"What did he say?"

"That neither fire or murder was an excuse for interrupting him, and if I did it again I would have to—"

"Quite so," interrupted Malcolm Sage, desirous of saving the old servitor the humiliation of explaining that he had been threatened with dismissal.

"So you are confident in your own mind that no amount of knocking at the door would have caused your master to open it?"

"Quite certain, sir," the butler said with deep conviction. "If he had heard me murdering Mrs. Graham he wouldn't have come out," he added gravely. "He used to say that man is for the moment; but research is for all time. He was a very wonderful man, sir," he added earnestly.

"So that to get into the laboratory someone must have had a duplicate key?"

"No, sir, the professor always bolted the door on the inside."

"Then he must have opened it himself?"

"He wouldn't, sir. I'm sure he wouldn't."

"But how did Sir Jasper get in?"

"He was expected, sir, and when he went to the laboratory, the master always ordered extra food. He was very absent–minded, sir; but he always remembered that. He was very considerate, sir, too. He never forgot my birthday," and he broke down completely, his frail body shaken by sobs.

Rising, Malcolm Sage placed his hand upon the old man's shoulder. As if conscious of the unspoken message of sympathy inspired by the touch, the butler clasped the hand in both his own.

Inspector Carfon looked surprised.

"He was so kind, sir, so kind and thoughtful," he quavered. "I don't know what I shall do without him." There was in his voice something of the querulous appeal of a little child.

"Were letters ever taken to the laboratory?" enquired Malcolm Sage, walking over to the window and gazing out.

"Never, sir," was the reply. "Everything was kept until the professor returned to the house, even telegrams."

"Then he was absolutely cut off?" said Malcolm Sage returning to his seat.

"That was what he used to say, sir, that he wanted to feel cut off from everybody and everything."

"You have seen the body?"

"Yes, sir."

"Did you notice anything remarkable about it?"

"He was more like he was some thirty years ago, sir."

"Rejuvenated, in fact."

"I beg pardon, sir?"

Malcolm Sage, Detective

"He seemed to have become suddenly a much younger man?" explained Malcolm Sage.

"Yes, sir. I've been with him over thirty years, and he looked very much as he did then, except, of course, that his hair remained grey."

"Apart from the food not being taken in, you noticed nothing else that struck you as strange?" queried Malcolm Sage.

The old man puckered up his eyebrows, as if genuinely anxious to remember something that would please the man who had shown him so much sympathy.

"I can't think of anything, sir," he said at length, apologetically, "only the marmalade, and that, of course, wouldn't—"

"The marmalade?" Malcolm Sage turned quickly.

"It was nothing, sir," said the old man. "Perhaps I oughtn't to have mentioned it; but the morning before we found him, the master had not eaten any marmalade, and him so fond of it. I was rather worried, and I asked Mrs. Graham if it was a new brand, thinking perhaps he didn't like it; but I found it was the same he always had."

For fully a minute Malcolm Sage was silent, gazing straight before him.

"He never smoked?" he asked at length.

"Never, sir, not during the whole thirty years I've been with him."

"Who cleaned the laboratory? It did not look as if it had been unswept for a week."

"No, indeed, sir," was the reply, "the professor was very particular. He always swept it up himself each morning. It was cleaned by one of the servants once a month."

"You're sure about the sweeping–up?" Malcolm Sage enquired, with a keen glance that with him always meant an important point.

"Quite certain, sir."

Malcolm Sage, Detective

"That, I think, will be all."

"Thank you, sir," said the butler, rising. "Thank you for being so kind, and—and understanding, sir," and he walked a little unsteadily from the room.

"I was afraid you wouldn't get anything out of him, Mr. Sage," said Inspector Carfon, with just a suspicion of relief in his voice.

"No," remarked Malcolm Sage quietly, "nothing new; but an important corroboration of the doctor's evidence."

"What was that?"

"That it was the murderer and not Professor McMurray who ate Wednesday's breakfast, luncheon and dinner."

"Good Lord!" The inspector's jaw dropped in his astonishment.

"I suspect that for some reason or other he returned to the laboratory; that accounts for the rough marks upon the door—fastenings as if someone had first torn them off and then sought to replace them. After his second visit the murderer evidently stayed too long, and was afraid of being seen leaving the laboratory. He therefore remained until the following night, eating the professor's meals. Incidentally he knew all about his habits."

"Well, I'm blowed if he isn't a cool 'un!" gasped the inspector.

Malcolm Sage rose with the air of one who has concluded the business on hand.

"Can I run you back to town, Carfon?" he asked, as he walked towards the door.

"No, thank you," said the inspector. "I must go over to Strinton and see Brewitt. He's following up a clue he's got. Some tramp who was seen hanging about here for a couple of days just before the murder," he added.

"Unless he is tall and powerful, left—handed, with something more than a layman's knowledge of surgery, you had better not trouble about him," said Malcolm Sage quietly.

"You might also note that the murderer belongs to the upper, or middle class, has an iron nerve, and is strongly humanitarian." For a moment Inspector Carfon stared at Malcolm Sage with lengthened jaw. Then suddenly he laughed, a laugh of obvious relief.

"At first I thought you were serious, Mr. Sage," he said "till I saw what you were up to. It's just like the story–book detectives," and he laughed again, this time more convincingly.

Malcolm Sage shrugged his shoulders. "Let me have a description of the man when you get him," he said, "and some of the tobacco he smokes. Try him with marmalade, Carfon and plenty of it. By the way, you make a great mistake in not reading The Present Century," he added. "It can be curiously instructive," and without another word he crossed the hall and, a moment later, entered his car.

"Swank!" murmured Inspector Carfon angrily, as he watched Tims swing the car down the drive at a dangerous rate of speed, "pure, unadulterated, brain–rotting swank," and he in turn passed down the drive, determined to let Malcolm Sage see what he could do "on his own."

Three weeks passed and there was no development in the McMurray Mystery. Malcolm Sage had heard nothing from Inspector Carfon, who was busily engaged in an endeavour to trace the tramp seen in the neighbourhood of "The Hollows" on the day previous to the murder.

Sir John Dene had called several times upon Malcolm Sage, whom he had come to regard as infallible, only to be told that there was no news. He made no comment; but it was obvious that he was greatly disappointed.

Interest began to wane, the newspapers devoted themselves to other "stunts," and the McMurray Mystery seemed fated to swell the list of unfathomed crimes with which, from time to time, the Press likes to twit Scotland Yard.

Suddenly the whole affair flared up anew, and Fleet Street once more devoted itself and its columns to the death of Professor James McMurray.

Malcolm Sage, Detective

A brief announcement that a man of the vagrant class had been arrested in London whilst endeavouring to sell a gold watch believed to be that of Professor McMurray, was the first spark. Later the watch was identified and the man charged with the murder. He protested his innocence, saying that he had picked up the watch by the roadside, just outside Gorling, nearly a month before. There were bloodstains on his clothes, which he explained by saying he had been fighting with another man who had made his nose bleed.

Inspector Carfon, unable to keep a note of triumph out of his voice, had telephoned the news to Malcolm Sage, who had asked for particulars of the man, his pipe, and a specimen of his tobacco; but day after day had passed without these being forthcoming. Finally the man, against whom the police had built up a damaging case, had been committed for trial.

Two weeks later he was found guilty at the assizes and sentenced to death.

Then it was that Malcolm Sage had written to Inspector Carfon curtly asking him to call at eleven on the following day, bringing with him the information for which he had asked. At the same time he wrote to Sir John Dene and Sir Jasper Chambers.

Punctually at eleven on the following morning the inspector called at the Malcolm Sage Bureau.

"Sorry, Mr. Sage," he said, as he entered Malcolm Sage's room, "I've been so rushed that I haven't been able to get round," and he dropped into the chair on the opposite side of the table.

Malcolm Sage pushed across the cigar box. "That's his tobacco–box," said Inspector Carfon, placing on the table a small tin–box.

Opening it, and after a swift glance at the contents, Malcolm Sage raised it to his nose: "Cigarette–ends," he remarked without looking up.

"And that's his pipe." The inspector laid on the table a black clay pipe, with some two inches of stem attached to the bowl.

Malcolm Sage scarcely glanced at it. Pulling out a drawer he produced a small cardboard box, which he opened and pushed towards the inspector.

"That is the tobacco smoked by the murderer. The makers are prepared to swear to it."

"Where the deuce did you get it?" gasped the inspector. "Grain by grain from the linoleum in the laboratory," replied Malcolm Sage. "That is why it was necessary to be sure it was swept each day. It also helped me to establish the man as middle or upper class. This tobacco is expensive. What is the man like who has been condemned?"

"A regular wandering willie," replied the inspector. "Oldish chap, gives his age as sixty−one. Five foot three and a half thin as a rake, twenty−nine inch chest. Miserable sort of devil. Says he picked up the watch about a quarter of a mile from 'The Hollows' early one morning."

"Does he eat marmalade?"

"Eat it!" the inspector laughed. "He wolfs it. I remembered what you said and took a pound along with me to Strinton, just for fun." He looked across at Malcolm Sage a little shamefacedly. "I afterwards heard that there was only the jar and the label left; but I don't see what all this has to do with it. The fellow's got to swing for it and—"

"Carfon, you've made a fool of yourself."

The inspector started back in his chair as if someone had struck him.

"I gave you a description of the man who had killed Professor McMurray; yet you proceed to build up a fantastical case against this poor devil."

"But—" began the inspector. He was interrupted by the door being burst violently open and Sir John Dene shot into the room.

For a moment he stood staring at the two men, Gladys Norman and William Johnson framed in the doorway behind him.

"Sir Jasper's killed himself," he cried.

144

Malcolm Sage, Detective

"Moses' aunt!" cried the inspector, starting to his feet.

Malcolm Sage sat immovable at his table, his eyes upon his outstretched hands. Slowly looking up he motioned to Miss Norman to close the door, then nodded towards a chair into which Sir John Dene sank. The inspector resumed his own seat. It was obvious that the news had considerably shaken him.

"You knew?" Sir John Dene interrogated, his voice a little unsteady.

"I expected it," said Malcolm Sage quietly.

"But how, Mr. Sage?" enquired Inspector Carfon in a whisper, his throat dry with excitement.

"Because I wrote to him yesterday saying that I could not allow the condemned man to be sacrificed. It was Sir Jasper Chambers who killed Professor McMurray."

For a moment Inspector Carton's eyes looked as if they would start out of his head. He turned and looked at Sir John Dene, who with unsteady hand was taking a cheroot from his case. Malcolm Sage drew his pipe from his pocket and proceeded to fill it—"On the Tuesday night," he began, "it is obvious that Professor McMurray admitted some one to the laboratory. That man was Sir Jasper Chambers.

"When the two had dined together a week before," proceeded Malcolm Sage, "an appointment was obviously made for a week later. The professor's last words were significant: 'Anyway, Chambers, you will be the first to know.' If the experiments had proved fatal, how could Sir Jasper be the first to know unless an appointment had been made for him to call at the laboratory and discover for himself the result?"

The inspector coughed noisily.

"'When Sir Jasper learned of the unqualified success of the experiments, and saw by the professor's changed appearance proof of his triumph, he remembered the article in The Present Century. He realised that in the lengthening of human life a terrible catastrophe threatened the world. Humanitarianism triumphed over his affection for his friend, and he killed him."

Malcolm Sage, Detective

Sir John Dene nodded his head in agreement. The inspector was leaning forward, his arms on the table, staring at Malcolm Sage with glassy eyes.

"The assailant was clearly a tall, powerful man and left–handed. That was shown by the nature of the blow. That he had some knowledge of physiology is obvious from the fact that he made no attempt at a second blow to ensure death, as a layman most likely would have done. He knew that he had smashed the occipital bone right into the brain. In his early years Sir Jasper studied medicine.

"The crime committed, Sir Jasper proceeded to cover his tracks. With the poker he loosened the sockets of the bolts and that of the lock in order to give an impression that the door had been burst open from without. He then left the place and, to suggest robbery as a motive for the crime, he took with him the professor's gold watch, which he threw away. This was found a few hours later by the tramp whom you, Carfon, want to hang for a crime of which he knows nothing." There was a note of sternness in Malcolm Sage's voice.

"But—" began the inspector.

"I suspect," continued Malcolm Sage, "that after he had left the laboratory. Sir Jasper suddenly realised that the professor had probably recorded in his book all his processes. He returned, discovered the manuscript, and was for hours absorbed in it, at first smoking continuously, later too interested in his task to think of his pipe. It must be remembered that he had studied medicine."

The inspector glanced across at Sir John Dene, who sat rigidly in his chair, his eyes fixed upon Malcolm Sage.

"I rather think that he was aroused from his preoccupation by the ringing of the bell announcing the arrival of the professor's breakfast. He then realised that he could not leave the place until nightfall. He therefore ate that meal, carefully avoiding the marmalade, which he disliked, and subsequently he consumed the luncheon, and dinner, passed through the wicket."

Malcolm Sage paused to press down the tobacco in his pipe.

"He burned the manuscript, tearing up letters and throwing them into the waste–paper basket to give the appearance of Professor McMurray having had a clearing–up. He then destroyed all the test–tubes he could find. Finally he left the laboratory late on the Wednesday night, or early Thursday morning."

"But how did you find out all this?" It was Sir John Dene who spoke.

"First of all. Sir Jasper and the murderer smoke the same[tobacco, 'Ormonde Mixture.' I verified that by picking Inspector Carfon's pocket." Taking a tobacco–pouch from a drawer Malcolm Sage handed it across the table. "You will remember Sir Jasper lent me his pouch. I had picked up some tobacco on the floor and on the hearth. Secondly, the murderer was left–handed, and so is Sir Jasper. Thirdly, the murderer does not eat marmalade and Jasper had the same distaste."

"But how—?" began the inspector.

"I telephoned to his housekeeper in the name of a loca grocer and asked if it would be Sir Jasper who had ordered some marmalade, as an assistant could not remember the gentleman's name. That grocer, I suspect, got into trouble, as the housekeeper seemed to expect him to know that Sir Jasper disliked marmalade.

"Well, you seem to have got the thing pretty well figured out," remarked Sir John Dene grimly.

"Another man's life and liberty were at stake," was the" calm reply, "otherwise—" he shrugged his shoulders.

"As Sir Jasper did not come forward I wrote to him yesterday giving him until noon to–day to make a statement," continued Malcolm Sage, "otherwise I should have to take steps to save the man condemned."

Then after a short pause he continued: "In Sir Jasper Chambers you have an illustration of the smallness of a great mind. He has devoted his vast wealth to philanthropy; yet be was willing to allow another man to be hanged for his crime."

"And this, I take it," said Sir John Dene, "is his reply," and he handed a letter across to Malcolm Sage.

"Read it out," he said.

Malcolm Sage glanced swiftly through the pages and then read:

'MY DEAR DENE,

By the time you receive this letter I shall be dead. I have just received a letter from Mr. Malcolm Sage, which shows him to be a man of remarkable perception, and possessed of powers of analysis and deduction that I venture to think must be unique. All he says is correct, but for one detail. I left the laboratory in the first instance with the deliberate intention of returning, although I did not realise the significance of the manuscript until after I had tampered with the fastenings of the doors. Had my servants found that my bed had not been slept in, suspicion might have attached itself to me. I therefore returned to remedy this, and I left a note to say that I had gone out early for a long walk, a thing I frequently do.

In his experiments McMurray had succeeded beyond his wildest imaginings, and I foresaw the horrors that must inevitably follow such a discovery as his. I had to choose between myself and the welfare of the race, and I chose the race.

I did not come forward to save the man condemned for the crime, as I regarded my life of more value to the community than his.

Will you thank Mr. Sage for the very gentle and humane way in which he has written calling upon me to see that justice be not outraged.

I am sending this letter by hand. My body will be found in my study. I have used morphia as a means of satisfying justice.

Very sincerely yours,

JASPER CHAMBERS.'

"It was strange I should have made that mistake about the reason for his leaving the laboratory," said Malcolm Sage meditatively. "I made two mistakes, one I corrected; but the other was unpardonable."

And he knocked the ashes from his pipe on to the copper tray before him with the air of a man who is far from satisfied.

"And I might have arrested an O.M.," murmured Inspector Carfon, as he walked down Whitehall. "Damn!"

CHAPTER XIII. THE GYLSTON SLANDER

"IT'S all very well for the Chief to sit in there like a five guinea palmist," Gladys Norman cried one morning, as after interviewing the umpteenth caller that day she proceeded vigorously to powder her nose, to the obvious interest of William Johnson; "but what about me? If anyone else comes I must speak the truth. I haven't an unused lie left."

"Then you had better let Johnson have a turn," said a quiet voice behind her.

She spun round, with flaming cheeks and white–flecked nose to see the steel grey eyes of Malcolm Sage gazing on her quizzically through gold–rimmed spectacles. There was only the slightest fluttering at the corners of his mouth.

As his activities enlarged, Malcolm Sage's fame had increased, and he was overwhelmed with requests for assistance. Clients bore down upon him from all parts of the country; some even crossing the Channel, whilst from America and the Colonies came a flood of letters giving long, rambling details of mysteries, murders and disappearances, all of which he was expected to solve.

Those who wrote, however, were as nothing to those who called. They arrived in various stages of excitement and agitation, only to be met by Miss Gladys Norman with a stereotyped smile and the equally stereotyped information that Mr. Malcolm Sage saw no one except by appointment, which was never made until the nature of the would–be client's business had been stated in writing.

Malcolm Sage, Detective

The Surrey cattle–maiming affair, and the consequent publicity it gave to the name of Malcolm Sage, had resulted in something like a siege of the Bureau's offices.

"I told you so," said Lady Dene gaily to her husband, and he had nodded his head in entire agreement.

Malcolm Sage's success was largely due to the very quality that had rendered him a failure as a civil servant, the elasticity of his mind.

He approached each problem entirely unprejudiced, weighed the evidence, and followed the course it indicated, prepared at any moment to retrace his steps, should they lead to a cul–de–sac.

He admitted the importance of the Roman judicial interrogation, "cui bono?" (whom benefits it?); yet he realised that there was always the danger of confusing the pathological with the criminal.

"The obvious is the correct solution of most mysteries," he had once remarked to Sir James Walton; but there is always the possibility of exception.

The Surrey cattle–maiming mystery had been a case in point. Even more so v/as the affair that came to be known as "The Gylston Slander." In this case Malcolm Sage arrived at the truth by a refusal to accept what, on the face of it, appeared to be the obvious solution.

It was through Robert Freynes, the eminent K.C., that he first became interested in the series of anonymous letters that had created considerable scandal in the little village of Gylston.

Tucked away in the north–west corner of Hampshire, Gylston was a village of some eight hundred inhabitants. The vicar, the Rev. John Crayne, had held the living for some twenty years. Aided by his wife and daughter, Muriel, a pretty and high–spirited girl of nineteen, he devoted himself to the parish, and in return enjoyed great popularity.

Life at the vicarage was an ideal of domestic happiness. Mr. and Mrs. Crayne were devoted to each other and to their daughter, and she to them. Muriel Crayne had grown up among the villagers, devoting herself to parish work as soon as she was old enough to do so. She seemed to find her life sufficient for her needs, and many were the comparisons drawn by other parents in Gylston between the vicar's daughter and their own restless offspring.

A year previously a new curate had arrived in the person of the Rev. Charles Blade. His frank, straightforward personality, coupled with his good looks and masculine bearing had caused him to be greatly liked, not only by the vicar and his family, but by all the parishioners.

Suddenly and without warning the peace of the village was destroyed. One morning Mr. Crayne received by post an anonymous letter, in which the names of his daughter and the curate were linked together in a way that caused him both pain and anxiety.

A man with a strong sense of honour himself, he cordially despised the anonymous letter–writer, and his first instinct had been to ignore that which he had just received. On second thoughts, however, he reasoned that the writer would be unlikely to rest content with a single letter; but would, in all probability, make the same calumnious statements to others.

After consulting with his wife, he had reluctantly questioned his daughter. At first she was inclined to treat the matter lightly; but on the grave nature of the accusations being pointed out to her, she had become greatly embarrassed and assured him that the curate had never been more than ordinarily attentive to her.

The vicar decided to allow the matter to rest there, and accordingly he made no mention of the letter to Blade.

A week later his daughter brought him a letter she had found lying in the vicarage grounds. It contained a passionate declaration of love, and ended with a threat of what might happen if the writer's passion were not reciprocated.

Although the letter was unsigned, the vicar could not disguise from himself the fact that there was a marked similarity between the handwriting of the two anonymous letters and that of his curate. He decided, therefore, to ask Blade if he could throw any light on the matter.

Malcolm Sage, Detective

At first the young man had appeared bewildered; then he had pledged his word of honour, not only that he had not written the letters, but that there was no truth in the statements they contained. With that the vicar had to rest content; but worse was to follow.

Two evenings later, one of the churchwardens called at the vicarage and, after behaving in what to the vicar seemed a very strange manner, he produced from his pocket a letter he had received that morning, in which were repeated the scandalous statements contained in the first epistle.

From then on the district was deluged with anonymous letters, all referring to the alleged passion of the curate for the vicar's daughter, and the intrigue they were carrying on together. Some of the letters were frankly indelicate in their expression and, as the whole parish seethed with the scandal, the vicar appealed to the police for aid.

One peculiarity of the letters was that all were written upon the same paper, known as "Olympic Script." This was supplied locally to a number of people in the neighbourhood, among others, the vicar, the curate, and the schoolmaster.

Soon the story began to find its way into the newspapers, and Blade's position became one full of difficulty and embarrassment. He had consulted Robert Freynes, who had been at Oxford with his father, and the K.C., convinced of the young man's innocence, had sought Malcolm Sage's aid.

"You see, Sage," Freynes had remarked, "I'm sure the boy is straight and incapable of such conduct; but it's impossible to talk to that ass Murdy. He has no more imagination than a tin–linnet."

Freynes's reference was to Chief Inspector Murdy, of Scotland Yard, who had been entrusted with the enquiry, the local police having proved unequal to the problem.

Although Malcolm Sage had promised Robert Freynes that he would undertake the enquiry into the Gylston scandal, it was not until nearly a week later that he found himself at liberty to motor down into Hampshire.

One afternoon the vicar of Gylston, on entering his church, found a stranger on his knees in the chancel. Note–book in hand, he was transcribing the inscription of a monumental brass.

As the vicar approached, he observed that the stranger was vigorously shaking a fountain–pen, from which the ink had evidently been exhausted.

At the sound of Mr. Crayne's footsteps the stranger looked up, turning towards him a pair of gold–rimmed spectacles above which a bald conical head seemed to contradict the keenness of the eyes and the youthful lines of the face beneath

"You are interested in monumental brasses?" enquired the vicar, as he entered the chancel, and the stranger rose to his feet. "I am the vicar," he explained. There was a look of eager interest in the pale grey eyes that looked out from a placid, scholarly face.

"I was taking the liberty of copying the inscription on this," replied Malcolm Sage, indicating the time–worn brass at his feet, "only unfortunately my fountain–pen has given out."

"There is pen and ink in the vestry," said the vicar, impressed by the fact that the stranger had chosen the finest brass in the church, one that had been saved from Cromwell's Puritans by the ingenuity of the then incumbent, who had caused it to be covered with cement. Then as an afterthought the vicar added, "I can get your pen filled at the vicarage. My daughter has some ink; she always uses a fountain–pen."

Malcolm Sage thanked him, and for the next half–hour the vicar forgot the worries of the past few weeks in listening to a man who seemed to have the whole subject of monumental brasses and Norman architecture at his finger–ends.

Subsequently Malcolm Sage was invited to the vicarage, where another half–hour was occupied in Mr. Crayne showing him his collection of books on brasses.

As Malcolm Sage made a movement to depart, the vicar suddenly remembered the matter of the ink, apologised for his remissness, and left the room, returning a few minutes later with a bottle of fountain–pen ink. Malcolm Sage drew from his pocket his pen, and proceeded to replenish the ink from the bottle. Finally he completed the transcription of the lettering of the brass from a rubbing produced by the vicar.

Reluctant to allow so interesting a visitor to depart, Mr. Crayne pressed him to take tea; but Malcolm Sage pleaded an engagement.

As they crossed the hall, a fair girl suddenly rushed out from a door on the right. She was crying hysterically. Her hair was disordered, her deep violet eyes rimmed with red, and her moist lips seemed to stand out strangely red against the alabaster paleness of her skin.

"Muriel!"

Malcolm Sage glanced swiftly at the vicar. The look of scholarly calm had vanished from his features, giving place to a set sternness that reflected the tone in which he had uttered his daughter's name.

At the sight of a stranger the girl had paused, then, as if realising her tear–stained face and disordered hair, she turned and disappeared through the door from which she had rushed.

"My daughter," murmured the vicar, a little sadly, Malcolm Sage thought. "She has always been very highly strung and emotional," he added, as if considering some explanation necessary. "We have to be very stern with her on such occasions. It is the only way to repress it."

"You find it answers?" remarked Malcolm Sage.

"She has been much better lately, although she has been sorely tried. Perhaps you have heard."

Malcolm Sage nodded absently, as he gazed intently at the thumb–nail of his right hand. A minute later he was walking down the drive, his thoughts occupied with the pretty daughter of the vicar of Gylston.

At the curate's lodgings he was told that Mr. Blade was away, and would not return until late that night.

As he turned from the gate, Malcolm Sage encountered a pale–faced, narrow–shouldered man with a dark moustache and a hard, peevish mouth.

Malcolm Sage, Detective

To Malcolm Sage's question as to which was the way to the inn, he nodded in the direction from which he had come and continued on his way.

"A man who has failed in what he set out to accomplish," was Malcolm Sage's mental diagnosis of John Gray, the Gylston schoolmaster.

It was not long before Malcolm Sage realised that the village of Gylston was intensely proud of itself. It had seen in the London papers accounts of the mysterious scandal of which it was the centre. A Scotland Yard officer had been down, and had subjected many of the inhabitants to a careful cross-examination. In consequence Gylston realised that it was a village to be reckoned with.

The Tired Traveller was the centre of all rumour and gossip. Here each night in the public-bar, or in the private-parlour, according to their social status, the inhabitants would forgather and discuss the problem of the mysterious letters. Every sort of theory was advanced, and every sort of explanation offered. Whilst popular opinion tended to the view that the curate was the guilty party, there-were some who darkly shook their heads and muttered, "We shall see."

It was remembered and discussed with relish that John Gray, the schoolmaster, had for some time past shown a marked admiration for the vicar's daughter. She, however, had made it clear that the cadaverous, saturnine pedagogue possessed for her no attractions.

During the half-hour that Malcolm Sage spent at The Tired Traveller, eating a hurried meal, he heard all there was to be heard about local opinion.

The landlord, a rubicund old fellow whose baldness extended to his eyelids, was bursting with information. By nature capable of making a mystery out of a sunbeam, he revelled in the scandal that hummed around him.

After a quarter of an hour's conversation, the landlord's conversation, Malcolm Sage found himself possessed of a bewildering amount of new material.

"A young gal don't have them highsterics for nothin'," mine host remarked darkly. "Has fits of 'em every now and then ever since she was a flapper, sobbin' and cryin' fit to break 'er heart, and the vicar that cross with her."

Malcolm Sage, Detective

"That is considered the best way to treat hysterical people." remarked Malcolm Sage.

"Maybe," was the reply, "but she's only a gal, and a pretty one too," he added inconsequently.

"Then there's the schoolmaster," he continued, "'ates the curate like poison, he does. Shouldn't be surprised if it was him that done it. 'E's always been a bit sweet in that quarter himself, has Mr. Gray. Got talked about a good deal one time, 'angin' about arter Miss Muriel," added the loquacious publican.

By the time Malcolm Sage had finished his meal, the landlord was well in his stride of scandalous reminiscence. It was with obvious reluctance that he allowed so admirable a listener to depart, and it was with manifest regret that he watched Malcolm Sage's car disappear round the curve in the road.

A little way beyond the vicarage, an admonitory triangle caused Tims to slow up. Just by the bend Malcolm Sage observed a youth and a girl standing in the recess of a gate I giving access to a meadow. Although they were in the shadow cast by the hedge, Malcolm Sage's quick eyes recognised in the girl the vicar's daughter. The youth looked as if he might be one of the lads of the village.

In the short space of two or three seconds Malcolm Sage noticed the change in the girl. Although he could not see her face very clearly, the vivacity of her bearing and the ready–laugh were suggestive of a gaiety contrasting strangely with the tragic figure he had seen in the afternoon.

Muriel Crayne was obviously of a very mercurial temperament, he decided, as the car swung round the bend.

The next morning, in response to a telephone message, Inspector Murdy called on Malcolm Sage.

"Well, Mr. Sage," he cried, as he shook hands, "going to have another try to teach us our job," and his blue eye twinkled good–humouredly.

156

Malcolm Sage, Detective

The inspector had already made up his mind. He was a man with many successes to his record, achieved as a result of undoubted astuteness in connection with the grosser crimes, such as train–murders, post–office hold–ups and burglaries. He was incapable, however, of realising that there existed a subtler form of law–breaking, arising from something more intimately associated with the psychic than the material plane.

"Did you see Mr. Blade?" enquired Malcolm Sage.

"Saw the whole blessed lot," was the cheery reply. "It's all as clear as milk," and he laughed.

"What did Mr. Blade say?" enquired Malcolm Sage, looking keenly across at the inspector.

"Just that he had nothing to say."

"His exact words. Can you remember them?" queried Malcolm Sage.

"Oh, yes!" replied the inspector. "He said, 'Inspector Murdy, I have nothing to say,' and then he shut up like a real Whitstable."

"He was away yesterday," remarked Malcolm Sage, who then told the inspector of his visit. "How about John Gray, the schoolmaster?" he queried.

"He practically told me to go to the devil," was the genial reply. Inspector Murdy was accustomed to rudeness; his profession invited it, and to his rough–and–ready form of reasoning, rudeness meant innocence; politeness guilt.

He handed to Malcolm Sage a copy of a list of people who purchased "Olympic Script" from Mr. Grainger, the local Whiteley, volunteering the information that the curate was the biggest consumer, as if that settled the question of his guilt.

"And yet the vicar would not hear of the arrest of Blade." murmured Malcolm Sage, turning the copper ash–tray round with his restless fingers.

The inspector shrugged his massive shoulders. "Sheer good nature and kindliness, Mr. Sage," he said "'He's as gentle as a woman."

"I once knew a man," remarked Malcolm Sage, "who said that in the annals of crime lay the master–key to the world's mysteries, past, present and to come."

"A dreamer, Mr. Sage," smiled the inspector. "We haven't time for dreaming at the Yard," he added good–temperedly, as he rose and shook himself like a Newfoundland dog.

"I suppose it never struck you to look elsewhere than at the curate's lodgings for the writer of the letters?" enquired Malcolm Sage quietly.

"It never strikes me to look about for someone when I'm sitting on his chest," laughed Inspector Murdy.

"True," said Malcolm Sage. "By the way," he continued, without looking up, "in future can you let me see every letter as it is received? You might also keep careful record of how they are delivered."

"Certainly, Mr. Sage. Anything that will make you happy."

"Later I may get you to ask the vicar to seal up any subsequent anonymous letters that reach him without allowing anyone to see the contents. Do you think he would do that?"

"Without doubt if I ask him," said the inspector, surprise in his eyes as he looked down upon the cone of baldness beneath him, realising what a handicap it is to talk to a man who keeps his eyes averted.

"He must then put the letters in a place where no one can possibly obtain access to them. One thing more," continued Malcolm Sage, "will you ask Miss Crayne to write out the full story of the letters as far as she personally is acquainted with it?"

"Very well, Mr. Sage," said the inspector, with the air or one humouring a child. "Now I'll be going." He walked towards the door, then suddenly stopped and turned. "I suppose you think I'm wrong about the curate?"

"I'll tell you later," was the reply.

"When you find the master–key?" laughed the inspector, as he opened the door.

"Yes, when I find the master–key," said Malcolm Sage quietly and, as the door closed behind Inspector Murdy, he continued to finger the copper ash–tray as if that were the master–key.

CHAPTER XIV. MALCOLM SAGE PLAYS PATIENCE

MALCOLM SAGE was–seated at a small green–covered table playing solitaire. A velvet smoking–jacket and a pair of wine–coloured morocco slippers suggested that the day's work was done.

Patience, chess, and the cinema were his unfailing sources of inspiration when engaged upon a more than usually difficult case. He had once told Sir James Walton that they clarified his brain and co–ordinated his thoughts, the cinema in particular. The fact that in the surrounding darkness were hundreds of other brains, vital and active, appeared to stimulate his own imagination.

Puffing steadily at a gigantic meerschaum, he moved the cards with a deliberation which suggested that his attention rather than his thoughts was absorbed in the game.

Nearly a month had elapsed since he had agreed to take up the enquiry into the authorship of the series of anonymous letters with which Gylston and the neighbourhood had been flooded; yet still the matter remained a mystery.

A celebrated writer of detective stories had interested himself in the affair, with the result that the Press throughout the country had "stunted" Gylston as if it had been a heavyweight championship, or a train murder.

For a fortnight Malcolm Sage had been on the Continent in connection with the theft of the Adair Diamonds. Two days previously, after having restored the famous jewels to Lady Adair, he had returned to London, to find that the Gylston affair had developed a new and dramatic phase. The curate had been arrested for an attempted assault upon Miss

Malcolm Sage, Detective

Crayne and, pleading "not guilty," had been committed for trial.

The incident that led up to this had taken place on the day that Malcolm Sage left London. Late that afternoon Miss Crayne had arrived at the vicarage in a state bordering collapse. On becoming more collected, she stated that on returning from paying a call, and when half–way through a copse, known locally as "Gipsies Wood", Blade had sprung out upon her and violently protested his passion. He had gripped hold of her wrists, the mark of his fingers was to be seen on the delicate skin, and threatened to kill her and himself. She had been terrified, thinking he meant to kill her. The approach of a farm labourer had saved her, and the curate had disappeared through the copse.

This story was borne out by Joseph Higgins, the farm labourer in question. He had arrived to find Miss Crayne in a state of great alarm and agitation, and he had walked with her as far as the vicarage gate. He did not, however, actually see the curate.

On the strength of this statement the police had applied for a warrant, and had subsequently arrested the curate. Later he appeared before the magistrates, had been remanded, and finally committed for trial, bail being allowed.

Blade protested his innocence alike of the assault and the writing of the letters; but two handwriting experts had testified to the similarity of the handwriting of the anonymous letters with that of the curate. Furthermore, they were all written upon "Olympic Script," the paper that Blade used for his sermons.

Malcolm Sage had just started a new deal when the door opened, and Rogers showed in Robert Freynes. With a nod, Malcolm Sage indicated the chair opposite. His visitor dropped into it and, taking a pipe from his pocket, proceeded to fill and light it.

Placing his meerschaum on the mantelpiece, Malcolm Sage produced a well–worn briar from his pocket, which, having got into commission, he proceeded once more with the game.

"It's looking pretty ugly for Blade," remarked Freynes, recognising by the substitution of the briar for the meerschaum that Malcolm Sage was ready for conversation.

"Tell me."

Malcolm Sage, Detective

"It's those damned handwriting experts," growled Freynes. "They're the greatest anomaly of our legal system. The judge always warns the jury of the danger of accepting their evidence; yet each side continues to produce them. It's an insult to intelligence and justice."

"To hang a man because his 's' resembles that of an implicating document," remarked Malcolm Sage, as he placed a red queen on a black knave, "is about as sensible as to imprison him because he has the same accent as a footpad."

"Then there's Blade's astonishing apathy," continued Freynes. "He seems quite indifferent to the gravity of his position. Refuses to say a word. Anyone might think he knew the real culprit and was trying to shield him," and he sucked moodily at his pipe.

"The handwriting expert," continued Malcolm Sage imperturbably, "is too concerned with the crossing of a 't,' the dotting of an 'i,' or the tail of a 'g' to give time and thought to the way in which the writer uses, for instance, the compound tenses of verbs. Blade was no more capable of writing those letters than our friend Murdy is of transliterating the Rosetta Stone."

"Yes; but can we prove it?" asked Freynes gloomily, as with the blade of a penknife he loosened the tobacco in the bowl of his pipe. "Can we prove it?" he repeated and, snapping the knife to, he replaced it in his pocket.

"Blade's sermons," Malcolm Sage continued, "and such letters of his as you have been able to collect, show that he adopted a very definite and precise system of punctuation. He frequently uses the colon and the semicolon, and always in the right place. In a parenthetical clause preceded by the conjunction 'and,' he uses a comma after the 'and,' not before it as most people do. Before such words as 'yet' and 'but,' he without exception uses a semicolon. The word 'only,' he always puts in its correct place. In short, he is so academic as to savour somewhat of the pomposity of the eighteenth century."

"Go on," said Freynes, as Malcolm Sage paused, as if to give the other a chance of questioning his reasoning.

"Turning to the anonymous letters," continued Malcolm Sage, "it must be admitted that the handwriting is very similar; but there all likeness to Blade's sermons and correspondence ends. Murdy has shown me nearly all the anonymous letters, and in the whole series there is not one instance of the colon or the semicolon being used. The punctuation is of the vaguest, consisting largely of the dash, which after all is a literary evasion.

"In these letters the word 'but' frequently appears without any punctuation mark before it. At other times it has comma, a dash, or a full stop."

He paused and for the next two minutes devoted himself to the game before him. Then he continued: "Such phrases as 'If only you knew,' 'I should have loved to have been,' 'different than,' which appear in these letters! would have been absolutely impossible to a man of Blade's literary temperament."

At Malcolm Sage spoke, Robert Freynes's brain had been working rapidly. Presently he brought his hand down wit a smack upon his knee.

"By heavens, Sage!" he cried, "this is a new pill for the handwriting expert. I'll put you in the box. We've got a fighting chance after all."

"The most curious factor in the whole case," continued Malcolm Sage, "is the way in which the letters were delivered. One was thrown into a fly on to Miss Crayne's lap, she tells us, when she and her father were driving home after dining at the Hall. Another was discovered in the vicarage garden. A third was thrown through Miss Crayne's bedroom window. A few of the earlier group were posted—in the neighbouring town of Whitchurch, some on days that Blade was certainly not there."

"That was going to be one of my strongest points," remarked Freynes.

"The letters always imply that there is some obstacle existing between the writer and the girl he desires. What possible object could Blade have in writing letters to various people suggesting an intrigue between his vicar's daughter and himself; yet these letters were clearly written by the same hand that addressed those to the girl, her father and her mother."

Freynes nodded his head comprehendingly.

"If Blade were in love with the girl," continued Malcolm Sage, "what was there to prevent him from pressing his suit along legitimate and accepted lines? Murdy frankly acknowledges that there has been nothing in Blade's outward demeanour to suggest that Miss Crayne was to him anything more than the daughter of his vicar."

"What do you make of the story of the assault?"

"As evidence it is worthless," replied Malcolm Sage, "being without corroboration. The farm–hand did not actually see Blade."

Freynes nodded his agreement.

"Having convinced myself that Blade had nothing to do with the writing of the letters, I next tried to discover if there were anything throwing suspicion on others in the neighbourhood, who were known to use "Olympic Script" as note–paper.

"The schoolmaster, John Gray, was one. He is an admirer of Miss Crayne, according to local gossip; but it was obvious from the first that he had nothing to do with the affair. One by one I eliminated all the others, until I came back once more to Blade.

"It was clear that the letters were written with a fountain–pen, and Blade always uses one. That, however, is not evidence, as millions of people use fountain–pens. By the way, what is your line of defence?" he enquired.

"Smashing the handwriting experts," was the reply. "I was calling four myself, on the principle that God is on the side of the big battalions; but now I shall depend entirely on your evidence."

"The assault?" queried Malcolm Sage.

"There I'm done," said Freynes, "for although Miss Crayne's evidence is not proof, it will be sufficient for a jury. Besides, she's a very pretty and charming girl. I suppose," he added, "Blade must have made some sort of declaration, which she, in the light of the anonymous letters, entirely misunderstood."

"What does he say?"

163

"Denies it absolutely, although he admits being in the neighbourhood of the 'Gypsies Wood', and actually catching sight of Miss Crayne in the distance; but he says he did not speak to her."

"Is he going into the witness–box?"

"Certainly," then after a pause he added, "Kelton is prosecuting, and he's as moral as a swan. He'll appeal to the jury as fathers of daughters, and brothers of sisters."

Malcolm Sage made no comment; but continued smoking mechanically, his attention apparently absorbed in the cards before him.

"If you can smash the handwriting experts," continued the K.C., "I may be able to manage the girl's testimony."

"It will not be necessary," said Malcolm Sage, carefully placing a nine of clubs upon an eight of diamonds.

"Not necessary?"

"I have asked Murdy to come round," continued Malcolm Sage, still intent upon his game. "I think that was his ring."

A minute later the door opened to admit the burly inspector more blue–eyed and genial than ever, and obviously in the best of spirits.

"Good evening, Mr. Sage," he cried cheerfully. "Congratulations on the Adair business. Good evening, sir," he added as he shook hands with Freynes.

He dropped heavily into a seat, and taking a cigar from the box on the table, which Malcolm Sage had indicated with a nod, he proceeded to light it. No man enjoyed a good cigar more than Inspector Murdy.

"Well, what do you think of it?" he enquired, looking from Malcolm Sage to Freynes. "It's a clear case now, I think." He slightly stressed the word "now."

Malcolm Sage, Detective

"You mean it's Blade?" enquired Malcolm Sage, as he proceeded to gather up the cards.

"Who else?" enquired the inspector, through a cloud of smoke.

"That is the question which involves your being here now, Murdy," said Malcolm Sage dryly.

"We've got three handwriting experts behind us," said the inspector complacently.

"That is precisely where they should be," retorted Malcolm Sage quietly. "In the biblical sense," he added.

Freynes laughed, whilst Inspector Murdy looked from one to the other. He did not quite catch the allusion.

"You have done as I suggested?" enquired Malcolm Sage, when he had placed the cards in their box and removed the card–table.

"Here are all the letters received up to a fortnight ago," said the inspector holding out a bulky packet. "Those received since have each been sealed up separately by the vicar, who is keeping half of them, whilst I have the other half; but really, Mr. Sage, I don't understand—"

"Thank you, Murdy," said Malcolm Sage. as he took the packet. "It is always a pleasure to work with Scotland Yard. It is so thorough." The inspector beamed; for he knew the compliment was sincere.

Without a word Malcolm Sage left the room, taking the packet with him.

"A bit quaint at times, ain't he, sir?" remarked Inspector Murdy to Freynes; "but one of the best. I'd trust him with anything."

Freynes nodded encouragingly.

"There are some of them down at the Yard that don't like him," he continued. "They call him 'Sage and Onions'; but most of us who have worked with him swear by Mr. Sage.

Malcolm Sage, Detective

He's never out of the limelight himself, and he's always willing to give another fellow a leg–up. After all, it's our living," he added, a little inconsequently.

Freynes appreciated the inspector's delicacy in refraining from any mention of the Gylston case during Malcolm Sage's absence. After all, they represented respectively the prosecution and the defence. For nearly half an hour the two talked together upon unprofessional subjects. When Malcolm Sage returned, he found them discussing the prospects of Dempsey against Carpentier.

Handing back the packet of letters to Inspector Murdy, Malcolm Sage resumed his seat, and proceeded to re–light his pipe.

"Spotted the culprit, Mr. Sage?" enquired the inspector, with something that was very much like a wink in the direction of Freynes.

"I think so," was the quiet reply. "You might meet me at Gylston Vicarage tomorrow at three. I'll telegraph to Blade to be there too. You had better bring the schoolmaster also."

"You mean—" began the inspector, rising.

"Exactly," said Malcolm Sage. "It's past eleven, and we all require sleep."

The next afternoon the study of the vicar of Gylston presented a strange appearance.

Seated at Mr. Crayne's writing–table was Malcolm Sage, a small attache–case at his side, whilst before him were several piles of sealed packets. Grouped about the room were Inspector Murdy, Robert Freynes, Mr. Gray, and the vicar.

All had their eyes fixed upon Malcolm Sage; but with varying expressions. Those of the schoolmaster were frankly cynical. The inspector and Freynes looked as if they expected to see produced from the attache–case a guinea–pig or a white rabbit, pink–eyed and kicking; whilst the vicar had obviously not yet recovered from his surprise at discovering that the stranger, who had shown such a remarkable knowledge of monumental brasses and Norman architecture, was none other than the famous investigator about whom he had read so much in the newspapers.

Malcolm Sage, Detective

With quiet deliberation Malcolm Sage opened the attache—case and produced a spirit lamp, which he lighted. He then placed a metal plate upon a rest above the flame. On this he imposed a thicker plate of a similar metal that looked like steel; but it had a handle across the middle, rather resembling that of a tool used by plasterers.

He then glanced up, apparently unconscious of the almost feverish interest with which his every movement was being watched.

"I should like Miss Crayne to be present," he said.

As he spoke the door opened and the curate entered, hi dark, handsome face lined and careworn. It was obvious that he had suffered. He bowed, and then looked about him without any suggestion of embarrassment.

Malcolm Sage rose and held out his hand. Freynes followed suit.

"Ask Miss Muriel to come here," said the vicar to the maid as she was closing the door.

The curate took the seat that Malcolm Sage indicated bedside him. Silently the six men waited.

A few minutes later Miss Crayne entered, pale but self possessed. She closed the door behind her. Suddenly she caught sight of the curate. Her eyes widened, and her paleness seemed to become accentuated. A moment later it was followed by a crimson flush. She hesitated, her hands clenched at her side, then with a manifest effort she appeared to control herself, and with a slight smile and inclination of her head, took the chair the schoolmaster moved towards her. Instinctively she turned her eyes towards Malcolm Sage.

"Inspector Murdy," he said, without raising his eyes, "will you please open two of those packets." He indicated the pile on his left. "I should explain," he continued, "that each of these contains one of the most recent of the series of letters with which we are concerned. Each was sealed up by Mr. Frayne immediately it reached him, in accordance with Inspector Murdy's request. Therefore, only the writer, the recipient and the vicar have had access to these letters."

Malcolm Sage, Detective

Malcolm Sage turned his eyes interrogatingly upon Mr. Crayne, who bowed.

Meanwhile the inspector had cut open the two top envelopes, unfolded the sheets of paper they contained, and handed them to Malcolm Sage.

All eyes were fixed upon his long, shapely fingers as he smoothed out one of the sheets of paper upon the vicar's blotting–pad. Then, lifting the steel plate by the handle, he placed it upon the upturned sheet of paper.

The tension was almost unendurable. The heavy breathing of Inspector Murdy seemed like the blowing of a grampus. Mr. Gray glanced across at him irritably. The vicar coughed slightly, then looked startled that he had made so much noise. Everyone bent forward, eagerly expecting something; yet without quite knowing what. Malcolm Sage lifted the metal plate from the letter. There in the centre of the page, in bluish–coloured letters, which had not been there when the paper was smoothed out upon the blotting–pad, appeared the words:

Malcolm Sage, August 15th, 1919. No. 138.

For some moments they all gazed at the paper as if the mysterious blue letters exercised upon them some hypnotic influence.

"Secret ink!"

It was Robert Freynes who spoke. Accustomed as he was to dramatic moments, he was conscious of a strange dryness at the back of his throat, and a consequent huskiness of voice.

His remark seemed to break the spell. Instinctively everyone turned to him. The significance of the bluish–coloured characters was slowly dawning upon the inspector; but the others still seemed puzzled to account for their presence.

Immediately he had lifted the plate from the letter, Malcolm Sage had drawn a sheet of plain sermon paper from the tray before him. This he subjected to the same treatment as the letter. When a few seconds later he exposed it, there in the centre appeared the same words: ' Malcolm Sage, August 12th, 1919', but on this sheet the number was 203.

Then the true significance of the two sheets of paper seemed to dawn upon the onlookers.

Suddenly there was a scream, and Muriel Crayne fell forward on to the floor.

"Oh! father, father, forgive me!" she cried, and the next moment she was beating the floor with her hands in violent hysterics.

* * * * *

"From the first I suspected the truth," remarked Malcolm Sage, as he, Robert Freynes and Inspector Murdy sat smoking in the car that Tims was taking back to London at its best pace. "Eighty–five years ago a somewhat similar case occurred in France, that of Marie de Morel, when an innocent man was sentenced to ten years' imprisonment, and actually served eight before the truth was discovered."

The inspector whistled under his breath.

"This suspicion was strengthened by the lengthy account of the affair written by Miss Crayne, which Murdy obtained from her. The punctuation, the phrasing, the inaccurate use of auxiliary verbs, were identical with that of the anonymous letters.

"Another point was that the similarity of the handwriting of the anonymous letters to Blade's became more pronounced as the letters themselves multiplied. The writer was becoming more expert as an imitator."

Freynes nodded his head several times.

"The difficulty, however, was to prove it," continued Malcolm Sage. "There was only one way; to substitute secretly marked paper for that in use at the vicarage.

"I accordingly went down to Gylston, and the vicar found me keenly interested in monumental brasses, his pet subject, and Norman architecture. He invited me to the vicarage. In is absence from his study I substituted a supply of marked Olympic Script in place of that in his letter–rack, and also in the drawer of his writing–table. As a further precaution, I arranged for my fountain–pen to run out of ink. He kindly supplied me with a bottle, obviously belonging to his daughter. I replenished my pen, which was full of a

169

chemical that would enable me, if necessary, to identify any letter in the writing of which it had been used. When I placed my pen, which is a self–filler, in the ink, I forced this liquid into the bottle." The inspector merely stared. Words had forsaken him for the moment.

"It was then necessary to wait until the ink in Miss Crayne's pen had become exhausted, and she had to replenish her supply of paper from her father's study. After that discovery was inevitable."

"But suppose she had denied it?" questioned the inspector.

"There was the ink which she alone used, and which I could identify," was the reply.

"Why did you ask Gray to be present?" enquired Freynes.

"As his name had been associated with the scandal it seemed only fair," remarked Malcolm Sage, then turning to Inspector Murdy he said, "I shall leave it to you, Murdy, to see that a proper confession is obtained. The case has had such publicity that Mr. Blade's innocence must be made equally public."

"You may trust me, Mr. Sage," said the inspector. "But why did the curate refuse to say anything?"

"Because he is a high–minded and chivalrous gentleman," was the quiet reply.

"He knew?" cried Freynes.

"Obviously," said Malcolm Sage. "It is the only explanation of his silence. I taxed him with it after the girl had been taken away, and he acknowledged that his suspicions amounted almost to certainty."

"Yet he stayed behind," murmured the inspector with the air of a man who does not understand. "I wonder why?"

"To minister to the afflicted, Murdy," said Malcolm Sage. "That is the mission of the Church."

"I suppose you meant that French case when you referred to the 'master–key,' remarked the inspector, as if to change the subject.

Malcolm Sage nodded.

"But how do you account for Miss Crayne writing such letters about herself?" enquired the inspector, with a puzzled expression in his eyes. "Pretty funny letters some of them for a parson's daughter."

"I'm not a pathologist, Murdy," remarked Malcolm Sage drily, "but when you try to suppress hysteria in a young girl by sternness, it's about as effectual as putting ointment on a plague–spot."

"Sex–repression?" queried Freynes.

Malcolm Sage shrugged his shoulders; then after a pause during which he lighted the pipe he had just re–filled, he added:

"When you are next in Great Russell Street, drop in at the British Museum and look at the bust of Faustina. You will see that her chin is similar in modelling to that of Miss Crayne. The girl was apparently very much attracted to Blade, and proceeded to weave what was no doubt to her a romance, later it became an obsession. It all goes to show the necessity for pathological consideration of certain crimes."

"But who was Faustina?" enquired the inspector, unable to follow the drift of the conversation.

"Faustina," remarked Malcolm Sage, "was the domestic fly in the philosophical ointment of an emperor," and Inspector Murdy laughed; for, knowing nothing of the marriage or the Meditations of Marcus Aurelius, it seemed to him the only thing to do.

CHAPTER XV. THE MISSING HEAVYWEIGHT

MR. DOULTON, sir. Very important." Rogers had carefully assimilated his master's theory of the economy of words, sometimes even to the point of obscuring his meaning.

Taking the last piece of toast from the rack, Malcolm Sage with great deliberation proceeded to butter it. Then, with a nod to the waiting Rogers, he poured out the last cup of coffee the pot contained.

A moment later the door opened to admit a clean–shaven little man of about fifty, prosperous in build and appearance; but obviously labouring under some great excitement. His breath came in short, spasmodic gasps. His thin sandy hair had clearly not been brushed since the day before, whilst his chin and upper lip bore obvious traces of a night's growth of beard. He seemed on the point of collapse.

"He's gone–disappeared!" he burst out, as Rogers closed the door behind him. Malcolm Sage rose, motioned his caller to a chair at the table, and resumed his own seat.

"Had breakfast?" he enquired quietly, resuming his occupation of getting the toast carefully and artistically buttered.

"Good God, man!" exploded Mr. Doulton, almost hysterically. "Don't you understand? Burns has disappeared!"

"I gathered as much," said Malcolm Sage calmly, as he reached for the marmalade.

"Pond telephoned from Stainton," continued Mr. Doulton. "I was in bed. I got dressed, and came round here at once. I—" he stopped suddenly, as Rogers entered with a fresh relay of coffee. Without a word he proceeded to pour out a cup for Mr. Doulton, who, after a moment's hesitation, drank it greedily.

Rogers glanced interrogatingly from the dish that had contained eggs and bacon to Malcolm Sage, who nodded.

When he had withdrawn, Mr. Doulton opened his mouth to speak, then closed it again and gazed at Malcolm Sage, who, having superimposed upon the butter a delicate amber film of marmalade, proceeded to cut up the toast into a series of triangles. Apparently it was the only thing in life that interested him.

For weeks past the British and American sporting world had thought and talked of nothing but the forthcoming fight between Charley Burns and Bob Jefferson for the heavyweight championship of the world. The event was due to take place two days hence at the Olympia for a purse of 40,000 offered by Mr. Montague Doulton, the prince of impresarios.

Never had a contest been looked forward to with greater eagerness than the Burns v. Jefferson match. A great change had come over public opinion in regard to prize–fighting, thanks to the elevating influence of Mr. Doulton. It was no longer referred to as "brutalising" and "debasing." Refined and nice–minded people found themselves mildly interested and patriotically hopeful that Charley Burns, the British champion, would win. In two years Mr. Doulton had achieved what the National Sporting Club had failed to do in a quarter of a century.

Long and patiently he had laboured to bring about this match, which many thought would prove the keystone to the arch of Burns's fame, incidentally to that of the impresario himself.

"And now he's disappeared–clean gone." Mr. Doulton almost sobbed.

"Tell me."

Malcolm Sage looked up from his plate, the last triangle of toast poised between finger and thumb.

In short staccatoed sentences, like bursts from a machine–gun, Mr. Doulton proceeded to tell his story.

That morning at six o'clock, when Alf Pond, Burns's trainer, had entered his room to warn him that it was time to get up, he found it unoccupied. At first he thought that Burns had gone down before him; but immediately his eye fell on the bed, and he saw that it had not been slept in, he became alarmed.

Going to the bedroom door, he had shouted to the sparring–partners, and soon the champion's room was filled with men in various stages of deshabille.

Only for a moment, however, had they remained inactive. At Alf Pond's word of command they had spread helter–skelter over the house and grounds, causing the early morning air to echo with their shouts for "Charley."

When at length he became assured that Burns had disappeared, Alf Pond telephoned first to Mr. Doulton and then to Mr. Papwith, Burns's backer.

"I told Pond to do nothing and tell no one," said Mr. Doulton, in conclusion, "and when I left my rooms my man was trying to get through to Papwith to ask him to keep the story to himself."

Malcolm Sage nodded approval.

"Now, what's to be done?" He looked at Malcolm Sage with the air of a man who has just told a doctor of his alarming symptoms, and almost breathlessly awaits the verdict.

"Breakfast, a shave, then we'll motor down to Stainton," and Malcolm Sage proceeded to fill his briar, his whole attention absorbed in the operation.

A moment later Rogers entered with a fresh supply of eggs and bacon. Mr. Doulton shook his head. Instinctively his hand had gone up to his unshaven chin. It was probably the first time in his life that he had sat at table without shaving. He prided himself upon his personal appearance. In his younger days he had been known as "Dandy Doulton."

"The car in half an hour, Rogers," said Malcolm Sage, as he rose from the table. "When you've finished," he said, turning to Mr. Doulton, "Rogers will give you hot water, a razor and anything else you want. By the time you have shaved I shall be ready."

"But don't you see—Think what it—" began Mr. Doulton.

"An empty stomach neither sees nor thinks," was Malcolm Sage's oracular retort, and he went over to the window and seated himself at his writing–table.

For the next half–hour he was engaged with his correspondence, and in telephoning instructions to his office.

By the time Mr. Doulton had breakfasted and shaved, the car was at the door.

During the run to Stainton both men were silent. Mr. Doulton was speculating as to what would happen at the Olympia on the following night if Burns failed to appear, whilst Malcolm Sage was occupied with thoughts, the object of which was to prevent such a catastrophe.

"They're sure to say it's a yellow streak," Mr. Doulton burst out on one occasion; but, as Malcolm Sage took no notice of the remark, he subsided into silence, and the car hummed its way along the Portsmouth Road.

Burns's training–quarters were situated at Stainton, near Guildford. Here, under the vigilant eye of Alf Pond, and with the help of a large retinue of sparring–partners, he was getting himself into what had come to be called "Burns's condition," which meant that he would enter the ring trained to the minute. Never did athlete work more conscientiously than Charley Burns.

As the car turned into a side road, flanked on either hand by elms, Mr. Doulton tapped on the wind–screen, and Tims pulled up. Malcolm Sage had requested that the car be stopped a hundred yards before it reached "The Grove," where the training quarters were situated.

"Wait for me here," he said, as he got out.

"It's the first gate on the right," said Mr. Doulton.

Walking slowly away from the car, Malcolm Sage examined with great care the road itself. Presently he stopped and taking from his pocket a steel spring–measure, he proceeded to measure a portion of the surface of the dusty roadway. Having made several entries in a note–book, he then turned back to the car, his eyes still on the road.

Instructing Tims to remain where he was, Malcolm Sage motioned to Mr. Doulton to get out.

"This way," said Malcolm Sage, leading him to the extreme left–hand side of the road. Turning into the gates of "The Grove," they walked up the drive towards the house. In front stood a group of men in various and nondescript costumes.

175

Malcolm Sage, Detective

As Malcolm Sage and Mr. Doulton approached, a man in a soiled white sweater and voluminous grey flannel trousers generously turned up at the extremities, detached himself from the group and came towards them. He was puffy of face with pouched eyes and a moist skin; yet in his day Alf Pond had been an unbeatable middle–weight, and the greatest master of ring–craft of his time; but that was nearly a generation ago.

In agonised silence he looked from Mr. Doulton to Malcolm Sage, then back again to Mr. Doulton. There was in his eyes the misery of despair.

The preliminary greetings over, Alf Pond led the way round to a large coach–house in the rear, which had been fitted up as a gymnasium. Here were to be seen all the appliances necessary to the training of a boxer for a great contest, including a roped ring at one end.

"He was here only yesterday." There was a world of tragedy and pathos in Alf Pond's tone. Something like a groan burst from the sparring–partners.

With a quick, comprehensive glance, Malcolm Sage seemed to take in every detail.

"It's a bad business, Pond," said Mr. Doulton, who found the mute despair of these hard–living, hard–hitting men rather embarrassing.

"What'd I better do?" queried Alf Pond.

"I've put the whole matter in Mr. Sage's hands," said Mr. Doulton. "He'll find him, if anyone can."

A score of eyes were turned speculatively upon Malcolm Sage. In none was there the least ray of hope. All had now made up their minds that Jefferson would win the fight by default.

Slowly and methodically Malcolm Sage drew the story of Burns's disappearance from Alf Pond, the sparring–partners occasionally acting as a chorus.

When all had been told, Malcolm Sage gazed for some moments at the finger–nails of his left hand.

"You were confident he would win?" he asked at length.

"Confident!" There was incredulity and wonder in Alf pond's voice. Then, with a sudden inspiration, "Look at Kid!" he cried—"look at him!" and he indicated with a nod a fair—haired giant standing on his right.

Malcolm Sage looked.

The man's face showed the stress and strain of battle. His nose had taken on something of the quality of cubism, his right eye was out of commission, there was an ugly purple patch on his left cheek, and his right ear looked as if a wasp had stung it.

"He did that in one round, and him the third. Kid asked for it, and he got it, same as Jeff would," explained Alf Pond proudly, a momentary note of elation in his voice. There was also something of pride in the grin with which Kid stood the scrutiny of the others.

"Do you know of any reason why Burns should have left his room?" Malcolm Sage looked from one to the other interrogatingly.

"There wasn't any," was Alf Pond's response, and the others nodded their concurrence.

"He knew no one in the neighbourhood?"

"No one to speak of. A few local gents would drop in occasional to see how he was getting on, and then a lot o' newspaper chaps came down from London." There was that in Alf Pond's tone which seemed to suggest that in his opinion such questions were foolish.

"Did he receive any letters or telegrams yesterday?" was the next question.

"Letters!" Alf Pond laughed sardonically. "Shoals of 'em. He'd turn 'em all over to Sandy Lane," indicating a red—headed man on the right.

"He wasn't much at writing letters," said Sandy Lane, by way of explanation.

"His hands were made for better things," cried Alf Pond scornfully, and the sparring–partners nodded their agreement

"Did he turn over to you the whole of his correspondence?" asked Malcolm Sage, turning to Sandy Lane.

"Sometimes he'd keep a letter," broke in Alf Pond, "but not often. Sort of personal," he added, as if to explain the circumstance.

"From a woman, perhaps?" suggested Malcolm Sage, taking off his hat and stroking the back of his head.

"Woman!" cried Alf Pond scornfully; "Charley hadn't no use for women, or he wouldn't have been the boxer he was."

"He was quite himself, quite natural, yesterday?" asked Malcolm Sage.

"Quite himself," repeated Alf Pond deliberately; then, once more indicating Kid, he added, "Look at Kid; that's what he done in one round." There was in his tone all the contempt of knowledge for ignorance.

Malcolm Sage resumed his hat and, taking his pipe from his pocket, proceeded to stuff it with tobacco, as if that were the only problem in the world. On everything he did he seemed to concentrate his entire attention to the exclusion of all else.

"No smokin' here, if you please," said Alf Pond sharply.

Malcolm Sage returned his pipe to his pocket without comment.

"Now, what are you going to do?" There was challenge in Alf Pond's voice as he eyed Malcolm Sage with disfavour. In his world men with bald, conical heads and gold–rimmed spectacles did not count for much.

"How many people know of the disappearance?" enquired Malcolm Sage, ignoring the question.

"Outside of us here, only Mr. Papwith," was the response. For fully a minute Malcolm Sage did not reply. At length he turned to Mr. Doulton.

"Can you arrange to remain here to meet Mr. Papwith?" he enquired.

"I propose doing so," was the reply.

"You want to find Burns, I suppose?" Malcolm Sage asked of Alf Pond, in low, level tones.

Alf Pond and his colleagues eyed him as if he had asked a most astonishing question.

"You barmy?" demanded the trainer, putting into words the looks of the others.

"You will continue with the day's work as if nothing had happened," continued Malcolm Sage. "No one outside must now that—"

"But how the hell are we going to do that with Charley gone?" broke in Alf Pond, taking a step forward with clenched fists.

"Your friend here," indicating Kid, "can pose as Burns," was Malcolm Sage's quiet reply, as he looked into the trainer's eye without the flicker of an eyelash.

"You, Mr. Doulton, I will ask to remain here with Mr. Papwith until I communicate with you. On no account leave the training–quarters, even if you have to wait here until to–morrow evening."

"But—" began Alf Pond; then he stopped and gazed at the sparring–partners, blinking his eyes in stupid bewilderment.

"Have I your promise?" enquired Malcolm Sage of Mr. Doulton.

"As far as I am concerned, yes," was the response, "and I think I can answer for Papwith. It's very inconvenient, though."

"Not so inconvenient as having to explain things at the Olympia to-morrow night," remarked Malcolm Sage dryly. "Now," he continued, turning once more to Alf Pond, "I suppose you've all got something on this fight."

"Something on it!" cried Alf Pond; then, turning to the sparring-partners, he cried, "He asks if we've got somethink on it. My Gawd!" he groaned, "we got our shirts on it. That's what we got on it, our shirts," and his voice broke in something like a sob.

"You had better post someone at the gate to tell all enquirers that Burns is doing well and is confident of winning," said Malcolm Sage to Mr. Doulton, "and keep an eye on the telephone. Tell anyone who rings up the same; in fact—"–and he turned to the others–"as far as you are concerned, Burns is still with you. Do you understand?"

They looked at one another in a way that was little suggestive of understanding.

"Did Burns wear the same clothes throughout the day?" asked Malcolm Sage of the trainer.

"Course he didn't!" Alf Pond made no effort to disguise the contempt he felt. "In the daytime he used to wear flannel trousers an' a sweater, same as me, except when he–was sparrin', then he put on drawers. Always would have everythink same as it was goin' to be, would Charley–seconds referee, timekeeper. Said it made him feel at home when the time came. Quaint he was in some of his ideas."

"Then from the time he got up until bedtime he wore the same clothes?" queried Malcolm Sage, without looking up from the inevitable contemplation of his finger-nails.

"No he didn't." Alf Pond spat his boredom at these useless questions into a far corner. "He was always a bit of a nib, was Charley. After he'd finished the day's work he'd put on a suit o' dark duds, a white collar, a watch on his wrist, an' all that bunko. Then we'd play poker or billiards till half-past eight, when we'd all turn in." The look with which Alt Pond concluded this itinerary plainly demanded if there were any more damn silly questions coming.

"Now I should like to see Burns's room."

Malcolm Sage, Detective

Malcolm Sage and Mr. Doulton followed Alf Pond upstairs to a large room on the first floor, as destitute of the attributes of comfort as a guardroom. A bed, a wash–hand stand, and a chest of drawers comprised the furniture. A few articles of clothing were strewn about, and in one corner lay a pair of dumb–bells.

The windows were open top and bottom; Malcolm Sage passed from one to the other and looked out. He examined carefully each of the window–ledges.

"Are these the clothes he wore when he got up?" he enquired, indicating a sweater and a pair of flannel trousers that lay on a chair.

Alf Pond nodded.

Swiftly Malcolm Sage felt in the pockets. There was nothing there. A minute later he left the room, followed by the others. Descending the stairs, he passed along the hall and out on to the short drive, accompanied by Mr. Doulton and Alf Pond.

Half–way towards the gate Malcolm Sage stopped.

"You will hear from me some time to–day or to–morrow," he said. "Do exactly as I have said and, if I don't telephone before to–morrow evening, go to the Olympia as if Burns were to be there. You might have sent out to my car a pair of drawers and boots in case I find him."

"You're going to find him then?" Alf Pond suddenly gripped Malcolm Sage's arm with what was almost ferocity. Malcolm Sage shrugged his shoulders.

"If you do as I tell you, it will help. By the way," he added, "if you have time, you might put twenty–five pounds on Burns for me. Mr. Doulton will be responsible for the amount. Now I want to look about me," and with that Malcolm Sage walked a few steps down the drive, leaving two men staring after him as if he had either solved or propounded the riddle of the universe.

For some minutes he stood in the centre of the drive, looking about him. Stepping to the right, he glanced back at the house, and then towards the road. Finally he made for a large clump of rhododendrons that lay between the road and the house.

Motioning the others to remain where they were on the gravelled drive, he walked to a clear space of short grass between the rhododendrons and the hedge bordering the road.

Going down upon his knees, he proceeded to examine the ground with great care and attention. For nearly half an hour he crawled from place to place, absorbed in grass, shrub, and flower–bed. Finally he penetrated half into the privet–hedge that bordered the road.

The sparring–partners had now joined the other two on the drive, and the group stood watching the strange movements of the man who, in their opinion, had already shown obvious symptoms of insanity.

Presently Malcolm Sage emerged from the hedge, in his hand a long cigar, round the centre of which was a red–and–gold band. For fully a minute he stood examining this with great care. Then, taking a letter–case from his pocket, he carefully placed the cigar in the hinge, returned the case to his pocket, and rejoined the group of wide–eyed spectators.

"Found anythink?" enquired Alf Pond eagerly.

"Several things," replied Malcolm Sage.

"What?" The men grouped themselves round him, breathless with interest.

"By the way," said Malcolm Sage, turning to Alf Pond, "does Burns happen to smoke long Havana cigars with a red—"

"Smoke!" yelled Alf Pond in horror. "Him smoke! You blinkin' well barmy?" he demanded, looking Malcolm Sage up and down as if meditating an attack upon him. "I'd like to see the man who'd so much as dare to strike a match here," and he glared about him angrily, whilst the sparring–partners shuffled their feet and murmured among themselves. There was just the suspicion of a fluttering at the corners of Malcolm Sage's mouth.

"I'm afraid Pond is rather excited just at present," said Mr. Doulton tactfully. By now he had entirely regained his own composure. "Burns is a great lover of tobacco, and Pond

182

takes no risks. You were saying that you had discovered several things?"

Again the group of men drew closer to Malcolm Sage, their heads thrust forward as if fearful of missing a word.

"For one thing, Burns left his room last night to meet a woman by—"

"It's a lie!" cried Alf Pond heatedly. "It's a damned lie! I don't believe it."

"A rather dainty creature, small and well dressed. She was accompanied by several men, one of them rather stout, very careful of his clothes, and an inveterate smoker. The others were bigger, rougher men. They all came in a car, which arrived after the motor bicycle, which in turn arrived later than the small car."

The sparring–partners exchanged glances, whilst Alf Pond stared.

"Subsequently they drove off in a very great hurry. Incidentally they took Burns with them; but against his will. On the way down the girl was in the tonneau; but on the return journey she sat beside the driver. As Burns was in the tonneau, it was no doubt a precaution."

"I don't believe a word," interrupted Alf Pond. "He's makin' it all up."

Without appearing to notice the remark, Malcolm Sage turned and walked towards the gate, Mr. Doulton following a step in the rear.

"Liar!" growled Alf Pond, as he turned towards the house. "Ruddy liar!" he added, as if finding consolation in the term. "He'll never find old Charley."

"Tell me, Sage, were you serious?" asked Mr. Doulton, as they reached the gate.

"Entirely."

"I'm afraid poor Pond thought you were making game of us," he added apologetically. "Do you mind explaining how you arrived at your conclusions?"

Malcolm Sage, Detective

"Behind that clump of rhododendrons," began Malcolm gage, "there is written a whole history. The marks of boots, or shoes, with very high heels suggest a woman, the size and daintiness of the footwear tell the rest. As Burns appeared, she stepped towards him. Her very short steps indicate both fashionable clothes and smallness of stature."

"And the man who was careful about his clothes?"

"He stood behind a holly–bush with an umbrella—"

"But how did you know?"

"He had been leaning upon it, and there was the mark where it had sunk into the soft turf up to the point where the silk joins the stick. A man who carries an umbrella on a kidnapping adventure must be habitually in fear of rain–none but a well–dressed man would fear rain.

"Then, as he had a cigar in his hand with the end bitten off, it shows the habitual smoker. He was only waiting for the end of the drama before lighting up. His height I get from his stride, and his size by the fact that, like Humpty–Dumpty, he had a great fall. I'll tell you the rest later. I'm afraid it's an ugly business."

"But the girl riding beside the driver?" burst out Mr. Doulton, bewildered by the facts that Malcolm Sage had deduced from so little.

"At the edge of a side–road there is invariably a deposit of dust, and the marks where they all got out and in are clearly visible. The hurry of departure is shown by the fact that the car started before one of the men had taken his place, and his footsteps running beside it before jumping on to the running–board are quite clear. I'll ring you up later. I cannot stay now." And with that he hurried away.

"Back along your own tracks, Tims," said he on reaching the car. He then walked on to the main road.

With head over right shoulder, Tims carefully backed the car, Malcolm Sage signalling that he was to turn to the right.

Malcolm Sage, Detective

Instructing Tims to drive slowly, Malcolm Sage took his seat beside him, keeping his eyes fixed upon the off–side of the road. He stopped the car at each cross–road, and walked down it some twenty or thirty yards, his eyes bent downwards as if in search of something. At the end of half an hour he instructed Tims to drive back to London at his best speed.

That afternoon in his office Malcolm Sage worked without cessation. Both telephones, incoming and outgoing, were continually in use. Telegraph girls and messenger boys came and went.

Gladys Norman had ceased to worry about the shininess of her nose, and William Johnson was in process of readjusting his ideas as to lack of the dramatic element at the Malcolm Sage Bureau as compared with detective fiction and the films.

About three o'clock a tall, clean–shaven man was shown into Malcolm Sage's room. He had a hard mouth, keen, alert eyes, and an air suggestive of the fact that he knew the worst there was to be known about men and acted accordingly.

With a nod Malcolm Sage motioned him to a seat. Six months before he had saved Dick Lindler from the dock by discovering the real criminal in whose stead Lindler was about to be charged with a series of frauds. Since then Malcolm Sage had always been sure of such "inside" information in the bookmaking world as he required.

"How's the betting now?" enquired Malcolm Sage.

"Nine to two on Jefferson offered; and no takers," was the reply. "There's something up, Mr. Sage; I'll take my dying oath on it," he said, leaning across the table and dropping his voice.

"Any big amounts?" enquired Malcolm Sage.

"No, that's what troubles me. The money's being spread about so. The funny thing is that a lot of it is being put on by letter. I've had a dozen myself to–day."

Malcolm Sage nodded slowly as he filled his pipe, which with great deliberation he proceeded to light until the whole surface of the tobacco glowed. Then, as if suddenly realising that Lindler was not smoking, he pulled open a drawer, drew out a cigar-box, and pushed it across, watching him closely from beneath his eyebrows as he did so.

Lindler opened the box, then looked interrogatingly at Malcolm Sage.

"Didn't know you smoked the same poison-sticks as the 'Downy One'," he said, picking up a long cigar with a red and gold band, and examining it.

"Who's he?"

"Old Nathan Goldschmidt, the stinking Jew."

"I'm sorry," said Malcolm Sage; "that should not have been there. Try one of the others."

Lindler looked across at him curiously.

"Personally, myself," he said, "I believe he's at the bottom of all this heavy backing of Jefferson."

Malcolm Sage continued to smoke as if the matter did not interest him, whilst Lindler bit off the end of the cigar he had selected and proceeded to light it.

"Several of his crowd have been around this morning trying to load me up," he continued presently, when the cigar was drawing to his satisfaction. "Must have stayed up all night to be in time," he added scathingly.

"Have you seen Goldschmidt himself?"

"Not since yesterday afternoon."

"Does he usually carry an umbrella?"

Lindler laughed.

"The boys call him 'Gampy Goldschmidt,'" he said.

186

Malcolm Sage, Detective

"You really think that the Goldschmidt gang is backing Jefferson?"

"They've been at it for the last week," was the response. "They know something, Mr. Sage. Somebody's going to do the dirty, otherwise they wouldn't be so blasted clever about it."

"Clever?"

"Putting on all they can on the Q.T.," was the response.

"Find out all you can about Goldschmidt and his friends. Keep in touch with me here if you learn anything. Incidentally, keep on the water-wagon until after the fight."

"Right-o!" said Lindler, rising; "but I wish you'd tell me—"

"I have told you," said Malcolm Sage, and with that he took the proffered hand and, a moment later, Dick Lindler passed through the outer door. As he did so, he almost collided with Thompson, who had just jumped out of Malcolm Sage's car and was dashing towards the door. Thompson rushed across the outer-office, through the glass-panelled door, and passed swiftly into Malcolm Sage's room.

"It's the car right enough. Chief," he said, making an effort to control his excitement. "I picked it up outside Jimmy Dilk's. There were three men in it."

Malcolm Sage nodded, then, opening a drawer, produced a sealed packet.

"If I'm not back here by half-past four," he said, "ring up Inspector Wensdale, and ask him to come round at once with a couple of men and wait in the outer office. Give him this packet. There's a letter inside. If he's not there, get anyone else you know."

Thompson stared. In spite of long association with Malcolm Sage, there were still times when he failed to follow his chief's line of reasoning.

"If I telephone or write cancelling these instructions, ignore anything I say. Do you understand?"

Malcolm Sage, Detective

"I understand, Chief," said Thompson.

Malcolm Sage picked up his hat and stick and left the room. Tims, who had been waiting at the outer door, sprang to his seat and, almost before the door of the car had closed, it jerked forward and was soon threading its sinuous way towards Coventry Street.

Five minutes later Malcolm Sage pressed a bell-push on the fifth floor of a large block of flats known as Coventry Mansions. The door was opened by a heavily-built, ill-favoured man. In response to Malcolm Sage's request to see Mr. Goldschmidt, he was told that he couldn't.

"Tell him," said Malcolm Sage, fixing his steel-grey eyes upon the man in a steady gaze, "that Mr. Malcolm Sage wishes to see him about something that happened last night, and about something more that is to happen to-morrow night. He'll understand."

A sudden look of apprehension in the man's eyes seemed to suggest that he at least understood. He hesitated for a moment, then, with a gruff "Wait there," shut the door in Malcolm Sage's face. Three minutes later he opened it again and, inviting him to enter, led the way along a passage, at the end of which was a door, which the man threw open.

Malcolm Sage found himself in a darkened room, from which the light was excluded by heavy curtains. For a moment he looked about him, unable to distinguish any object. When his eyes became accustomed to the gloom, he saw seated in an arm-chair a man with a handkerchief held to his face.

"Mr. Goldschmidt?" he interrogated, as he seated himself in the centre of the room.

"Well, what is it?" was the thickly spoken retort.

"I came to ask your views on the fight to-morrow night, and to enquire if you think the odds of nine to two on Jefferson are justified."

There was an exclamation from the arm-chair.

"If you've got anything to say," said the thick voice angrily, "get it off your chest and go-to hell," he added, as an afterthought. "What do you want?" the voice demanded, as

Malcolm Sage, Detective

Malcolm Sage remained silent.

"I want you to take a little run with me in my car," said Malcolm Sage evenly. "Fresh air will do your nose good."

"What the—" the man broke off, apparently choked with passion, then, recovering himself, added, "Here, cough it up, or else I'll have you thrown out into the street! What is it?"

"I want either you, or one of your friends, to come with me to where Charley Burns has been taken."

There was a stifled exclamation from the chair, then a howl of agony as the hand holding the handkerchief dropped. At the same moment three men burst into the room. Malcolm Sage's back was to the door. He did not even turn to look at them.

Somebody switched on the light, and Malcolm Sage saw before him the puffy face of a man of about sixty, in the centre of which was a hideous purple splotch that had once been a nose. A moment later the handkerchief obscured the unsavoury sight.

"What the hell's all this about?" shouted one of the men, advancing into the room, the others remaining by the door.

Slowly Malcolm Sage turned and regarded the three men, whose appearance proclaimed their pugilistic calling.

"I was just asking Mr. Goldschmidt to be so good as to accompany me to where Charley Burns is—"

He was interrupted by exclamations from all three men.

"What the hell do you mean?" demanded he who had spoken, a dark, ill—favoured fellow with a brow like a rainy sky.

"I will tell you," said Malcolm Sage. "Last night Mr. Goldschmidt, accompanied by certain friends, went to Burns's training—quarters to keep an appointment made in the

189

name of a girl friend of Burns. He came out quite unsuspectingly, was overpowered, and subsequently taken in Mr. Goldschmidt's car to a place with which I am unacquainted, so that he shall not appear at the Olympia to—morrow night."

He drew his pipe from his pocket and proceeded to fill it. His air was that of a chess player who knows that he can mate his opponent in two moves.

"It's a damned lie!" roared one of the men, whilst Goldschmidt shrieked something that was unintelligible.

"You drove out by way of Putney Hill, Esher, and Clandon Cross Roads. You backed the car to within two hundred yards of 'The Grove', where you all got out with the exception of the driver. You then entered 'The Grove', taking cover behind a large clump of rhododendrons."

"It's a damned lie," choked Goldschmidt.

"By the way," continued Malcolm Sage, "your fair friend drove out in the tonneau; but returned seated beside the driver, and one of you was nearly left behind and entered the car after it had started."

The men looked at one another in bewilderment.

"You, Goldschmidt, carried an umbrella," continued Malcolm Sage, "and took cover behind the holly bush; but you came out a little too soon, hence that nose. Burns was playing 'possum. You were rather anxious for a smoke too. I am a smoker myself."

A stream of profanity burst from Goldschmidt's lips.

"You see I am in a position to prove my points," said Malcolm Sage calmly.

"Oh! you are, are you?" sneered the spokesman, as he moved a little closer to Malcolm Sage, "and I am in the position to prove that we're four to one."

"Three to one," corrected Malcolm Sage quietly. "Your friend," indicating Goldschmidt, with a nod, "is scarcely—"

190

Malcolm Sage, Detective

He was interrupted by a stifled oath from the armchair.

"Good old Nigger!" murmured one of the men by the door.

"Well, and what about it?" demanded Nigger.

"If Burns is delivered over to me within two hours, unharmed and in fighting trim, and a cheque for 1,000 is paid to St. Timothy's Hospital by noon tomorrow, there will be no prosecution, and I will not divulge your names. If not, during the next twenty–four hours, London will probably have its first experience of lynch–law."

With that Malcolm Sage struck a match and proceeded to light his pipe.

"That all?" sneered the man. "Ain't there nothink else you'd like?"

"I cannot recall anything else at the moment," said Malcolm Sage imperturbably, as he looked across at the fellow over the top of the burning match.

"You dirty nark," burst out the man by the door, who had hitherto remained silent. "A pretty sort of stool–pigeon you are."

"Spyin' on us, wasn't you?" demanded Nigger, edging nearer to Malcolm Sage.

"It's ten minutes past four," remarked Malcolm Sage coolly, as he glanced at his wrist–watch.

"Oh, it is, is it?" was the retort, "and in another hour it'll be ten minutes past five."

"I have to be back at my office by half–past four." Malcolm Sage looked about for some receptacle in which to throw the spent match.

"You don't say so." Again Nigger edged a little nearer; but Malcolm Sage appeared not to notice it.

"Well, I may as well tell you that you don't leave here until eleven o'clock to–morrow night, see?"

There were murmurs of approval from the others.

"Then, perhaps, you will send out and buy me a tooth–brush," was Malcolm Sage's quiet rejoinder.

CHAPTER XVI. THE GREAT FIGHT AT THE OLYMPIA

NEVER had the Olympia seen such a crowd as was gathered to watch the fight between Charley Burns of England and Joe Jefferson of America. Never in its career of hybrid ugliness had it witnessed such excitement.

For thirty–six hours the wildest rumours had been current. Charley Burns had broken down, run away, committed suicide, and refused to fight. He had broken a leg, an arm, a finger, and had torn more tendons than he possessed. He had sprained ankles, wrung withers, been overtrained, had contracted every known disease in addition to manifesting a yellow streak.

The atmosphere was electrical. The spectators whispered among themselves, exchanging views and rumours. The most fantastical stories were related, credited, and debated with gravity and concern.

If some ill–advised optimist ventured to question a particularly lugubrious statement, he was challenged to explain the betting, which had crept up to six to one on Jefferson offered with no takers.

The arrival of the Prince of Wales gave a welcome vent for pent–up excitement. Accustomed as he was to enthusiastic acclamation, the Prince seemed a little embarrassed by the warmth and intensity of his greeting.

The preliminary bouts ran their course, of interest only to those immediately concerned, who were more truly alone in the midst of that vast concourse than some anchorite in the desert of Sahara.

The heat was unbearable, the atmosphere suffocating. Men smoked their cigars and cigarettes jerkily, now indulging in a series of staccatoed puffs, now ignoring them until they went out.

Slowly the time crept on as by the bedside of death. If those ridiculously bobbing figures in the ring would only cease their caperings!

"Break! Break!" The voice of the referee suddenly split through a "pocket" of silence. Everyone seemed startled, then the curtain of sound once more descended and wrapped the assembly in its impenetrable folds. The gong sounded the beginning and the end of each round, and so it went on.

Mr. Papwith sat in the front row near the Prince. Smiling, smiling, for ever smiling. He was a dapper little man, with a fiery, clean–shaven face, and a fringe of grizzled hair above his ears that gave the lie to the auburn silkiness with which his head was crowned. Next to him was Mr. Doulton, who chatted and smiled, smiled and chatted; but his eyes moved restlessly over the basin of faces, as if in search of an answer to some unuttered question.

At length the preliminary bouts were ended. As the combatants had arrived unheralded, so they departed unsung. Although no one appeared to be watching, a sudden hush fell over the assembly. The dramatic moment had arrived. A few minutes would see the rumours confirmed or disproved. Men, seasoned spectators of a hundred fights, found the tension almost unbearable.

The M.C. climbed through the ropes and looked fussily about him. He appealed to the spectators for silence during the actual rounds and for the discontinuance of smoking. A black cardboard box, sealed as if it contained duelling–pistols instead of gloves, was thrust into the ring. Men took a last fond draw at their cigars and cigarettes before mechanically extinguishing them.

All eyes were directed towards the spot where the combatants would appear.

The referee turned expectantly in the same direction. A group of men in flannels and sweaters was seen moving towards the ring. Among them was a sleek, dark–haired man in a long dressing–gown of bottle green. It was Joe Jefferson.

Suddenly a great roar burst out, echoing and re–echoing continuously as the group approached the ring and Jefferson climbed through the ropes.

Then came another hush. A second group of men was observed approaching the ring. There was a shout as those nearest recognised Alf Pond among them. It developed into a roar, then died away as if strangled, giving place to a hum of suppressed inquiry. Everyone was either asking, or looking, the same question.

"Where is Burns?"

Alf Pond and his associates moved to the ringside as if bound for a funeral.

Their gloom seemed suddenly to pervade the whole vast concourse. Men talked to one another mechanically, their eyes fixed upon the group.

There was a strange hush. The men reached the ringside and stood looking at one another. The audience looked at them. What had happened?

None seemed to notice three men moving down the opposite gangway towards the ring. The man in the centre was muffled in a heavy overcoat that reached to his heels, a soft felt hat was pulled down over his eyes. One or two spectators in their immediate neighbourhood gave them a hasty, curious glance.

Suddenly Alf Pond gave a wild whoop and, breaking away from his fellows, dashed towards the three strangers. In a moment the overcoat and muffler were thrown aside and the hat knocked off, revealing the fair–haired and smiling Charley Burns.

Gripping Burns's hand, Alf Pond broke down. Tears streamed down his battle–seared features, and he sobbed with the choking agony of a strong man.

Then suddenly everything became enveloped in a dense volume of sound. Men and women stood on their chairs and waved frantically, madly, anything they could clutch hold of to wave. The whole Olympia appeared to have gone mad. Noble peers, grave judges, sedate generals and austere philosophers acted as if suddenly bereft of the restraining influences of civilisation and decorum.

Hugged and fondled by his seconds, Burns reached the ring and climbed into it. The black cardboard box was opened, the men's hands bandaged, the gloves donned. Still the pandemonium raged, now dying down, now bursting out again with increased volume.

Jefferson and Burns shook hands. The referee stood in the middle of the ring and, with arms extended aloft, appeared to be imploring the blessing of heaven. The crowd, however, understood, and the great uproar died down to a hum of sound.

Then for the first time it was noticed that, in place of the habitual smile that had made Burns the idol he was, there was a grim set about his jaw that caused those nearest to the ring to wonder and to speculate.

Charley Burns's "battle—smile" had become almost a tradition.

"If he'd only fight more and box less," Alf Pond would say complainingly, "he'd beat the whole blinkin' world with one hand."

Suddenly a hush fell upon the assembly, a hush as pronounced as had been the previous pandemonium. The referee took a final look round. Behind Burns, Alf Pond could be seen sponging his face over a small bucket. He was once more himself. There were things to be done.

Almost before anyone realised it the gong sounded; the fight bad begun.

"God!" The exclamation broke involuntarily from Alf Pond, as he dropped the sponge and gazed before him with wide—staring eyes.

"He's fighting," he cried, almost dancing with excitement. "Did ever you see the like, Sandy?" But Sandy's eyes were glued upon the ring. His hands and feet moved convulsively—he was a fighter himself.

Discarding his traditional opening of boxing with swift defensive watchfulness, Charley Burns had darted at his man. Before anyone knew what was happening his left crashed between Jefferson's eyes, a blow that caused him to reel back almost to the ropes.

195

Before he could recover, a right hook had sent him staggering against the ropes themselves. For a second it looked as if he would collapse over them. Pulling himself together, however, he strove to clinch; but Burns was too quick for him. Stepping back swiftly, he feinted with his left, and Jefferson, expecting a repetition of the first blow, raised his guard. A white right arm shot out to the mark, and Jefferson went down with a crash.

The timekeeper's voice began to drone the monotonous count; at eight Jefferson gathered himself together; at nine he was on his feet.

Once more Burns was upon him, and Jefferson saved himself by clinching. It was clear that he was badly shaken.

Three times during the first round Burns floored his man. The onlookers were mad with excitement.

Back in his own corner, Charley Burns was sitting, a hard set look in his eyes, his jaw square and firm.

Alf Pond fussed about him like a hen over a chick.

"Shut up, Alf! I know what I'm doing," said Burns sharply.

"He knows what he's doing," repeated Alf Pond ecstatically. "Hear that. Sandy? He knows what he's doing, and so does Jeff, I'll lay a pony to a pink pill," he added.

Once more the gong sounded; once more Burns sprang up and darted at his man. Jefferson tried first to dodge and then to clinch; but without avail. He was unnerved. His strategy and tactics had been planned in view of Burns's usual methods; but here was an entirely different man to deal with—a great fighter.

Twice more Jefferson went down, taking a count of nine on each occasion. He seemed to share with the spectators the knowledge that there would be no third round.

On rising the second time he seemed determined to change his tactics. He rushed forward, fighting gamely, apparently in the hope of getting a lucky knock—out blow.

196

Without giving an inch, Burns threw off the blows and, feinting with his left, crashed his right full on the point of his opponent's jaw. Jefferson's hands fell, and for a second he stood gazing stupidly before him; then his knees sagged and, with a deliberation that seemed almost intolerable, he crashed forward on his face, one arm outstretched as if in protest.

Again the timekeeper's voice was heard monotonously counting. Burns turned to his corner without waiting for the conclusion of the count. He knew the strength behind that blow.

Later that night, just as Big Ben was taking breath preparatory to his supreme effort, Malcolm Sage was seated in his big arm—chair smoking a final pipe before bed, and turning over in his mind the happenings of the day and the probable events of the morrow.

His train of thought was suddenly interrupted by a hammering at the outer door of his chambers, followed by the sound of loud and hilarious voices as Rogers answered the summons.

A moment later the door of the sitting—room burst open, and there flowed into the room Charley Burns and his entourage, all obviously in the best of spirits. In the background stood Rogers, with expressionless face, looking towards his master.

Malcolm Sage rose and shook hands with Burns, Mr. Doulton and Mr. Papwith, Alf Pond and his assistants.

"Sorry, Mr. Sage," cried Burns, with a laugh; "but the boys wouldn't wait, although I told them calling time was four till six," and he laughed again, the laugh of a man who has not a care in the world. He also gripped Malcolm Sage's hand with a heartiness that made him wince. The others in turn shook hands in a way that caused Malcolm Sage to wonder why America had not long since ceased to be a Republic.

The men dropped into chairs in various parts of the room, and Rogers, who had disappeared at a signal from Malcolm Sage, now returned with a tray of glasses, syphons, and decanters. Soon the whole company was drinking the health of Malcolm Sage with an earnestness which convinced him that on the morrow there would be trouble with

197

Colonel Sappinger, who lived above and cherished Carlyle's hatred of sound.

"And now, Mr. Sage," said Alf Pond, "we want to know how you found Charley. He won't tell us anythink. Wonderful, I call it," he added, and there was a murmur of assent from the others, as they proceeded to light the cigars that Rogers handed round.

"It was not very difficult," said Malcolm Sage, stuffing tobacco into his pipe from a terra–cotta jar beside him. As he applied a light to the bowl the others exchanged glances.

"From the first," he continued, "it was obvious that some message, or letter, had been conveyed to our friend Burns." He gazed across at the champion, who looked uncomfortable.

"As he had not mentioned the fact to any of his friends," continued Malcolm Sage, a little slyly, "it seemed obvious to assume that there was a lady in the case."

Alf Pond looked reproachfully at Burns, who reddened beneath the united gaze of seven pairs of eyes.

"That the appointment had been for the evening," proceeded Malcolm Sage, "was obvious from the fact that Burns disappeared in the blue suit he always changed into after the day's work."

Alf Pond looked across at Mr. Doulton, nodding his approval of the reasoning.

"It was Kitty, or I thought it was," burst out Burns. "She said something terrible had happened and that she must see me," he added.

Kitty Graham was shortly to become Mrs. Charley Burns, but during the period of training she had been rigorously excluded from all intercourse with her fiance by order of the autocratic Alf Pond.

"The meeting was arranged for the further side of the large clump of rhododendrons, which acted as a screen," continued Malcolm Sage. "When Burns arrived there, he saw a girl standing a little distance away. Before he could reach her, however, he was seized and a chloroformed pad held over his mouth. The suddenness of the attack dazed him; he did not struggle, but held his breath; he—"

"How the blazes did you know that, Mr. Sage?" burst out Burns.

"You are always a quick–thinker in the ring," said Malcolm Sage, "and you were a quick–thinker then. You smelt chloroform, held your breath and thought. It was a sort of instinctive ring–craft."

"But you—" began Burns.

"There were no marks of a struggle where you were seized. You probably realised that your only chance lay in letting the enemy think you were losing consciousness."

Burns nodded.

"Seeing that there was no sign of trouble," continued Malcolm Sage, "the principal in this little affair stepped out from where he had been taking cover just at the moment when Burns broke loose and let out. Movement has always a primary attraction for the eye, and Burns got this man full on the nose and ruined it. He also sent him clean into the privet–hedge, where he collapsed."

"Who was it?" demanded Alf Pond fiercely.

"There were, however, too many of them for Burns," continued Malcolm Sage, ignoring the question. "They had planned the attack very carefully, each clinging to a limb. Soon they had him unconscious and bound in the car. Then they turned their attention to their leader."

"Yes; but how did you find Burns?" asked Mr. Doulton eagerly.

"I didn't," said Malcolm Sage. "They showed me where he was."

"But—" began Mr. Papwith, whose shiny, clean–shaven face, normally suggestive of a Turner sunset, now looked like a conflagration.

Malcolm Sage, Detective

"After half an hour's fruitless effort to track the car down side–roads, I returned to London as fast as my man could take me," proceeded Malcolm Sage, "and I immediately set enquiries on foot as to the betting on the Stock Exchange, at Tattersall's, the National Sporting Club, and other places. By three o'clock that afternoon I knew pretty well who it was that had been laying heavily against Burns. That simplified matters."

Alf Pond and Burns exchanged admiring glances.

"As you know, for more than a week previously the betting had made it clear that heavy sums were being laid on Jefferson. In the course of ten days it had veered round from 5 to 4 on Burns to 9 to 2 against. As there were no rumours detrimental to his condition or state of health, this could only mean that a lot of money was being put on Jefferson. I found out the names of the principal layers and the amounts. I discovered that all were extremely active with the exception of one. That I decided was the man with the umbrella."

"Who's he?" demanded Sandy, whose mouth had not ceased to gape since Malcolm Sage began his story.

"The man Burns knocked out. He had been leaning rather heavily on the handle whilst taking cover behind a holly–bush, and the metal cap at the base of the silk was clearly marked on the ground. He was also holding an unlit cigar in his hand, which he left in the hedge. By great good chance this was recognised by someone I happen to know as a brand smoked by a certain backer of Jefferson."

"Well, I'm damned!" broke in Alt Pond, with intense earnestness.

"So you see, I had quite a lot to help me. I was searching for a well–dressed man—"

"But how did you know he was well–dressed?" queried Mr. Doulton.

"His footprints showed that he wore boots of a fashionable model," explained Malcolm Sage. "He also carried an umbrella, even on an occasion such as this.

"I had to look for a well–dressed man who always carried an umbrella, and who smoked large and expensive cigars and, most important of all, whose nose had been smashed out

200

of all recognition."

"But how could you tell I got him on the nose?" demanded Burns, leaning forward eagerly.

"There was quite a pool of blood beneath the hedge," explained Malcolm Sage. "He was probably there for some minutes while his friends were making sure of you, Burns. Blood would not have flowed so generously as a result of a blow from the fist except from the nose."

"You're a knock—out, that's what you are, Mr. Sage," said Alf Pond, with admiring conviction. "I'd never have thought of it all," he added, with the air of one desiring to be absolutely fair.

"Finally," continued Malcolm Sage, "there was the car. It was a large car, a defect in one of the tyres enabled me to determine that by a steel rule. It was obviously heavily laden and the near back—wheel was out of track. This fact, of course, was of no help on the high—road, where other cars would blot out the track; but if I could show that someone who had been heavily backing Jefferson had a nose badly damaged, and a car with a near back—wheel out of track in just the same way that this particular wheel was out of track, and that its tyres were the same as those of the car that drew up outside Burns's training—quarters, then I should have a wealth of circumstantial evidence that it would be almost impossible to confute.

"From a friend at Scotland Yard I obtained the number of the car belonging to the man whom this evidence involved.

"As Stainton is off the Portsmouth Road, I telephoned to the Automobile Association patrols at Putney Hill, Esher, and Clandon Cross Roads. I was told that on the previous evening this particular car was seen going in the direction of Guildford. These patrols take the numbers of all cars that pass. As it had not passed Liss, where the next patrol is stationed, it was another link in the chain."

"Well, I'm blowed!" The exclamation broke involuntarily from Kid.

Malcolm Sage, Detective

"As the patrols go off duty at dusk, I could get no further help from them," continued Malcolm Sage. "I sent a man to watch Jefferson's training–quarters, although I was fairly certain that he and his party were in no way involved."

Malcolm Sage went on to narrate his call upon Nathan Goldschmidt, carefully omitting any mention of the name or address. His hearers listened with breathless interest.

"I concluded that they had taken their prisoner to some lonely, empty house," he explained, "but there was not time to search all the empty houses in the home counties, so the man with the damaged nose had to come with me in my car, and his friends followed in his."

"But how did you manage it?" gasped Mr. Papwith. .

"At first they showed fight," said Malcolm Sage, "and threatened to keep me prisoner until after the fight."

"Gee!" exclaimed Kid.

"I anticipated some such move, and had instructed my people that unless I were back by half–past four, they were to deliver certain packets to the editors of well–known London papers. In these packets was told the story as far as I had been able to trace it. This I informed them."

"What did they say to that?" asked Mr. Doulton.

"They insisted that I telephone countermanding my orders; but as I explained that I had told my man Thompson he was to disregard any telephone message, or written instructions, he might receive from me, they realised that the game was up. I also informed them that Inspector Wensdale and two of his men were waiting at my office in anticipation of a possible hold–up."

"Well, I'm blessed," exclaimed Alf Pond. "If you ain't It."

"I pointed out," continued Malcolm Sage, "that whereas by producing Burns they would have a fight for their money, if the truth became known, not only would their bets most

202

likely be forfeited; but they would probably have to go to law to recover their stake–money. I further pledged Mr. Doulton, Mr. Papwith, and Burns not to take any legal action. I rather suspect that in this I was technically conspiring to defeat the ends of justice."

"But weren't you afraid they'd do a double cross?" asked Burns.

"They heard me instruct one of my assistants that unless I were back by nine o'clock that evening, the notes I had written and addressed were to be delivered. Incidentally the inspector was present, unofficially of course."

"You oughter been in the ring with a head like that," said Alf Pond sorrowfully.

"We found Burns fairly comfortable in the wine–cellar of an empty house near Ripley. They had left him food and water and beer. In all probability on awakening to–morrow morning, had we not found him, he would have discovered the door unlocked and himself no longer a prisoner." Malcolm Sage paused with the air of one who has told his story.

"But why did you keep Papwith and me at Stainton until late this afternoon?" enquired Mr. Doulton.

"In the first instance, to be in charge and to see that Burns's disappearance was kept secret. It was obvious that every endeavour would be made to put a lot of money on Jefferson before the fact became known. This would lead to rumour, and later to enquiry. Subsequently I decided that you were both better out of London, as you would have been interviewed and bound to give something away, in spite of the utmost caution."

"And now, Mr. Sage," said Mr. Doulton, "who are the scoundrels?"

"I have promised not to give their names," was the quiet reply.

"Not give their names?" cried several of his hearers in unison.

Malcolm Sage then proceeded to explain that unless the gang had seen a loop–hole of escape they would not have thrown up the sponge. "Had exposure been inevitable in any case they would have brazened it out, knowing that, whatever happened to themselves,

Burns could not appear at the Olympia. The knowledge that their identity would not be divulged tempted them to risk the loss of their money. Apart from this," he added, "the details I was able to give seemed to convince them that they had either been watched or given away.

"You must remember that they have lost enormous sums of money," Malcolm Sage went on, "and there will be another 1,000 pounds for St. Timothy's Hospital. It was further understood that, if I could discover any one of them had inspired a covering bet, I was released from my promise. That is why the odds got to six to one. Incidentally they ensured the defeat of their man. When Burns entered the ring to–night, it was to fight, not to box."

"That's true," said Alf Pond, nodding his head and reaching for another cigar. "He never fought like it before in all his puff."

"And where were you last night?" enquired Mr. Papwith of Burns.

"In my bed," said Malcolm Sage, "and my friend Inspector Wensdale of Scotland Yard and I slept here. Burns has never been out of Wensdale's sight until we handed him over this evening."

"I've been having police protection," laughed Burns.

"Still, you didn't oughter have gone two days without doing anythink," said Alf Pond.

"Oh! I had a bit of sparring with Mr. Sage," said Burns, "in spite of the glasses. If you want to see some pretty foot–work, Alf, you get him to put the gloves on."

"I knew it," cried Alf Pond, with conviction; then, turning to the others, "Didn't I say he oughter been in the ring?"

And Malcolm Sage found relief from the admiring eyes of his guests in gazing down at the well–bitten mouthpiece of his briar.

"But why did you let me think that Jefferson and his crowd were in it?" enquired Burns, with corrugated brow.

"Well," said Malcolm Sage slowly, "as I had put twenty–five pounds on you to steady Pond's nerves, I didn't want to lose it."

And Alf Pond winked gleefully across at Mr. Doulton.

CHAPTER XVII. LADY DENE CALLS ON MALCOLM SAGE

"LADY DENE wishes to see you, Miss."

"Sure the Archbishop of Canterbury isn't with her, Johnnie dear?" asked Gladys Norman sweetly, without looking up from the cleaning of her typewriter. In her own mind she was satisfied that this was a little joke inspired by Thompson.

"No, Miss, she's alone," replied the literal William Johnson.

"Show her Ladyship in," she said, still playing for safety. "Dash!" she muttered as, having inadvertently touched the release, the carriage slid to the left, pinching her finger in its course.

William Johnson departed, his head half turned over his right shoulder in admiration of one who could hear with such unconcern that a real lady had called to see her.

As her door opened for a second time, Gladys Norman assiduously kept her eyes fixed upon her machine.

"No, Johnnie," she remarked, still without looking up. "It's no good. Lady Denes don't call upon typists at 9.30 a.m., so buzz off, little beanlet. I'm—"

"But this Lady Dene does."

Gladys Norman jumped to her feet, knocking over the benzine bottle and dropping her brush into the vitals of the machine.

Before her stood a fair–haired girl, her violet eyes brimming with mischievous laughter, whilst in her arms she carried a mass of red roses.

"I'm so sorry," faltered Gladys Norman, biting her lower lip, and conscious of her heightened colour and the violet–stained gloves that had once been white. "I thought Johnnie was playing a joke."

Lady Dene nodded brightly, whilst Gladys Norman stooped to pick up the benzine bottle, then with a motion of her head indicated to William Johnson that his presence was no longer required. Reluctantly the lad turned, and a moment later the door closed slowly behind him.

"I want you to help me," said Lady Dene, dropping the roses on to the leaf of Gladys Norman's typing–table. "These are for Mr. Sage."

"For the Chief?" cried Gladys Norman in astonishment. Then she laughed. The idea of a riot of red roses in Malcolm Sage's room struck her as funny.

"You see," said Lady Dene, "this is the birthday of the Malcolm Sage Bureau, and I'm going to decorate his room."

"I don't—" began Gladys Norman hesitatingly, when Lady Dene interrupted her.

"It's all right," she cried, "I'll take all the responsibility."

"But we've got no vases," objected Gladys Norman.

"My chauffeur has some in the car, and there are heaps more roses," she added.

"More?" cried Gladys Norman aghast.

"Heaps," repeated Lady Dene, dimpling with laughter at the consternation on Gladys Norman's face. "Ah! here they are," as the door opened and a mass of white roses appeared, with a florid face peering over the top.

"Put them down there, Smithson," said Lady Dene, indicating a spot in front of Gladys Norman's table. "Now fetch the vases and the rest of the roses."

"The rest!" exclaimed Gladys Norman.

Lady Dene laughed. She was thoroughly enjoying the girl's bewilderment. "He's not come yet?" she interrogated.

The girl shook her head. "He won't be here for half–an–hour yet," she said. "He had to go down into the city."

"That will just give us time," cried Lady Dene, stooping and picking up an armful of the white roses. "You bring the red ones," she cried over her shoulder, as she passed through Malcolm Sage's door, just as Smithson entered with several purple vases.

Picking up the red roses, Gladys Norman followed the others into Malcolm Sage's room. Her feelings were those of someone constrained to commit sacrilege against her will.

"Now get some water, Smithson."

"Water, my Lady?" repeated Smithson, looking about him vaguely, as Moses might have done in the wilderness.

"Yes; ask the lad. Be quick," cried Lady Dene, with deft fingers beginning to arrange the roses in the vases. "Oh! please help me," she cried turning to Gladys Norman, who had stood watching her as if fascinated.

"But——" she began, when Lady Dene interrupted her.

"Quick!" cried Lady Dene excitedly, "or he'll be here before we've finished."

Then, convinced that it was the work of Kismet, or the devil, Gladys Norman threw herself into the task of arranging the flowers.

When Thompson arrived some ten minutes later, he stood at the door of Malcolm Sage's room "listening with his mouth," as Gladys Norman had expressed it. When he had regained the power of speech, he uttered two words.

"Jumping Je–hosh–o–phat!" but into them he precipitated all the emotion of his being.

Malcolm Sage, Detective

"Go away, Tommy, we're busy," cried Gladys Norman over her shoulder. "Do you hear; go away," she repeated, stamping her foot angrily as he made no movement to obey, and Thompson slid away and closed the door, convinced that in the course of the next half–hour there would be the very deuce to pay.

He knew the Chief better than Gladys, he told himself, and if there were one thing calculated to bring out all the sternness in his nature it was flippancy, and what could be more flippant than decorating the room of a great detective with huge bowls and vases of red and white roses.

Regardless of Thompson's forebodings, Lady Dene smiled to herself as she put the finishing touches to the last vase, whilst Gladys Norman gathered up the litter of leaves and stalks that lay on the floor, throwing them into the fireplace. She then removed the last spots of water from Malcolm Sage's table.

Lady Dene took from her bag a small leather case, which she opened and placed in the centre of the table opposite Malcolm Sage's chair. It was a platinum ring of antique workmanship, with a carbuchon of lapis lazuli.

"Oh, how lovely!" cried Gladys Norman, as she gazed at the ring's excellent workmanship.

Presently, the two girls stepped back to gaze at their handiwork. In a few minutes they had transformed an austere, business–man's room into what looked like a miniature rose–show. From every point red and white roses seemed to nod their fragrant heads.

"I—" began Gladys Norman, then she stopped suddenly, arrested by a slight sound behind her. She span round on her heel. Malcolm Sage stood in the doorway, with Thompson and William Johnson a few feet behind him.

Slowly and deliberately he looked round the room; then his eyes rested on Lady Dene.

"How do you do, Lady Dene," he said quietly, extending his hand.

For a moment she was conscious of an unaccustomed sensation of fear. "You're not cross?" she interrogated, looking up at him quizzically, her head a little on one side. "You see, it's the Bureau's birthday and—" She stopped suddenly.

Malcolm Sage had dropped her hand and walked over to his table. Picking up the ring he examined it intently, then turned to Lady Dene, interrogation in his eyes.

"It's from my husband and me," she said simply. "You have such lovely hands, and–and we should like you to wear it."

Without a word he removed the ring from the case and put it on the third finger of his right hand, which he then extended to Lady Dene, who took it with a little laugh of happiness.

"You're not really cross," she said, looking up at him a little anxiously.

"To me they stand for so much, Lady Dene," he said gravely, "that I am not even speculating as to their probable effect upon the faith of my clients."

And Malcolm Sage smiled.

It was that smile Gladys Norman saw as she closed the door behind her, and which Thompson resolutely refused to believe.

CPSIA information can be obtained at www.ICGtesting.com
Printed in the USA
LVOW03*1550300414

383886LV00014B/415/P